OVERTIME

Overtime

KAT MIZERA

HeartEyes Press

For my writer pals — Jami, Kelly, and Tess. Thanks for being my friends, my motivation, my tribe.

CONTENTS

PATRICK

Sixteen seconds on the clock.

The score was tied at two, and I wasn't going to be happy if we had to go to overtime. The team I played for had lost to these guys during this particular New Year's tournament for the last ten years. Tonight, we were going to win it. At least, we were if I had anything to say about it.

I cut my gaze over to my twin brother, Paxton, and gave him a little signal. It was something we'd been doing for years, since we were six or seven years old, and when I winked twice, he knew exactly what I had in mind. He skated behind the other team's goalie, but instead of carrying the puck with him to the other side, he stopped behind the net like he was looking to make a pass. To everyone's surprise but mine, he flipped the puck over the top of the net, dumping it right into the slot—where I was waiting. I one-timed it over the goalie's left shoulder and with ten seconds left in the game, I saw that gorgeous red light go off.

My teammates immediately surrounded me, arms in the air. We'd just pulled ahead and if we could keep it away from them for ten more seconds, we'd actually beat these guys for the first time in years.

I skated to the bench and let the D-men handle it, and nine seconds later, we had our arms in the air once again.

Fuck yeah.

"You rock, Trick!" Lex Vonne, one of my teammates, called me by my nickname as he shook his head. "You and Pax freak me right out when you do that twin shit."

"Damn twins." Another teammate, Tate Adler, grinned at us.

Paxton didn't say much—he never did—and just smiled as he walked back toward the locker room. I followed behind him, my heart still thumping with excitement. This had been a great tournament and winning always made it that much better. Scoring the winning goal made the whole event epic.

I was in such a good mood, I didn't notice someone coming up behind me.

"Patrick. I need to talk to you." Bart Keller, the team's gruff, no-nonsense head coach, motioned for me to follow him.

Shit. This couldn't be good.

"What's up, Coach?" I had a feeling I knew what was coming, but I'd been hoping getting the game-winning goal would deter him. Apparently not.

"I just got a list of players with bad grades. You're on it." He met my eyes, and there wasn't an ounce of sympathy in his. "I don't care if you make the game-winning goal every game for the rest of your college career—if you don't keep your grades up next semester, you're benched. If you're failing a single class, you're off the team. Starting now, I want notes from every one of your professors, weekly."

"Coach, I—" I started to defend myself but he cut me off.

"Save it. Get a tutor. Beg your brother to help you. I don't care how you do it, but I need weekly progress reports as soon as classes resume. And anything less than a B, you're benched."

"Wait, what?" I stared at him. "I can't get less than a B? But—"

"My team, my rules. That's all." He turned away and I scowled, my heart dropping to my feet. I was so screwed.

My grades this past semester had been awful. I'd barely

2

scraped by, but studying had never been my thing, and with a contract in the big leagues looming before me, marketing and statistics really weren't on my radar. It's not like I'd ever use any of that stuff as a professional hockey player, so taking time to study seemed like a waste. Hell, even if I didn't play hockey for some reason, I was never going to use statistics in the real world.

"What happened?" Paxton fell into step beside me when we finally headed out to the bus that would take us back to campus.

I relayed the conversation and he grimaced.

"Told you all that partying was going to catch up to you." We sank down next to each other when we got on the bus.

"Thanks, bro. Way to kick your twin when he's down."

"You need a tutor."

"Duh."

"I think I know someone." Paxton was the studious one, so I'd half thought he would volunteer.

"Besides you?" I asked, arching a brow.

He chuckled. "I have my own studying to do, plus I have a girlfriend who requires my attention. And anyway, you never listen to me. You need someone you can't easily tell to fuck off."

I gave a half-hearted laugh. "There is that."

"Ellie."

"Huh?"

"Ellie McGinn. You know who she is, right?"

"She's that super-genius teenager… Isn't she a kid?"

"Not really. I think she's nineteen now, and anyway, her age is irrelevant because she's brilliant. She's also not your type, so you won't spend the whole time trying to get in her pants."

"Why isn't she my type?" I asked, frowning. If I was honest, almost all women were my type. As long as they were hygienic and stuff, I wasn't that picky. I mean, sure, I had my choice of girls most of the time as captain of the Burlington University—affectionately known as Moo U—varsity hockey team, but I didn't have a type, per se.

"Well, she's shy and nerdy, for one thing. Super smart, studies all the time, and definitely not the kind of girl who'll fawn over you. And you seem to like that."

"Whatever." I shook my head, taking his teasing in stride. "I need help getting my grades up, so I don't really care what she looks like, as long as she's smart, competent, and won't completely break the bank."

"She's smart, all right." He pulled out his phone. "I'm going to text her now, ask her if she's available."

"Thanks." I leaned back in the seat and closed my eyes.

Happy fucking New Year.

Despite the bad news for me, a couple of my teammates and I headed to a party not long after we got back to school. Paxton went home to meet up with Naomi, his girlfriend, but Tate and I didn't waste any time getting to the party. He was looking for his girlfriend, and I was looking for a distraction, so the timing was good. Honestly, I didn't know how the guys who lived in what we called the hockey house could put together a party while still on the road, but they'd managed to. We were some of the first people there and cars were already lining the street. This was obviously going to be a good one.

I headed inside and went right through the house and onto the back deck. That was always where the kegs were, and tonight was no exception. I grabbed a red plastic cup and filled it up before going back inside and taking stock of who was there. Half the team had shown up, most with dates, though a few were on the prowl, but I didn't see any fresh blood. I'd already hooked up with most of the cute single girls on campus and had gotten a little bored with that whole scene. Mostly, I wanted to get my degree and get the hell out of dodge.

I'd loved college to date, probably a little too much if my grades were any indication, and I'd had more than my fair share of fun. In fact, I'd spotted one of my two favorite ways to spend a

4

weekend, dancing on the other side of the room. I had two friends with benefits that I hooked up with fairly regularly, but I was getting tired of it. And them. I'd hoped they wouldn't be here tonight, but they always were. The goal now was to try to avoid that kind of thing. Four months until the end of the school year. Four months until I had to make a big decision.

A flash of blond hair distracted me and I thought it was Desi at first, one of my two favorite hookups, but the girl who turned was younger and softer than Desi, giving me pause. I squinted, trying to get a better look at her through the throngs of people dancing. I didn't recognize her, so I took a few steps in her direction in an attempt to check her out. It wasn't often someone new showed up at a hockey house party, so I was curious.

She had a red plastic cup in her hand and was talking to someone I didn't know, but the closer I got, the cuter she was. Long blond hair, cute figure, and an adorable, little upturned nose. I couldn't tell what color her eyes were, but from where I stood, she was extremely attractive and had a great laugh. Her ass looked fantastic in a pair of tight black jeans, and though it didn't appear she had much in the way of a chest, her trim body made my mouth water.

How did I not know this girl?

Well, I was going to rectify that situation right now. I'd almost reached her when her eyes met mine. There was a moment of...*something*, and then warm, wet lips suddenly fastened to mine.

"Patrick! You're here." Cheryl Bernard had her arms around my neck and was pressing her perfect thirty-four double Ds against my chest. "Why didn't you tell me you were back?"

"Oh. Hey." Now that I'd spotted someone new, I was a lot less interested in Cheryl, but she already had one hand in my pocket, groping me through the fabric of my jeans.

"Let's go upstairs," she whispered. "We haven't hooked up in weeks...and I'm *soooo* horny."

"I just got here," I protested mildly, tugging her hand out of my pocket. "Let me finish a beer, okay?"

"Fine." Her lower lip protruded a little as she watched me. She was still practically fused against my chest, and short of giving her a shove, I couldn't dislodge her, so I half walked, half dragged her outside. She hated being cold, and if I took my time, she'd go inside without me.

"Paaaatttyyy…" she whined, shivering. "Why are we out here?"

I hated when she called me Patty.

"I'm getting more beer," I responded. "You want one?"

"I hate beer," she muttered.

"Okay." I toyed with the tap, pretending something was wrong with it, hoping she'd get bored and go away.

"I'll meet you inside," she said with a scowl, abruptly turning away.

Thank god.

I took my time refilling my beer, and instead of going back in through the kitchen, I jumped off the deck and walked around to the front of the house. I was freezing my balls off, but it would be worth it if I could lose Cheryl for a while. Normally, I was good with a quickie with Cheryl, Desi, or both of them together, but tonight I had other shit on my mind.

Like the blonde who'd made eye contact with me across the dance floor. That kind of thing was a big part of the reason I was in the trouble I was in—I had no self-control. Dammit. Not when it came to women and partying, anyway. The problem was that after two and a half years of mindless hookups, I was tired of it. They all looked alike, felt alike, tasted alike. I wanted something different. Someone different. Someone who might actually keep my interest beyond thirty minutes of foreplay and a few rounds in the sack.

I ran my hands through my too-long hair and made a mental note to get it cut. I'd let a lot of things go lately with all the partying I'd been doing, so I made the spontaneous decision to avoid women altogether for the rest of the night and hang out with my friends and teammates instead. Lex was here now and I moved in his direction. He lived here at the hockey house, which was a Victorian-style mansion that they'd converted into a fraternity house type of place, with a huge living area for parties, a big-ass kitchen and deck, and what seemed like a thousand bedrooms. It was probably only five, but I'd never counted them, so I wasn't sure.

I'd almost made it to Lex when I saw her again.

The blonde.

She wasn't dancing anymore. She was just standing against a wall, looking a little lost and forlorn, as if the happy-go-lucky personality I'd seen when she'd been dancing had been an act. I wasn't sure why I thought that, but my gut told me there was more to this girl than a great ass and a sweet face.

I approached her with a friendly smile.

"Hi." I leaned against the wall so we were facing each other. "You want to dance?"

She hesitated a fraction of a second and then nodded. "Sure."

We moved into the middle of the room, since there wasn't an official dance floor, and she closed her eyes as we started to move. She was delightful to look at, her features delicate and feminine. She had fair skin and her hair was a delicious honey-blond color, reminding me of summer sunshine. It flowed around her shoulders as she danced, soft waves that made me want to run my fingers through it.

The song came to an end and a slow one came on. Without saying a word, she moved into my arms and I put one arm around her lower back and used the hand of my other arm to hold one of her hands. Her eyes met mine, an unspoken question in them, but I didn't want to talk. Not yet. I wanted to enjoy the feel of her slender body against mine and lose myself in someone with no expectations. Maybe she knew who I was and was angling for a hookup, but I didn't get that vibe. She hadn't been giving me inviting looks, hadn't approached me, and there hadn't been any recognition in her eyes at all. My gut told me she didn't know who I was any more than I knew who she was.

When the song came to an end, I reluctantly let her go and she smiled.

"Thank you for the dances," she said. She was yelling since a loud, fast song had come on and someone blasted the volume.

I didn't want to let her go just yet so I reached for her hand.

"Let's do a shot," I said, motioning to a table set up along one wall. It had originally been intended for food but had morphed into the shot table, with someone pouring them and placing them in rows by drink. Jägermeister, Jack Daniel's, and Fireball were the three I recognized, and I reached for the JD while she grabbed a Fireball.

"To a new year and new friends," I said, lifting the cup.

"Cops!" someone yelled.

"Shit! I have to get out of here," she said frantically. "My mom will kill me if I get caught drinking—again!"

"Come on." I grabbed her hand and tugged her through the kitchen, out onto the deck, and then I vaulted over the side into the snow. "Come on!" I yelled up at her. "I'll catch you. *Jump!*"

ELLIE

I had no idea who this gorgeous male specimen was, despite the fact that he seemed a little familiar, but he was asking me to jump over the side of a second-level deck. Probably to my death. But that would be preferable to what would happen if my mom found out I was underage drinking at a party tonight instead of tutoring someone like I'd told her I would be.

Someone yelled from inside the house, and after a quick glance in that direction, I panicked enough to do the unthinkable: I jumped.

Instead of me breaking all the bones in my body, the hottie I'd just been dancing with broke my fall and then immediately put me down and grabbed my hand. We made a run for the woods nearby and kept going until the lights from the house and noise from the party faded to nothing.

"Stop…" I panted. "I can't run in these boots."

"Sorry." He slowed to a walk and let go of my hand.

I paused, bending over and resting my hands on my thighs as I tried to catch my breath. I walked and did yoga once in a while, but running through the woods on snow-covered ground in boots with three-inch heels was way out of my comfort zone.

"You okay?" Hottie McHottie asked.

"Yeah. Give me a sec." I took a few deep breaths. "Thanks for catching me."

"Of course."

I really liked his voice. Deep but not gruff, with a warmth I hadn't expected from a stranger. Especially not a cute one since I had about as much game with guys as a rugby player might have in a dance studio.

"Hey." A couple more guys I didn't know caught up to us and paused, some catching their breath the way I was. "Cops swept the house. It's been ugly. We should keep moving."

"Great," I muttered.

"Don't worry," McHottie said. "I won't let them get us. Come on." He took my hand again and the group of us jogged off, going deeper into the woods.

Technically, I should have known better than to go into the woods with a group of guys I didn't know, but almost anything was preferable to getting in trouble again for drinking. I was only nineteen, and I'd gotten into my fair share of mischief the last couple of years, but this felt more serious. And for some strange reason, I trusted McHottie.

I'd gone home to my parents' house for the holiday break but had come back to tutor one of my regulars, a basketball player who couldn't figure out basic algebra to save his life. Except he'd stood me up and then invited me to the party at the hockey house. I'd been tempted to drive back to my parents' house in Brattleboro, but it had been snowing, so I'd decided what the hell? Now I regretted it. Well, not entirely. If I hadn't come to the party, I wouldn't have met McHottie.

Stealing a glance at him, he looked familiar, but I couldn't put my finger on it. He had dark hair that touched his shoulders and a beard, but his nose was straight, lips full and defined, and his body... Well, I wouldn't get started on that. I probably shouldn't have even looked. My inexperienced self had no business checking out his muscular arms or well-rounded ass.

"Where are we?" I panted. "I live in the dorms and walked to the party, so I can just go home." I groaned. "Shit. No, I can't. I left my purse at the party, so I don't have my keys."

"We're going to need to hang tight until the cops leave," McHottie said. "Then we can swing by and get our stuff. I don't even have a coat on." He turned to me. "Are you cold?"

"Not yet," I replied, "but I figure I will be once we stop moving."

"We can go this way." One of the other guys pointed. "It'll bring us on campus behind the library. I've got my key card, so we can get in and hang out there."

Thankfully, the library was open twenty-four seven.

We'd just come out of the woods and were on a path that led to campus when we ran into another group, including my friend Harley.

"Your mom will kill you if you get arrested," she said, laughing.

"How did you know where I was? You weren't at the party, were you?"

"I was actually on my way there when I saw the cops. I made a quick U-ey and then figured a handful of you would make a break for it through the woods." She paused, cocking her head. "I didn't think you'd be one of them, though."

"I just fell in with a group making a run for it." I glanced over at McHottie but he was talking to a group of guys.

"Cop car just turned the corner," someone called out.

Everyone started to scatter and I glanced over my shoulder to look for McHottie once more. He was moving in the other direction but he turned back at the same time. Yet again, our eyes met and temporarily locked, but then he shook his head.

"Go," he said, glancing down the street to where the police car was heading in our direction. As if he somehow understood I couldn't afford to get in trouble.

I didn't know what to do because I really, really wanted to talk to him, but I didn't want to get caught after we'd worked so hard to get away from the raid at the party.

"Go!" he repeated, motioning with his hand. He mouthed something else, but I couldn't tell what it was and before I could open my mouth to ask, he'd already turned and jogged after the others.

I didn't get back to my dorm room until nearly four in the morning, since it took almost that long before I could retrieve my purse and room key, but I was restless and tossed and turned a lot. I was spectacularly inexperienced with guys, but the one I'd met tonight had been different. Hotter than hot. Built. And nice. He'd gotten me out of there and then prompted me to get going when we were about to be separated.

Maybe I was just a romantic teenage girl who'd never had a boyfriend before, but there had been something between us. Our eyes had met across the crowded dance floor earlier in the evening and my entire body had become physically aware of him. I'd seen hot guys before and that had never happened, so this was something else. What it was, I had no idea, but I wasn't a big believer in coincidence, and the fact that he'd also turned out to be my knight in shining armor, gave me pause.

Of course, we hadn't even exchanged names, and Harley hadn't known who he was either. So the first interesting guy to really look at me had disappeared into the night and I had no way of finding him.

Just my luck.

I drove home when I got up, since school didn't start again for more than a week. My parents lived two hours away from Moo U and I usually went home on long weekends and breaks even though I didn't want to. They'd bought me an SUV for my eighteenth birthday, specifically so I could come home more often, and though they drove me crazy most of the time, I loved having my own vehicle. Of course, my mother threatened to take it away from me practically on a daily basis, so I had to be careful. That had been one of the main reasons I'd run from the party—she definitely would have taken the SUV if I'd been caught drinking at a party—so I took a minute to breathe as I pulled into the garage of my parents' house.

I was bound to have to answer a thousand questions about my weekend and I didn't feel like it. I also had to work on a big project, which I planned to turn in before spring break so I could coast through the rest of the semester. I'd never coasted through anything in my life, and despite the pressure on me to make a decision about medical school, I had a secret that made me giddily happy. Unbeknownst to anyone, I hadn't even applied to medical school. My parents thought I had, but I hadn't and didn't plan to. I wanted to continue with graduate school and get my Ph.D., but I didn't know in what field yet, despite my current track. All I knew for sure was that I didn't want to be a medical doctor.

Too bad I couldn't make them understand.

"Hi, honey." Mom looked up from where she was typing on her computer. She'd retired from teaching freshman English at Burlington University to write a book, and from what she'd told me, it wasn't going well. I tried not to ask too many questions, though.

"Hi, Mom." I smiled but kept moving up the stairs toward my room.

"Where are you going?"

"Homework," I called back.

"I was thinking we need to talk about—" she began.

"Not now!" I yelled back, closing my bedroom door behind me.

Medical school was her favorite topic and she brought it up at least twice a day when I was home. Not to mention every time we spoke on the phone. It was exhausting and I kept hoping she'd give me a little time to grow up and figure out who I was beyond academics. My whole life to date had been about studying, test scores, and accomplishments. No one ever asked what I wanted, or what made me happy, and sometimes it hurt. What more did they want from me and why was my future their problem? I had a general idea what I wanted and where I was going, but I was only nineteen. I had time. At least I should have had time.

I didn't date, I had a limited number of friends, and yet I rarely had time to myself. Mostly I studied or kept up with my students since I was a teaching assistant too. I also tutored part-time, which was really my only source of independence. I made a lot more money under the table than my parents knew about, and I'd been squirreling it away. For what, I wasn't sure, but it felt good to have something that was just mine.

"Ellie?" Mom stuck her head in the door and I managed not to sigh out loud, though I definitely did on the inside.

My mother and I had a difficult relationship. While a lot of mothers and daughters said that, it was intense at my house. I was an only child and not just the family's little princess, but also a literal genius. I was nineteen and already had two undergraduate degrees, but instead of being proud of me, my parents had professional expectations that were nothing like my own.

"Homework, Mom."

"I know." She came in and sat on the edge of the bed. "I just wanted to see if you'd heard from any of the medical schools you applied to." Mom wanted me to become a world-famous doctor, maybe with a focus in oncology, where I would potentially find a cure for cancer and win a Nobel Prize or something.

"Nothing."

Duh.

"You could stay at Moo U and—"

"I'm not staying at Moo U," I said quietly.

Our eyes met and she scowled. "You've been preparing for this your whole life," she said. "I understand you want to have fun and party, like other teens your age, but don't you see what a waste that would be? You have a gift, Ellie. You're *special*."

"I'm tired," I interjected, though it was more a state of mind than a physical issue. "There's so much more to life than academics and you don't let me explore any of it. It's not normal to live like this."

"Don't be a drama queen," she snapped. "I just told you—you're special. You have gifts very few people have. Letting you waste your incredible talents with teenage boys and frat house parties, or whatever other nonsense you're thinking about, would be criminal."

"Oh, please." I managed to keep from rolling my eyes since it always annoyed her and I didn't need to set her off. "I'm nineteen with two bachelor's degrees. I'm educated and even employable, so I have time to—"

"Employable doing what?" she demanded. "Teaching? That's ridiculous. With your talents, you'll be chief of staff at some hospital before you're thirty. You'll have the most illustrious and dignified career and make all of us proud."

"So you won't be proud of me if I become a college professor or a research scientist at the CDC who discovers a life-saving vaccine or something like that?"

She pursed her lips. "Well, of course, love, but you have to trust me to know what's best for you."

This time I did sigh and just looked back at my laptop. "Mom, I really do have homework to do. Can we not talk about this over the holidays? Can't we just be a family for once?"

She looked taken aback, but then nodded. "All right. I'll see you at dinner."

She let herself out and I closed my eyes. Every time we had this conversation, I wanted to cry. And never more so than right now.

3

PATRICK

The first week of classes was usually pretty easy, focusing more on buying the requisite books, checking out the syllabus and gauging how to juggle the workload with hockey. My classes this semester were kind of a bitch, though, and I had five of them. I'd done that by design, hoping to make my course load in my senior year lighter, but now I was regretting it. Statistics was probably going to be the death of me, and based on the dour expression on the professor's face as he'd given us an overview of the class, I wasn't looking forward to Tuesday and Thursday mornings at all.

My sociology class seemed pretty interesting, though, so at least I had that to look forward to, but I was stressed about the semester in general. There were no grades yet, but studying wasn't my thing and with Coach Keller requesting weekly progress reports, it would only take one fuck-up to get me benched.

Which was why I was heading to the library on Friday at lunchtime. My two morning classes were over and tonight's game was at home, so I was finally meeting up with that tutor Paxton had set me up with. I couldn't risk getting behind, so I was starting right now, at week one, even though it was going to cost money I didn't have. Paxton and I both worked during the summer to save up for the school year, but it was January and funds were starting to run low. Paying for tutoring was going to suck, but what choice did I have? I couldn't risk hockey.

I walked into the library and looked around. Ellie's text said she had long blond hair, was five foot five, and would be wearing a pink Taylor Swift hoodie. I spotted a blond ponytail on a girl wearing a pink hoodie but she had her back to me so I wasn't sure if that was her. There was something familiar about her though, and I approached gingerly, wondering why I had a sense of déjà vu.

"Excuse me, are you…" My voice trailed off as familiar blue eyes looked up at me.

We both froze. It was the chick from the party and, great fucking balls of fire, she had on a Taylor Swift hoodie.

"I'm Ellie." She stared at me for a moment, her eyes narrowing slightly. "Are you…"

"Patrick Graham." I held out my hand with a teasing grin. "Also known as the guy who helped you escape from the cops."

Her mouth opened as recognition slowly dawned. She stared at me a little longer, her hand resting in mine as our eyes remained locked. "It's really you… I mean, you cut your hair and shaved off your beard… Wait, now it all makes sense. You're Paxton's twin. That's why you looked so familiar but with the beard and long hair…"

I chuckled. "Yup."

"You left before I could get your name." Her tone was soft but it felt like a gentle admonishment.

"You needed to get out of there." I sank into the chair next to hers. "I told you I'd find you."

She frowned. "You did?"

"You didn't hear me?" I cocked my head a little. "After I told you to go, I called out that I'd find you."

"I knew you said something but couldn't hear it." She smiled, dipping her head almost shyly.

"So, uh, hi." I felt silly all of a sudden. "I guess I found you.

I'm Patrick." Geez, we'd already introduced ourselves. How lame was I?

"Ellie."

Our gazes met and there it was, that weirdly intense connection. I didn't understand it because even though I thought she was beautiful, Paxton had been right that she wasn't my usual type. She wasn't wearing makeup today, making her look a lot younger than she had at the party, and kind of innocent. She was a girl-next-door type while I typically went for the big-city-hottie types, but something happened every time we saw each other. Even now, without the benefit of alcohol and the party atmosphere, the air was charged with intensity.

"I feel like we should get a do-over from the other night," I said after a minute. "I was going to ask you your name, maybe get your number…"

"Way too much excitement for all that," she said with a laugh.

"Never jumped off a deck before?" I teased.

"Definitely not," she said, shaking her head. "I don't know what I was thinking… I could have broken my neck."

"I wouldn't have let you fall."

"Somehow I knew that." She cocked her head. "I don't know why I knew it, but I did."

"Sometimes you just know."

We were staring at each other like lovesick puppies or something. The last time I'd gazed into a girl's eyes without jumping her bones was high school. This was stupid. The whole reason Paxton had hooked us up was so she could *tutor* me. I wasn't supposed to be thinking about her bright blue eyes or pink lips. Or what she might look like naked.

Shit.

I tore my eyes away and fumbled to dig out my schedule. "Anyway, now that we've found each other, these are my classes: Sociology, Statistics, Global Business Practices, Marketing Management, and Database Management."

She nodded. "Okay, well, business isn't my thing, but I've

heard those classes aren't bad, so I can teach you study skills that will help you keep up with them. On the other hand, based on what Paxton told me, I'm guessing Statistics is going to be the bane of your existence."

I chuckled. "Yup. Sociology seems like fun, but stat is the class stressing me out. I've put it off as long as I could, but I've got almost enough credits to graduate so I had to take it."

"Aren't you a junior?" she asked.

"Yeah, but I started off with some AP credits thanks to my super-anal twin brother, and that got me ahead. Also, I've taken a class each of the last two summers, which put me a little more ahead. Technically, I'll only need three classes next year to graduate."

"Then why are you taking so many now?"

"Because I have a pending contract with the Las Vegas Sidewinders and if I decide to go pro at the end of the school year, I still want to be close enough to getting my degree, even if I have to take one online class per semester while playing professionally. That's also why I left a couple of easier classes for the end."

"You're thinking of leaving school early?"

"I want to get my degree, but my dad is pushing me to go pro, so I don't know what I'm going to do." I paused. I barely knew this girl and I was already telling her things I rarely even admitted to myself, much less a stranger.

"Sounds like me," she said quietly. She was staring down at the piece of paper with my schedule on it, tracing little circles on it with her finger, her voice thoughtful. "My parents want me to go to medical school but I want to stay in grad school and get a Ph.D. Personally, I want to stay as far under the radar as possible and stay away from people as much as possible as well. I was much happier doing research. My degrees are in biology and computer science, and the ultimate goal is to eventually get my Ph.D. in something like biotechnology. Then I got way off course with this damn computer science graduate program… And my mom isn't on board for anything."

"You're a doctor either way, though, right?" I asked curiously.

"Well, medical doctor versus doctor of philosophy, and I honestly have no interest in seeing patients. I want to do research, work in a lab, maybe do a little teaching, but only at the college level. Not, like, high school or anything."

"I get that," I responded.

"Anyway." She cleared her throat, as if she'd just realized the serious turn our conversation had taken. "You're done with classes by 10:45 or so Monday, Wednesday, and Friday, and by one o'clock on Tuesdays and Thursdays. What's your practice schedule?"

We discussed the logistics of my hockey schedule, including a lot of weekend travel, and she pulled out what appeared to be a thick, spiral-bound planner. She flipped it open and stared at the calendar.

"Okay, we can do Monday and Wednesday nights from seven to nine. Does that work for you?"

I immediately nodded. "Anything you've got works for me as long as I can get to class, hockey practice, and games. My coach is expecting weekly progress reports, so I can't get behind."

"Anything due right now? I know this was the first week of class, but there's usually something."

"Uh, I have some reading to do for Sociology and Global Business, and some practice problems to do in stat."

"Then let's start with stat. If that's going to be your biggest problem, we should make sure you're getting the concepts from day one."

"Okay." I looked at her, taking in her delicate profile as she made notes in her calendar. She was prettier than I'd initially thought, with soft features and creamy skin. She reminded me of old-fashioned ice cream sundaes and drive-in movies, which made no fucking sense, but that's what came to mind when I looked at her.

"You, um, want to start now?" she asked quietly.

"Sure." I pulled the textbook and a notebook out of my backpack and set them on the desk. If studying meant I got to spend more time with her, I was all in.

We talked and studied for the next hour, with her patiently explaining basic statistics concepts and me fighting to stay on task instead of asking her to go out on a date with me. I wasn't sure why it was so important, but I had to know if this magnetism between us was real or me just being a horndog.

"Are you going to the game tonight?" I asked when we started packing up. I had to start getting ready to go, no matter how much I wanted to continue hanging out with Ellie.

"Game?" She looked blank.

"The hockey game. You know, the team I'm the captain of. We're playing at home tonight."

"Oh." She shook her head. "I don't go to many. I'm usually studying."

"But you could go to one, right? I mean, as my tutor, you show me how good you are at academics. It's only fair you get to see what I'm good at."

ELLIE

I had a feeling he was good at a lot more than hockey, and the way he'd been looking at me made me a tiny bit uncomfortable and a whole lot excited. Uncomfortable because no one had ever looked at me like that before—as if he wanted to see inside of me —and excited because, well, no one had ever looked at me like that before. No one tall and blue-eyed and muscular. No one funny and strong with a warm voice and an easy, infectious laugh. He made me smile. It was weird, because we barely knew each other and I was a nerd of epic proportions, but he wasn't looking at me like a guy who thought I was dorky.

"I, um, I guess I could," I finally responded when I realized he'd been waiting for me to answer.

"Don't sound so glum," he said, laughing. "It'll be fun."

"I know, but I don't want to go by myself." I wrinkled my nose. "Maybe I could get my friend Harley to come with me. Let me see what she's doing."

I sent her a quick text and hoped she'd go with me. We hadn't been friends for long but she was fun and easy-going so she might be up for it.

"I really have to go," he said, standing up and throwing his backpack over his very broad shoulders. "But let's find each other after the game, okay? We can go get a coffee or something and you can tell me what you thought."

"I, um, cool." Holy shit, was he asking me out on a date?

"I'll see you later, Ellie." He reached out and squeezed my shoulder. "This was way more fun than I ever thought statistics could be."

"I'll do my best to keep it that way," I said, my shoulder burning from where he'd touched me.

"See you tonight." He winked and then turned and moved toward the exit.

Harley and I got to the arena early. Mostly because I wanted to check everything out and get a feel for what it was going to be like. I knew less than nothing about hockey, so I'd spent a couple of hours devouring everything I could find online about the sport. Not to mention videos on YouTube that featured Patrick freakin' Graham. You didn't have to know anything about hockey to see how gorgeous he was on the ice. His movements were smooth and fluid, but filled with speed and strength. Hockey was actually two sports in one, I realized, the game itself coupled with ice skating.

I could ice-skate, but definitely not like Patrick. It was as if he became one with the ice, and with each subsequent video I'd watched, I'd become that much more enthralled with him. Of course, he was also a huge deal among up-and-coming hockey players. He'd been in the top ten draft picks overall the year he'd been chosen by the team in Las Vegas. I didn't know much about how all of it worked, but it was a big deal.

"I can't believe we're going to a hockey game," Harley grumbled as we walked into the rink. "You hate sports."

"But I like Patrick," I pointed out.

"But why do I have to be here?"

"Because you're my friend?"

She laughed. "Okay, fine."

The arena was huge and we looked around, impressed. I felt kind of bad that I'd never been to a hockey game before, but I'd been fifteen when I'd gotten here and had been pretty intimidated by everything. Mostly, I hunkered down in my room and studied. My mom had made sure I didn't have any fun either, keeping tabs on me and showing up at my dorm room at all hours since she'd worked here my first year on campus. She'd calmed down once I'd been here for a year or so, but she still tried to control my life. Even now that I was a legal adult.

"Let's go down to the ice and watch them warm up," Harley suggested, heading in that direction.

I followed amiably since I figured it was as good an idea as any.

The team was on the ice, skating around, shooting the puck into the goal. My research told me Patrick wore the number fifty-one, and I scanned the jerseys, looking for him.

And there he was.

I'd liked him better with his hair long and with a beard, but he was gorgeous no matter what. Dark hair that was now cropped close to his head, blue eyes that made me a little weak in the knees, and though they were covered by his uniform now, I knew how well his shoulders filled out a Henley. I seemed to recall a great backside too, but I was trying not to think about that.

As a nineteen-year-old virgin, I had no business checking him out in such great physical detail, but I couldn't seem to help it. I'd thought of little else since the party two weeks ago, and seeing him earlier today had been epic. I'd been somewhat tongue-tied, as was usual with me when it came to guys, but he'd just kept staring at me and I'd had this strange urge to touch him. Not inappropriately, but to run my hands over the bulge of his biceps. Maybe across his flat stomach and—okay, that was a little inappropriate, but I'd never been in a situation like this where I was pretty sure the hottest guy I'd ever met liked me. Especially since it turned out he was the identical twin of my friend Paxton. The long hair and beard had thrown me off, and now I felt a little silly, but there was no mistaking the pull between us that was way different than anything I'd ever felt with Paxton.

I wasn't delusional, of course. Patrick was probably just looking to get me naked, but that was okay at this point in my life. My mother had kept me on such a tight leash, all I wanted was to taste a little freedom. If Patrick Graham could assist me in that endeavor, who was I to say no?

I was so lost in thought I almost missed him skating up to the glass and stopping, his eyes meeting mine. Those damn blue eyes of his. They were fixed on me and I was mesmerized. I think I smiled, but until he winked and skated away, I was pretty much rooted to the spot.

"Dude." Harley elbowed me, hard.

"Ow!" I turned to her in confusion. "What'd you do that for?"

"You were practically drooling. At least play a little hard to get."

I scowled. "I wouldn't even know how. Let's go find our seats."

The game was exciting as hell and when Patrick scored the first goal of the night, I was on my feet, screaming at the top of my lungs. I'd never been excited about a sporting event in my life, but this was different. It was fast-paced and exhilarating, and adding Patrick to the mix made it that much better.

"Okay, this was cooler than I thought," Harley admitted as we headed out of the arena with the crowd. "It was a little hard to follow the puck, but I definitely want to come to another one."

"Me too," I agreed.

"So you meeting up with your new boyfriend?"

"We're just friends," I said, though my face felt a little hot. I'd never had a boyfriend so I wasn't completely sure how I'd define it. Hell, I'd only gone out on a handful of real dates and they'd all been disasters.

"But are you meeting up with him?"

"He said we would." I dug in my pocket as my phone buzzed, and I saw a text from Patrick.

PATRICK: *Are you still here?*

ELLIE: I'm here!
PATRICK: Meet me in front of the arena in thirty minutes. I'll find you.
ELLIE: See you then.

I turned to Harley. "I guess we're meeting in half an hour."

"Okay, cool. Then I'm gonna head home because I have a hot date."

"You do?" My eyes widened. "With who? You didn't tell me you had a date!"

"He just texted. I met him in my accounting class this week. He's kinda dorky but has a great body. We'll see."

"Sounds interesting."

"I'll keep you posted," Harley said as we walked toward the exit. "But as for you, don't go giving up your V-card on the first date!"

I laughed. "He's probably not even interested in me and is just being nice to get a discount on tutoring or something. Don't worry. I'm kinda desperate but not desperate enough to make a fool of myself."

"Just have fun, Ellie." In a rare moment of sincerity, Harley turned to me, her dark eyes searching my face. "You let your mom and professors and everyone else put so much pressure on you— do something for yourself for once. Even if he's just looking for a free tutoring ride or whatever, he's the captain of the hockey team. He's hotter than the Mohave in July. You say he's nice. What else is there, and honestly, what do you have to lose? Enjoy it. One date, friendship, whatever it is."

"I'm going to try," I said softly.

Patrick found me twenty minutes later, coming from inside the arena. He had that same lighthearted smile on his face he'd had when we first met, even while his eyes blazed with intensity.

"Hey," he said.

"Hi!" I was a little breathless just looking at him and letting it sink in that he'd come to me, so I continued without missing a beat. "The game was amazing! I loved it. Watching you fly down the ice... There are no words for how cool it is. How do you *do* that?"

He seemed almost sheepish as he shrugged. "Dunno. Been skating and playing hockey my whole life. It's what I do. Kind of like how you do science."

Our eyes met and I bit my lip. "Well, it's cool as shit."

"Thanks."

"Thanks for inviting me. I had a great time."

"I'm glad." He paused. "So, you want to do something now? Go to a party? I know of one happening. Or maybe someplace quieter where we can talk? We could even go into town if you want to get an Uber."

"I have a car," I replied. "But I'm only nineteen, so not old enough to drink, which means we're limited on where we can go if we go into Burlington, but I'm game for just about anything."

"What about Tito's?"

Tito's Wood-Fired Pizza was a local place that served delicious Detroit-style deep-dish pizza.

"Oh, yum, pizza..." I nodded enthusiastically. "I skipped dinner, so that sounds good."

He offered me his elbow and I stared at it for a fraction of a second until I realized what he was doing and my heart skipped at least three beats. This was the equivalent of holding hands, right? Dammit, why was I so inept at this kind of thing? He was looking down at me curiously and I couldn't just stand here, so I slid my hand through his bent elbow as we started to walk.

"Why'd you skip dinner?" he asked.

"I was trying to get some homework done since I was going out tonight, and then it was late and I forgot." I wasn't going to admit I'd been too nervous to eat.

"You want to drive? It's a bit of a walk from here."

"Sure." I closed my fingers around his forearm as we continued through the parking lot to my car.

I dug out my keys and Patrick got into the passenger seat.

"Pepperoni on your pizza?" he asked.

"And sausage," I replied firmly.

"Girl after my own heart."

Those words made me stupidly happy.

Girl after his own heart? Be still *my* heart.

5

PATRICK

"I took a break from studying this afternoon to read up on the rules of hockey," Ellie said once we were seated and had ordered. "I'm going to need you to explain icing to me because no matter how many times I read the definition, I couldn't picture the reason for it in my head when I was watching the game."

"You took a break and already learned enough about hockey to ask questions about different calls?" I shook my head.

"I...um, sorta have a photographic memory," she said quietly, almost as if that embarrassed her. "I read a few articles for beginners so I wouldn't be completely lost."

I was more impressed than surprised since I already knew she was some kind of genius. It hadn't come up before now, and I certainly wasn't going to ask, but a photographic memory made sense. "Okay, so I think the easiest way to explain it is to tell you what it's intended to prevent. Suppose your team was putting on a big offensive push and really controlling the puck. If the other team gets it for a second and just fires it all the way down the ice without any repercussions, then they can get a line change and all your hard work is for nothing."

"But isn't that the point? To stop the other team from scoring?"

"Yes, but not by giving the other team an easy way out. Your opponent has to carry the puck at least over the center red line or it would just be a free-for-all, sending it up and down the ice."

"I see." She nodded. "That makes more sense. I have other questions, but I'm thinking we'll save offsides for another time."

I laughed. "Or I can explain it now. Whatever you prefer."

"I think I need to go to another game before I ask any more questions. That way, I'll have specific questions to specific events that are fresh in both our minds."

"I guess that means you're coming to tomorrow night's game too?"

"I think so." Her eyes met mine. "If you want me to."

"I do." I sat back as our drinks arrived. She'd ordered a root beer and I had a cola. I didn't drink much soda, but I could afford the calories and sugar after a game. Not to mention the five days a week I spent working out or practicing. It was a good thing I did, too, because I liked to eat.

Our food arrived then and I was glad for the distraction. The pizza here was awesome and the second the scent hit my nostrils, my stomach growled. They made both deep-dish and regular pizza, and they were all amazing. We'd gotten deep-dish and Ellie had already grabbed a piece.

"Do you eat here often?" Ellie was asking me as she lifted the first piece to her mouth.

"Not real often," I said. "I try to eat better than this, so I stick to the dining hall where I can get salads and grilled chicken or fish. Diet's an important part of playing at the level I do."

"I'll bet. Luckily, there are no such restrictions in academia." She lifted the pizza and opened her mouth, her tongue snaking out to circle a strand of melted cheese.

My zipper was suddenly uncomfortable as I imagined her doing other things with that tongue, and I quickly reached for my own slice of pizza, determined to distract myself. I took a bite and the flavor—all garlicky sauce and cheesy deliciousness—sent me down a more culinary path. That was probably good since Ellie appeared to be enjoying the hell out of hers.

Being on a date with someone who enjoyed her food was novel. Most women picked at their salads and drank too much, which had always been a turnoff for me. Of course, I didn't go out on real dates very often. I'd only been on a handful since getting to Moo U, and that was by design because my plan was to be untethered until I went pro.

Watching my twin fall in love this past fall must have rubbed off on me or something, because no matter what Paxton thought, Ellie was absolutely my type. Maybe not the type I usually hooked up with, but the type I could picture myself with beyond a roll in the sack. That was the difference with her. The weird thing was that I'd technically only known her a day, the night we'd met notwithstanding, and now I wanted to sit here and talk to her all night. That was weird, right?

We ate in silence for a while and finally she sat back and motioned for the waitress to bring us refills on our drinks.

"I'm stuffed," she said, "but it was so good. I could eat here every night and I don't think I'd ever get sick of it."

"Get sick of it? No. But I probably wouldn't be able to skate for shit with all the weight I'd gain."

She waved her hand. "Ah, whatever, you'd find ways to work it off."

The moment she said it, our eyes met and hers widened.

"I didn't mean it like that!" she said, before dissolving into giggles. Her face was bright red, which was both endearing and adorable, and I wondered if she was as innocent as she seemed.

"Uh-huh." I wasn't sure whether to tease her or let her off easy. It had been a long time since I'd been with a girl who blushed this easily.

"I meant with hockey," she said, shaking her head.

"If you say so." I grinned and took a sip of soda.

"Speaking of hockey," she said, delicately dabbing her mouth with her napkin even though she was done eating, "do you study at all on the weekends or is it all hockey?"

"All hockey," I admitted. "If we have away games, there's

travel involved, and I might do some reading or look at notes on the way home, but on the way there, I'm focused on the game. On a night like tonight, after a big win, there's no way I could concentrate on school stuff, I'm way too wound up, so Fridays and Saturdays aren't study days. Sunday could be an all-day thing, but usually I'm off doing something fun."

"Balance," she said with a grin. "A few hours of studying, a few hours of fun."

I made a face. "Yeah, I've never been good about that kind of balance, but I have to try because Coach won't be happy if my grades drop."

"We'll stay on top of them," she said. "In my experience, which is a lot when it comes to studying, you always do the stuff you like the least first. That way, doing the fun stuff is sort of like a reward. I used to do all the non-science stuff first because I don't love it, but I knew all the biology and harder topics were coming, which gave me the energy to keep going."

"For me, I don't love any of it. Some of it isn't as bad as others, but mostly I prefer sports."

"Why didn't you major in something sports-related?"

"Too much science," I quipped.

We both laughed.

"I might be offended," she said, though she was still smiling.

"Nah. I wish I was as smart as you."

She chewed her lip for a moment, all playfulness gone. "No, you really don't," she said after a moment. "You wouldn't believe the expectations once people realize you're smart. I can't ever get a B. *Ever.*"

"You've never gotten a B?" I couldn't even imagine.

"Nope. I got a ninety-four on a paper once and my mother was apoplectic. Luckily, now that I'm a legal adult and my education is free thanks to scholarships and my teaching, she doesn't have access to my grades, but I still feel that pressure. There's *always* pressure. Pressure about grades, about med school, about my career, my future, how many Nobel Prizes I might win..." Her voice trailed off. "Sorry. I might get bitter sometimes."

"Believe me, I get it." I nodded. "My dad played pro hockey but he got an injury that ended his career early on. He had no education, no skills other than hockey, so he wasn't very employable and it hurt our family financially. We always struggled, so now all he talks about is getting Pax and me to the big leagues. He wanted us to go pro without even going to college, but we pushed back on that. Now he's saying it's time, that we're ready, and even though he might be right, we both want to get our degrees. Paxton could graduate now. He took a thousand AP classes in high school and started with something like two semesters of credit. So he can graduate in May if he wants to. I still need three classes after this and I'm kind of afraid if I leave at the end of this year, I'll never finish."

"There's no hockey in the summer, right? You could take summer classes."

"I know. To be honest, I don't think about much else lately. My dad's voice is in my ear constantly, telling me to go pro. Then I look at Paxton, who's ready to graduate, and I could kick myself for not working as hard academically as he has, so I can graduate this spring too."

"Self-flagellation and regret about the past are counterproductive," she said. "The best way to move forward is to focus on what to do now. What do you want now? Go pro or stay in college? Make the money or get the degree so you have a backup plan? Which thing is most important to you?"

"Both," I admitted sadly. "I want the degree but I'm ready to go pro. And if Paxton leaves at the end of the year, it won't be the same without him. I can't imagine getting on the ice every night knowing he's playing in Seattle."

"I'll bet it's going to be hard for you guys to be separated," she said. "Does that make you nervous?"

I looked at her in surprise. No one had ever asked me what it might be like for us to be apart once we left college. We'd played together since we were practically babies, and that was one thing I'd tried not to think about too much, the idea that he and I would be playing not just on separate teams, but against each other sometimes. The media had asked us something like that back when we'd first been drafted, but it had been lighthearted and laced with excitement then. It was different now that it was closer to becoming a reality.

"It does," I said slowly. "Not nervous so much as sad. I've never been away from him for any length of time. And while that might sound kind of weird and needy, it's not about that. We don't *need* each other, so to speak, but we rely on each other in ways that are hard to explain. Our bond as twins is special. Our mom died when we were ten and we're not close to our dad, so it's going to take getting used to. Not having him on the ice will be one thing, but not being able to run things past him, or hang out after practice, well, that's not going to be easy."

"I can't even imagine," she said. "He's literally your other half —physically and emotionally. It makes sense that you're going to miss him."

"In a way, it's already started," I admitted. "Now that he has a girlfriend, and it's looking pretty serious, he's already moving in a different direction. It's weird."

"It's ironic because that's all I want," she said. "To move in a totally different direction than my life so far. I don't want to go to medical school, which has been the direction I've been heading since I was about fourteen. Now I want to explore a bunch of different options, maybe teach a few years, wrap my head around all this adulting stuff. I've only been an adult a little over a year, and so far, it's been really freakin' hard."

"I've been an adult three years and it's hard, so I think it takes a while. It's nice to know others are going through it too, though, so you don't feel so alone."

"I've always felt alone," she whispered.

"Not anymore," I said, putting one of my hands on top of hers. "Now you have me."

"That's so nice."

I hadn't thought about being nice to her, beyond a general modicum of manners, but the grateful look in her eyes made me feel good. Hell, everything about her made me feel good. And I hadn't been expecting that at all.

ELLIE

I hoped he wouldn't run screaming from the restaurant at the serious turn our conversation had taken, but he was so easy to talk to. We had a lot in common, which I never would have imagined. His overbearing father, my overbearing mother, and a lot of concern about this whole idea of adulting. He was twenty-one, and hadn't been nearly as sheltered as I had, but I heard a lot of the same insecurities in his voice that I often felt in myself.

We talked and drank soda until we were the last people in the restaurant and we finally paid the bill and walked out to my car. I didn't want this night to end but he had another game tomorrow and I needed to spend the whole day working on my research paper if I was going to go out again tomorrow night.

"Where do you live?" I asked him when we got into the car. It was a frigid January night and I shivered as I waited for the heat to kick in.

"In the apartments on Bellamy," he said.

I knew just where those apartments were located since a lot of Moo U students lived there and it wasn't far. I'd considered living there too but I got my room and board for free between being a resident assistant in the dorm and my teaching, and I liked the fact that I didn't have to count on my parents for housing. They already paid for my car, insurance, and phone, so I'd been willing to suck it up for the tiniest bit of freedom.

He told me where to drop him off and I pulled up to the curb.

"Tonight was great," he said, turning to me. "I'm really looking forward to doing it again tomorrow night."

"You are?" The words slipped out before I could stop them, and I mentally grimaced, wishing I knew how to be a little coy, a little flirty, instead of insecure and out of my league.

"Well, yeah." He frowned. "Aren't you?"

"I haven't dated anyone since I came to college," I blurted out. "I was only fifteen then, so I was too young for college guys, and now that I'm legal, most guys think I'm dorky. So I don't know how this works. If you're just trying to be nice so I'll tutor you, you don't have to because I'd do it anyway. As a favor to Paxton."

"You think this is about tutoring?" He looked both a little mad and a little sad, which confused me even more.

"I don't know why the captain of the hockey team—who can and does sleep with everything that moves—is interested in me when not a single guy on campus ever has been before."

There. I'd said it. It was out in the open now and if nothing else, he'd know I wasn't naïve enough to think he really wanted to date me.

"You haven't gone out on a single date the whole time you've been here?" he asked, ignoring everything else I'd said.

I shook my head. "Not a real date, like we had tonight. I've met guys at the library or for coffee, but never like this."

"Their loss is my gain." He reached out and pushed one side of my hair behind my ear. "I thought we had a connection," he said softly. "That night at the party. I think you're pretty and smart and sweet. It has nothing to do with tutoring or anything like that. I don't know what other guys see when they look at you, but I'll be honest and say that someone as smart as you is probably a little intimidating."

"And you're not, um, intimidated?" Why did I say "um" all the time? I sounded like a nervous twelve-year-old.

"No." He leaned forward, his eyes locked with mine. "Not even a little. And I think maybe the best way to prove that to you is like this."

Oh-shit-oh-shit-oh-shit—he was kissing me. His lips were lightly pressed to mine, caressing them as if they were made of glass. Gentle whispers of skin against my mouth, nothing like I'd imagined kissing a hottie like Patrick would be. I'd only been kissed a handful of times before and it had always been sloppy and wet; this was ridiculously sweet. And definitely not sloppy.

Not even when he slid his tongue along the seam of my lips, gently prying them apart. My mouth opened of its own volition, anxious for more, because nothing had prepared me for this. When our tongues finally met one another, it was like a magnetic force had drawn them together and I couldn't do anything but go along for the ride. It felt like my whole body was involved, instead of just my mouth, and I let myself get swept away.

I might have whimpered in protest when he finally pulled away, and the look in his eyes was one I'd only ever read about in books. I didn't know men actually looked at women that way. It didn't have to be love or anything that deep, but sheer, unadulterated desire? I'd never seen it outside of movies and this was way, way better because it was directed at me. The fact that I turned him on enough to put that look there, well, that was something new to me and it did all kinds of things to my nether regions.

"I should go," he said softly, still watching my face with that look that made me shiver all over.

"It's late," I said out loud, though I really wanted to sit here long enough for him to kiss me again.

"I had fun tonight. And I'd like to go out with you again after the game tomorrow…if you want to."

"I…yes." I almost said "um" again but caught myself. "Yes, I'd like to."

"Good night, Ellie." He pressed his lips to mine, chastely this time, and then got out of the car and bounded up the steps of his building.

I was in so much trouble.

For the first time in a long time, I had trouble studying the next day. I kept staring off into space, doodling Patrick's name on the notebook in front of me. I had most of my stuff on my laptop, but some of my notes were handwritten so I could reference different things while I worked. I also had textbooks open and Post-it notes everywhere. My research was all over the place, but I worked best that way, and normally, having everything spread out on my desk kept me focused.

My phone buzzed and I looked down to see a text from Harley.

> *HARLEY: Well?! Are you seriously keeping me in suspense?*
> *ELLIE: We had pizza and talked until Tito's closed. Then I took him home.*
> *HARLEY: That's it? No hanky-panky?*
> *ELLIE: There might have been a little hanky. No panky, though.*
> *HARLEY: What?!*
> *ELLIE: We kissed. That's all. Nothing earth-shattering.*
> *HARLEY: And?*
> *ELLIE: And what?*
> *HARLEY: Was it good? Did you like it? Are you going out again? I'm going to kill you if you don't tell me everything!*
> *ELLIE: LOL. We kissed good night. That's all. It was nice.*
> *HARLEY: Are you going to the game tonight?*
> *ELLIE: I am.*
> *HARLEY: Oh, shit's about to get real for you… I'll meet you there! We obviously need to talk.*
> *ELLIE: See you there.*

Harley took off right after the game and I waited in front of the arena for Patrick to get there. I'd spent a lot of time getting ready tonight, even though I was in jeans and a Moo U hoodie, but I'd been waffling between keeping my makeup light so Patrick could see the real me, or putting it on heavy, which was how it had been the night we'd met. He'd seen me both ways already, since I hadn't been wearing makeup when we'd met up on Friday, and I finally opted to wear a little mascara and lip gloss but to keep it simple. Either he liked me or he didn't, and the real me only wore makeup on special occasions or to a party or something. Most days, I put my hair in a ponytail, threw on a little mascara and ran out the door. I'd put in a little more effort than that for a date with Patrick, but I wasn't going to go nuts either.

I'd only recently learned about hair and makeup, and at nine-teen, I figured I was way behind the eight ball in this department. I'd gotten my braces off two years ago and started wearing lip gloss. From there, I'd learned to tame my frizzy mop with good hair products and a flat iron. Then I'd moved to mascara, eyeliner, and eventually a whole routine that included foundation and bronzer. Mom had been horrified, saying I had better things to do with my time, but she'd gotten quiet when I'd pointed out she never left the house without makeup. She'd never brought it up again and I'd spent a good part of last summer watching makeup tutorials on YouTube.

I didn't know much about much when it came to dating, but I knew enough not to be something I wasn't. I wanted to grow up and live a little, not change who I was. I assumed some change would happen organically, but I wasn't thinking that far ahead. Mostly, I wanted to spend as much time as possible looking into Patrick Graham's deep blue eyes while pretending I was someone else. Someone who had a hot hockey hunk for a boyfriend. There had been no Patrick Grahams in my fantasies, but now there was one in my life.

I was a little giddy as I waited for him, and though my rational mind warned me not to get attached, I couldn't help it. I'd never had a guy interested in me before, not a hot, sexy adult guy. There had been some childhood crushes, and a handful of guys who'd shown some half-hearted interest, but this was different. Patrick was a man. A sexy, virile one at that, and while I had zero real-life experience, I'd read a lot and even watched a little porn. I was curious about sex, of course, and having a bachelor's degree in biology, it was an important part of the field, but I'd assumed I'd be a virgin until I was thirty.

"Hey." The gentle tap on my shoulder made me jump and I turned to see those beautiful blue eyes looking down at me.

"Hi." I moved a little closer to him, tilting up my head in what I hoped was an inviting gesture. Sure enough, he bent his head and pressed a light kiss on my lips.

"I've been thinking about kissing you all day," he said softly.

"Me too."

He wrapped his fingers around mine and tugged my hand. "Let's get out of here. You want to go back to Tito's or do something else?"

"Let's go somewhere quiet," I replied. "Somewhere we can be alone."

PATRICK

Somewhere we could be *alone*? The last thing I wanted was to be alone with her. Don't get me wrong, I wanted to. I wanted to be alone with her more than I wanted to take my next breath of air, but that would be dangerous. Sex wasn't always my priority, but it was up there, and I already knew Ellie wasn't the kind of girl you just hooked up with. If we got to the sex portion of the program, there was going to be more to us than hooking up, and it was too soon to know that.

Jesus, who was I and where had that mature, responsible-sounding thought come from?

She was waiting for me to say something, though, and knowing I was the first guy she'd dated as an adult meant I had to be careful because I also didn't want her to think I wasn't into her.

"Could we get something to eat first?" I asked. "I'm starving."

"What if we picked up Tito's and brought it back to my dorm? That way we'll have some privacy, but you can still eat and I can keep an eye on the Saturday night shenanigans. Sometimes it gets rowdy."

"Uh, sure."

Shit. This was bad. This was really, really bad. But it also made sense for her to need to be in her dorm if she was an R.A. And I'd look like a jerk if I said I didn't want to. Especially since I did.

I could spend the evening doing nothing but kissing her, right? It had been a long time since I'd had to hold back, but Ellie wasn't like anyone I'd ever met. I'd never believed in love at first sight, but we had some heavy-duty chemistry going on that I'd never experienced with anyone else. And I liked it. Well, mostly, I liked her.

Luckily, I hadn't been lying about being hungry and by the time we got to her dorm room, I was genuinely thinking about the pizza. We settled at the small table she had in the corner, and she handed me a soda and a paper towel, and then sat across from me.

"I'm definitely not set up for company," she said, chuckling.

I looked around. "Maybe not, but your room is nicer than the one Paxton and I had our freshman year."

"Well, as an R.A., I get some perks. Not many, but a private room, private bathroom, and maybe five square feet more than everyone else."

"Better than nothing, right?"

"Especially since it's free."

"That's definitely a bonus. Paxton and I work together all summer, two jobs, so we can afford our apartment and some spending money during the school year. We're on athletic scholarships, but they don't cover everything and our dad can't afford to help."

"What two jobs?" she asked.

"Lifeguard on weekdays, and at the local rink at night and on weekends."

"And you took an online class too, right?"

I nodded.

"That's a lot, especially in the summer. I've never had a job beyond tutoring and teaching, but I take classes all summer too, so I never get a break either. Sometimes I just want to run away and backpack through Europe or go be a roadie for a rock band or something."

"All hundred pounds of you, huh? Lugging equipment around?"

"A hundred and ten," she corrected me primly. "And I'm stronger than I look."

"I have no doubt." I grinned at her and she grinned back.

We ate our pizza and talked about hockey some more, since she'd made a list of questions for me, which was pretty cool. I explained about offsides and spearing, gave her a few examples of boarding, and even demonstrated high-sticking using a wooden spoon as a hockey stick, and the whole ordeal had us collapsing on her bed laughing.

"So now that you've high-sticked me," she said, "does that mean you have to serve a penalty?"

"Sure." I grinned at her. "What's my punishment?"

"Hockey lessons."

I arched a brow. "For you?"

She nodded. "How about we trade tutoring for hockey lessons? I don't get enough exercise anyway, and I think it'll be fun."

"That's not exactly punishment."

"I know, but I don't actually want to punish you." She was looking at me expectantly. "I like you."

We were on her bed, close together, and she wanted me to kiss her. I knew women and there was no mistaking that look. My first taste of her last night had told me it was going to take a lot of restraint to go slow, so I'd been trying to avoid this, but now I didn't have a choice. This might kill me but I couldn't help myself. I needed another taste, even if it didn't go any further, and my lips had just touched hers when a pounding on the door made us both jump.

"Ellie! Open up!" The loud female voice sounded frantic.

"Harley?" Ellie quickly got up and went to the door, yanking it open. "Hey, what's wrong?"

"Fight on the second floor—it's bad this time. I called campus police but they're handling a disturbance somewhere else on campus, and sometimes you're the only one who can talk any sense into these guys."

"Carter and Tuck?" Ellie asked, sliding her feet into her Chucks. This was a different Ellie, all business now, grabbing her phone as she turned to me. "I have to handle something—this is what I meant by Saturday night shenanigans."

"Hey, I'm coming too." I jumped up and jammed my feet into my sneakers, following her and the girl she'd called Harley.

We took the stairs down two floors and heard the shouts even before we got into the hallways.

"Shit." Ellie took off running so I did too and when we got to the lounge area—there was a gathering area with chairs and tables on each floor for students to hang out in—a massive fight had broken out. Two guys I recognized from the wrestling team were throwing punches like their lives were at stake and I didn't even have time to wrap my head around what was going on before Ellie walked right into the melee. I called to her, terrified she'd get caught between punches, but it was too loud and all I could do was follow.

To my surprise, she climbed up on one of the only tables that remained upright and let out a loud, shrill whistle.

"Knock it off!" I would never have imagined someone as petite as Ellie could have a voice that loud, but she did.

Tuck and Carter momentarily stopped, turning their heads in her direction.

"I warned you about what would happen if campus police was called again, dammit," she said, putting her hands on her hips.

"But he—" Tuck began.

"Don't fucking lie!" Carter yelled, interrupting.

They started swinging again and Ellie whistled once more, this time even louder. "Campus police is on the way and you're both going to jail this time if you don't stop it, right fucking now."

They both turned to glare at her, chests heaving, blood dripping from Tuck's nose and a cut above Carter's right eye.

"I mean it," she said, tapping her foot impatiently. "Work out whatever it is this time, and then go get cleaned up. You're also going to come back here and clean up this mess."

"Aw, come on, El!" someone yelled out. "I've got ten bucks on Tuck!"

"Gambling is illegal on campus," she said. "Now get out of here—all of you."

There was grumbling and muttered curses, but people actually began to disperse, and Tuck and Carter went in opposite directions.

"The Thug Whisperer strikes again," Harley said, chuckling.

Ellie hopped down off the table and righted a few chairs that had been tipped over. She was certainly full of surprises.

"At least once a week," she muttered, shaking her head.

"They're both in love with Shauna Little," Harley said. "And she hooks up with both of them. Whenever the other finds out, they fight."

"They just want to fight," Ellie said. "They use Shauna as an excuse but it's like they can't stand going more than a week without throwing a few punches. As if they don't have any other outlet to burn off nervous energy or something. Except it always winds up happening here in the dorm and then I get in trouble because they say I can't handle it."

"Seems to me you handled it just fine," I said.

"Sometimes. Other times it's like pulling teeth to get them to settle down." She looked around. "I'm going to get a lecture about the two broken chairs, and if I do, those guys are going to be doing my laundry for the rest of the semester!"

"Oh, look, campus police are coming," Harley said, looking out the window. "A day late and a dollar short."

"I'm going back to my room," Ellie said. "They know where to find me if they need me."

We went back up to her room and she collapsed on her bed, flat on her back. "Aren't you glad you hung out with me tonight?"

"Actually, I am." Her legs were hanging over the edge of the bed and I plopped down beside her. "You're pretty badass."

She smiled. "I had to figure it out if I was going to become an R.A., so I probably cheated a little. Early in the semester, I did some free tutoring for my problem children, like Tuck and Carter, and got myself in their good graces. Even though they were grumpy tonight, they're both pretty protective of me, so they know that no matter how mad they are at each other, they don't want to upset me."

"That's pretty cool," I replied. "We all do what we have to do to get by. I think you're doing a great job. There was no doubt back there that you commanded respect."

"My mom said I'd never be able to handle it," she admitted softly. "So I do absolutely everything in my power to prove her wrong."

"Like me and my dad." I reached over and took her hand. Her much-smaller fingers curled around mine and we held them there between us. For the first time in probably ever, I was alone with an attractive young woman, on a bed, and the last thing on my mind was sex. I just wanted to talk to her. Listen to her. Laugh with her. Comfort her and let her comfort me.

It made no sense, but here I was, being a perfect gentleman.

"Do you ever wonder what it would be like to have parents who weren't overbearing and pushy?" she asked after a moment. "Like normal, supportive parents who think it's okay to screw up once in a while? Who just want you to be happy instead of trying to live vicariously through you?"

I sighed. "All the time."

Our eyes met and something intangible passed between us. An unspoken understanding of the kind of pressure most people our age—or maybe any age—had no idea about. While her mother was pressing her into a career she didn't want, my father was pushing me into one I wanted, but sooner than I wanted to do it.

"I'm so glad I met you, Patrick. You get me without even trying."

"Ditto." We turned on our sides and faced each other.

"I wouldn't wish it on anyone, but it's nice to know I'm not the only one with this kind of pressure. It's always been a little lonely, you know?"

"Well, it's not exactly the same for me because I have my twin, but yeah, I get it. That feeling of isolation, where you have to play both sides of the coin, to follow your heart while keeping other people happy."

"It's so hard sometimes. And there's no one I can talk to about it."

"Not anymore. Now you can talk to me."

"You're sweet." She searched my face. "Patrick?"

"Hmm?"

"Would you kiss me again?"

8

PATRICK

Oh, hell. Here went nothing. I was terrified that once we started, we'd never stop, but how could I resist such sweet innocence? And I had no doubt she was innocent. I'd have bet my left nut she was a virgin, which was a whole different type of terrifying, but right now, I wasn't thinking about anything except how soft her lips were. How it sounded when she sighed into my mouth. How trim and sexy her body was as it pressed against mine.

I could have kissed her all night. She was a little timid at first, but then she relaxed and let me guide her. Her mouth was soft and pliable, her lips tasting faintly of something fruity. When a lock of silky hair draped over my forearm, it was possibly the sexiest thing I'd felt in a long time. I wanted to dig my fingers in it, roll on top of her and devour her. But fuck, I didn't want to scare her off either.

I slowly and reluctantly pulled away, staring down into her pretty face. She was breathless and flushed, which probably described me as well, but I loved seeing it on her. The more I looked at her, the prettier she was, and the more I wanted to touch her.

"You're beautiful," I said softly, running my knuckles along her cheek.

"Thank you." She bit her lip, as if she didn't quite believe me and was going to protest but then thought better of it.

"What?" I asked. "You wanted to say something and then changed your mind."

She smiled faintly. "I just, well, I'm not... I mean, I've never done anything like this before."

"Like what? Making out in your dorm room?"

"Or, you know, making out anywhere." She blew out a breath. "It's kind of embarrassing."

"How come?"

"I *hate* not knowing how to do something!"

There was such frustrated determination on her face, I laughed. I couldn't help it. She was such a damn overachiever. I understood it, but in this context, it was pretty adorable. "I'm going to call foul on that and say you definitely know how to kiss."

"Liar." She made a face. "I was probably horrible at it when we first started."

"You were tentative. That's not the same as horrible."

"I'm way out of my element," she whispered. "And I know your reputation. I don't know if I'm...what you're used to."

"What am I used to?"

"You know." She looked away.

"I'm not looking for a casual hookup. I can get that at the rink after any game. I wouldn't risk screwing up with someone who's not just my tutor but also a friend of my brother's."

"But why me? You just said it—you can have your pick at the rink."

"Because there's something between us." I paused. "Isn't there?"

"I think so, but like I told you, this is my first time dating as an adult so I don't have anything to compare it to. Yet another reason I hate when I don't know how to do something."

"This is our second date and you're doing fine." I leaned over and pressed a kiss on the tip of her nose. "And anything you want to know, just ask."

"It feels so dorky!" she blurted out. "And you can't possibly understand how tired I am of being dorky."

"You think you're dorky?" I narrowed my eyes a little. "What are you talking about? You're a little shy, and I'll go so far as to call you inexperienced, but dorky? Why? Because you're smart? Ellie, a real man, at least a man like me, likes a woman with a brain. I guess I can't speak for all men, but for me? Your smarts are a huge turn-on. As are your big blue eyes. And your ass…" I sighed and blew out a breath, shaking my head a little. "I can't wait until the day you're ready to let me bite it."

Her mouth opened slightly and her eyes were glassy, but she had her usual shy smile playing on her lips. "You want to bite my butt?"

"Not hard," I whispered, leaning in. "Unless you ask me to." I kissed her again, taking her mouth gently but firmly, hopefully showing her how much I liked her.

We kissed for a while, but I kept my hands to myself, beyond resting one on her hip, and focused on making her forget all that nonsense about her being a dork. What made her think that? I didn't think she was dorky at all and couldn't imagine anyone thinking that about her. She was beautiful and had a smokin' hot body, so even guys who were turned off by how smart she was would still be interested in getting her into bed. Wouldn't they? Because I definitely was.

When we finally came up for air, I made a conscious decision to slow things down. I kept telling myself that, but then the minute she touched me, I'd forget my resolve, so I had to be stronger than this.

"You are *so* not dorky," I whispered.

"I so am." She was smiling when she said it this time, though.

"Wanna watch a movie?" I asked, trying to concentrate on anything other than my raging erection. "We can cuddle and stay warm."

"Sounds like fun." She got out her laptop and logged into Netflix. I let her choose the movie, thinking she'd pick a rom-com or something, but she chose an action-disaster flick I'd never seen. It was something about skyscrapers and tornadoes, and though it was pretty good, I was far more distracted by her. The side of her lithe body pressed against my side. Her long legs even though they were covered by jeans. Her sweet laugh. Even the small mounds made by her breasts. They weren't very big, but I had a feeling they would be perky and round and fit right in my hands.

I really needed to stop thinking about her body.

About sex.

About teaching her all the bedroom things.

Jesus, what kind of prick was I that I wanted to be the one to do that?

Stop it! I mentally chided myself. She wasn't ready and, frankly, I'd known her all of thirty-six hours. What the hell was wrong with me?

We fell asleep side by side on the bed, fully dressed, and the next time I opened my eyes, she was on her side with her head on my chest. Glancing toward the window, it was dark and gray outside, a heavy snow falling. Well, a good day to study since there wouldn't be much else to do.

"Hey." I gently nudged Ellie. "Wake up, sleepyhead."

"Hmm?" She blinked awake and then smiled. "Morning."

"Morning." I sat up. "I'm starving. Can we go get breakfast before we start studying?"

"Are we studying today?" she asked, quirking a brow.

"Hey, I'm all about having a good time," I laughed. "You want to skip studying, I'm in. We can make out all day."

She blushed. "You know we have to study. Let me freshen up and then we can go to breakfast."

We headed out ten minutes later and I took her hand as we walked. It was freezing today, probably close to zero degrees, but our gloved hands slid together easily. I had no desire to study, but I had every desire to spend more time with her, so I'd do whatever it took. If that helped me in the academic department, that was a cool bonus.

We'd just gotten to the dining hall entrance when a familiar voice called out, "Hey, you two." My twin was looking at me quizzically, his eyes briefly traveling down to where my hand was linked with Ellie's, and then back to my face.

"Hey." Ellie gave him a casual grin. "This must be Naomi."

"You two haven't met?" Paxton shook his head as he slid his arm around his girlfriend. "Babe, this is Ellie. Ellie, Naomi."

The ladies exchanged greetings.

"You guys want to eat with us?" Naomi asked.

"Sure." Ellie seemed happy about it and though I kind of wanted her all to myself, I went along amiably.

We separated once we were inside. I went to make an omelet and Ellie went toward the waffles. Paxton followed me, so I tried to keep my face neutral as I waited for the inevitable grilling. He was protective of his friends in general, and I had a feeling he would be even more so when it came to Ellie.

"Please tell me you didn't do what I think you did," he hissed under his breath.

"I can't read your mind," I replied easily, "so it's hard to say."

"Don't do that!" He gave me a look. "She's a *nice* girl. She's a friend of mine. Why would you do this?"

"Do what?"

"You didn't come home last night." His words held distinct meaning since we both knew what I usually did when I didn't come home at night.

"What does that mean?" I demanded, suddenly a little offended. Did he think that little of me, that I would do something to hurt Ellie?

"You're my brother," he said quietly, "and I'm cool with however you want to lead your life, but you're a man-whore with no limits when it comes to women and sex."

"Oh, because you were a fucking saint before Naomi?" I scowled at him.

"I wasn't, but I stuck to girls who knew what they were getting into. Ellie isn't like that."

"I know that!"

"So why'd you sleep with her? You know you're going to be bored with her in ten minutes, and I'm going to be pissed if you hurt her."

"First of all, who said I slept with her?" I demanded.

He paused, arching his brows. "You didn't come home last night... You weren't with Ellie?"

"I was." I met his gaze with a defiant look.

"And you didn't..." He seemed so confused, I wanted to laugh, but I was annoyed.

"It's been two days," I said. "We hung out and fell asleep watching movies. I like her and she likes me, but believe me, I'm not rushing anything."

Paxton continued to watch me and then sighed. "Okay, but I'm serious—don't be a dick."

"Thanks for the vote of confidence." I placed my order and then pulled out my phone, as if I was checking my email.

I was genuinely pissed, though. It took a lot to hurt my feelings, but Pax had kind of just done it. Who was he to judge? He'd been just as wild as I was, before Naomi. He studied more than I did, but he wasn't some virginal monk who'd been saving himself for marriage.

Burlington University was a great school and had a top-notch hockey team, which was why Paxton and I were here, but living in Vermont was kind of boring. It was beautiful in the fall, but winters were a bitch and since we didn't have a car, it was hard to go anywhere if we wanted to leave campus. There was no public transportation around here and very little to do that wasn't related to hockey, classes or parties. So that's what we'd done. Me more than him, but again, he'd had more than his share of women.

If he could fall in love with Naomi, why was it such a stretch that I might want to have a girlfriend too? I wasn't ready for anything serious, but Ellie was special. Even I could sense that. And our connection was so strong, there was no way I was going to do anything to fuck it up.

"Hey." Paxton was behind me as I picked up my omelet.

I didn't turn my head. "What?"

"I'm sorry. I didn't mean to piss you off. It's just that she's so young and sweet…and you have your choice of other chicks around campus. That's all. It wasn't meant as an insult."

"It's cool. I get it. I have a rep. But you don't have to worry. I like her."

"After two days?" He seemed dubious.

"Yes. That okay with you?"

He held up a hand in mock surrender. "Okay. Got it."

We headed back to the table where the girls were waiting for us, and I was a little uncomfortable. Now I had Pax's voice in my head, making me second-guess myself. What was I doing, spending a platonic night with a girl, double-dating with my brother and his, essentially, live-in girlfriend, and talking about my feelings? What was Ellie doing to me? In forty-eight hours, I'd become someone I didn't recognize.

Maybe Paxton was right and I needed to *not* do this with Ellie. I was interested but not in any position to be someone's boyfriend, so maybe it would be better to keep things simple. A little tutoring, a few hockey lessons since I'd promised, and no more sleepovers. I was ready for something more than sex, but not the forever stuff, and I had to be cognizant of the fact that Ellie literally had no experience with any of it. She wasn't the right girl to test the relationship waters with. Especially not with me potentially leaving in four months.

It was kind of a bummer, and as I looked into her bright blue eyes, I felt the first prickle of regret. She was laughing at something Naomi had said and I realized how addicted I'd gotten to the sound in just two goddamn days.

"Patrick?" Ellie had been talking to me and I'd been so lost in thought I'd missed it.

"Sorry, what?" I asked her.

"When are we having our first hockey lesson?" she asked, smiling. "Paxton and Naomi might join us."

"Oh." I paused, swallowing as I tried to think of a way to say what I was going to say. "I don't know. We both have a lot going on. There's no rush, is there?"

Her face fell a little, though she quickly masked it, and I felt like a world-class dick.

"Well, I guess I'll let you know," she told Naomi.

"Okay." Naomi changed the subject, but now I was in an even worse mood. My brother had ruined my day, my date, and my potential future relationship, all in a matter of two minutes in the omelet line.

I really wanted to deck him sometime.

ELLIE

I didn't know what I'd done or what had gone wrong at breakfast, but my gut told me it had something to do with Paxton. He and Patrick had talked and now Patrick was being weird.

Ugh. Why did people have to stick their noses in other people's business?

I knew it had come from a good place. Paxton and I were friends and he was probably looking out for me, but I already had an overprotective mother, so I didn't need that from my friends. Even if I got hurt, I wanted to spend time with Patrick, kiss him, be with him. For however long he wanted me around. I knew he was out of my league, but I was okay with getting to experience it. I'd rather be the girl Patrick Graham dumped than the girl who never knew what it was like to be with someone like him.

"We're going to the movies tonight," Naomi said. "You guys want to come with us?"

"I have studying to do," Patrick said.

"Me too," I said automatically, pulling on my coat and gloves.

"Okay, then I guess we'll see you later!" Naomi and Paxton headed in the opposite direction of my dorm and I eyed Patrick uneasily, wary of what was coming. I didn't need to know a lot about relationships to understand something had shifted over the last hour.

"I was thinking I should probably go home," he said after a moment.

"Because your brother warned you not to hurt me and you think I'm too nice of a girl?"

"Uh…maybe?" He looked uncomfortable but I didn't care. I was getting dumped before I even had a chance to enjoy having a boyfriend, and that pissed me right off.

"My virginity more than you can stand?" I asked wryly.

"What?" He looked startled. "Of course not!"

"Then what is it? And don't give me any bullshit about studying. If anything, you're going to go home, have a beer, and watch hockey."

He sighed, running a hand through the short hair on his head. "I didn't even know for sure you were a virgin," he said after a moment.

"Does it matter?"

"Kinda. Not that it's a bad thing," he added quickly, "but I might not be the guy you want to, you know, give that to."

"What kind of guy should I give it to? The dorky kid from the vegan fraternity who knows less about sex than I do? Or should I have a genuine one-night stand with a faceless stranger? Because, honestly, that's where I'm at with this." I waved an impatient hand. "You know what? Forget it. It doesn't matter. I'll see you tomorrow night for tutoring." I stepped into the cold and turned towards my dorm.

"Ellie, wait." He fell into step beside me. "Please."

"I get it," I replied, not slowing down. "You don't want any of the responsibility or emotions that come with that kind of thing, and that's cool. I'm sure there are other guys out there who have no such qualms."

"No, that's not it. It's just, you know, complicated. I'm really not a relationship kind of guy and I like you. A lot."

"That makes absolutely no sense."

"I know." He stuffed his hands in his pockets, falling into step beside me. "I like you more than I've liked anyone in a really long time. I can't stop thinking about you. I want to touch you every minute of the day. I fantasize about seeing you naked while simultaneously convincing myself to be a gentleman. It's not normal for me."

I slowed down and cocked my head. "That still makes no sense."

"It's scary to have so much intensity after two freakin' days," he said slowly. "This doesn't usually happen and I'm afraid it's going to burn itself out, leaving you singed. Or worse."

I rolled my eyes. "Give me a break, Patrick. Look, if you're having second thoughts because I'm not the easy lay you thought I'd be, just say so. Don't play games with me. I'd rather you say you were only interested in sex than make up some 'it's not you, it's me' crap."

We'd stopped walking and stared at each other a long time. He seemed to be at war with himself, emotions playing across his face as he struggled with whatever it was. Then, out of nowhere, he reached down and kissed me. His mouth found mine hungrily, his hands grabbing me around the waist and yanking me against him. Our tongues swirled together, deepening the kiss despite the frigid wind and amused laughter of passersby. And I was helpless to stop him. I already craved his kisses even though three days ago I hadn't known they existed. He was right that none of this was normal, but it felt so damn good.

"I'm already crazy about you," he whispered when we finally broke apart. "And it scares the shit out of me."

"I'm crazy about you too," I whispered back. "And it scares me just as much. But you have to decide if you want to risk it."

"You've already decided, haven't you?" He smiled faintly.

"Well, duh. Dorky genius gets chance to hook up with hunky hockey player... When am I *ever* going to get a chance like this again?"

"Is that all I am?" he asked, looking down into my face with a playful smile that lightened up the mood. "A hockey player for you to conquer?"

I bit back laughter. "Of course. What else could it be?"

He tried to hide laughter of his own. "You're something, Ellie McGinn."

"I know." I wrapped my arms around his neck. "And I believe you just said you like it."

"I do."

"Then let's just go back to my dorm and study."

"How about I go home, shower, and get some clean clothes in case we fall asleep again?" he asked. "I'll meet you there in an hour."

"Uh-oh. That's just enough time for Paxton to talk you out of it," I said.

He kissed me. "Not a chance. You and I have some things we need to talk about, but I'm not going to ghost you. I'll give you the 'it's not you, it's me' line before I do that."

I chuckled. "See you in an hour."

Part of me worried he wouldn't show up, but fifty-five minutes after we'd parted ways, he buzzed downstairs and I let him in. He had his backpack with him and he chucked it in the corner as he walked in, digging out a book and kicking off his boots.

He looked good enough to eat and I drank in the sight of him coming towards me in low-slung gray sweats, a black Henley that stretched tight across his broad chest, and a five o'clock shadow that made me itch to find out what it felt like against my skin. Damn, I had it bad for this guy, which meant I wasn't going to get anything done today on my paper. Thank god I was an over-achiever who always worked ahead and could afford to slack off here and there.

"Hey." He sat on the edge of my bed. "I know you have to

study, so I'm going to re-read everything and then do those stat problems again from scratch."

"If you're trying to impress me, it's working."

"Let's get shit done this afternoon so we don't have to do anything tonight but hang out and talk or whatever. Sound good?"

"Sounds perfect." I turned back to my monitor and forced myself to concentrate. I could do this. I had to do some coding, which was semi-mindless work I could do. Whether I wanted to admit it or not, most of my brain was focused on the blue-eyed hunk who was lying back on my bed, pillows under his head, textbook in his lap. Damn, a hockey player with a book was way hotter than I'd imagined it would be.

"Why are you staring at me instead of your computer screen?" he called out without looking up.

"Because there's never been a guy on my bed before."

"I beg to differ. In fact, I'm pretty sure there was a guy on your bed *all last night.*"

I threw a crumpled-up piece of paper at him and he caught it with one hand, still without looking up. I grinned and went back to work.

We worked through lunch, and by four o'clock I was hungry and done for the day. Patrick had finished his stat problems a while ago and was watching a hockey game on his phone without the sound on.

"Who's playing?" I asked, peering over his shoulder.

"Vegas and Seattle," he replied quietly.

"A preview for when you and Paxton are playing against each other in the pros, huh?" I sat beside him, looking down at the screen on his phone.

"Yeah." He didn't say anything else and I realized this was a bit of a sore spot for him.

"You should talk about it," I said after a moment. "I mean, not to me or anything, but you and him. I don't know your dynamic, but I assume as twins you're close and share things maybe other guys your age wouldn't."

He nodded. "Of course, but he already knows how I feel about this situation. He feels it too. We'd hoped we'd get drafted together, even though it was a long shot, but since it didn't happen, there's nothing to do but go forward. And in a way, it'll be good for us to be apart. We've done everything together, from the juniors to college, so it's probably time for us to do our own thing. Even if the adjustment will be hard in the beginning."

"You're going to be so busy, and so excited to be in Vegas, you're not going to have time to miss him," I whispered, leaning over and resting my head on his shoulder. "And then you're going to be a huge hockey superstar, so it'll be that much easier to bear."

"You're sweet." He kissed the top of my head. "Ready to call it a day with studying and go get some dinner?"

"Sure."

We held hands as we walked across campus, back to the dining hall, and it was like déjà vu. We'd done the same thing just this morning and then almost broken up. Except I wasn't even sure we were together enough to break up. It made sense that we were, that this qualified as dating even after such a short time. We'd spent more than forty-eight hours together almost nonstop, so it felt like we were. But I had to be sure because I was me and my analytical mind refused to accept things unless I had the facts.

"I have a question," I said to him.

"I will attempt to give you a satisfying answer," he replied.

I took a breath. "Are we dating?"

"Yes."

I cut a glance up at him. "That's it? A simple yes?"

"Er, should I have had a question mark in my voice, in case you weren't interested… You know, because you didn't already *tell me* you were interested."

I wrinkled my nose. "That was dumb, right?"

"Actually, it wasn't." He slid an arm around my shoulder. "It's kind of refreshing to be with someone who doesn't play games and isn't trying to mind-fuck me. So to speak."

He grimaced at his choice of words and then we both laughed.

"I'm definitely not trying to do anything like that," I said. "I just like to know things."

"I think you've mentioned that. So yes, we're dating."

"Okay."

"Anything else you want to talk about?"

"You mean, like my virginity?"

"Well, no, that wasn't what I meant, but if you want to talk about that, we can."

"It's embarrassing."

"Why? It's not a race or anything. And you've been kind of busy being a genius, getting all these degrees. When did you have time?"

I made a face. "I don't know, but I'm nineteen. I don't know any other nineteen-year-old virgins."

"There are probably more than you think."

"But not the girls you usually date."

He winced but shook his head. "No, but if it bothers you, let's talk about that."

"It's not that it bothers me," I said quietly. "It's just that I'm all screwed up. I know all the book things. More than some people ever learn their whole lives. With my photographic memory, I can learn entire lessons in a day. Even stuff like hockey, where I'm not physically able to play, I've already memorized three how-to books for beginners. I couldn't get on the ice and do it, but I could coach someone on *how* to do it. Based on those books, of course, but you know what I mean. Like, I learned the essentials of the sport in two days. That's not normal, right? And we've kind of come full circle with this—I'm definitely not normal and you are."

"If you're not normal, then I don't ever want to date someone normal again."

PATRICK

Damn, I'd tried to keep it light, but I didn't know exactly what to say. The fact that she'd memorized multiple beginning hockey books was impressive. I probably should have said something like that, but she was on a roll and didn't really give me a chance.

"I just want to be normal. I don't want to be that nerdy genius girl everyone stares at when I do something brilliant, and laughs at when I do something dumb. I know all the book things but very little about real life. Which is why I couldn't let you break up with me before we even really started dating."

She was staring at me intently, imploring me to understand something important to her. And this was about so much more than her virginity. I knew that instinctively. I probably should have made excuses and gotten the hell out of here, but I didn't want to. I'd had my first sexual experience a long time ago and hadn't been with a virgin since high school. Definitely not since getting to college. But again, this wasn't actually about her virginity. At least not entirely.

"Ellie, I won't pretend to understand what you've gone through, being forced to grow up so fast and not being able to be a kid or a teenager or even a regular college student. All I know is what's in front of me, and so far, I see a gorgeous girl who's spectacularly smart but also likes to laugh, with a touch of a dirty mind and probably a lot more layers than I've seen yet. I don't know what people have said in the past to make you think you're not normal, but I don't believe there's any such thing. Hell, what does *normal* even mean? Is it normal that I have the athletic skill to play hockey at the level I do? Technically, it's not. Less than one percent of the population has it. That doesn't make me a freak or whatever—it just makes me, well...*me*. It's part of what makes me Patrick Graham. And your smarts, your photographic memory, all of that makes you Ellie McGinn. If your definition of normal includes being like everyone else, then I'm really glad you're not because that would mean you would be just another random chick and we wouldn't have this incredible chemistry."

She stared at me for a minute and then she kissed me. And it wasn't the shy, tentative kissing we'd shared the first couple of times we'd done it. This time she was all fucking in, and it was a damn good thing we were in the middle of the campus compound in frigid weather with snow falling, or I might have pushed her up against the nearest wall and stuck my hand down her pants. I didn't know what was happening here or why agreeing that she wasn't exactly normal turned her on, but it obviously did and it was great.

"Okay, babe, I think that's enough of a show for the compound," I whispered, pulling away. "You want to continue this back in your room, let's go."

She smiled and we started to walk again. "We still have to talk about sex."

"Because you're ready or because you're not?"

"Ironically, both."

"Explain?" I had no idea what she meant.

"Mentally, I'm so ready it's not even funny. Emotionally, I think we need to work up to it. I haven't done *anything*, Patrick. Like what we've done, kissing and touching on the outside of our clothes? That's it."

"So you want to start at the beginning? We're still on first base and can probably get to second pretty easily. Then we work up to third and not even worry about going all the way until you decide the time is right."

"That works for me, but are you okay with that? When was the last time you dated someone who wasn't having sex with you?"

"Never," I said solemnly. "But you *are* having sex with me. Just not intercourse. It's not sex-sex, but it's still sex."

"Sex lite," she chortled.

"Diet sex," I agreed, laughing.

"Which means at some point, you're going to want to cheat on your diet," she said softly.

"When the time is right, we'll plan the cheat day together."

I slept over again but we'd gone to sleep early. I needed my rest because I worked hard six days a week. Sunday was usually my only day off and I hadn't gotten nearly enough sleep Saturday night, but I'd explained how intense my schedule was Monday through Saturday and she'd been on board. It was different to be having sleepovers with a girl I wasn't having intercourse with, but there was suddenly no rush. I had a lot going on and while I was hornier than fuck, the trade-off was spending time with someone unlike anyone I'd ever met. And at this early stage, I wasn't going to overthink it.

Practice that week was hardcore and I'd barely seen Ellie at all, though we'd texted and talked on the phone at night. I'd met her for a quick coffee yesterday but we'd barely had thirty minutes and were both distracted and busy. I was on my way to meet her now for our tutoring session and I was glad because, although I'd gone to classes and taken notes, I hadn't had time for much in the way of homework or studying. It was a damn good thing I'd done all the reading over the weekend because it helped keep me on track. There was a quiz tomorrow in statistics and I wanted to be ready.

"Hey." She smiled up at me from where she was sitting. We'd decided to meet in the library because being alone at her place would undoubtedly lead to distractions and we couldn't afford them during the week.

"Hi." I dropped a quick kiss on her upturned face and sank down next to her.

"How's your week going?" she asked.

"Not bad. Busy. How about yours?"

"Same."

"Quiz in stat tomorrow, so I need to kill it. My coach gets my first progress reports Friday, so if I tank it, I'm benched Friday night."

"We've got this." She pulled out a pencil. "Okay, let's see where you are."

We studied until almost eleven even though we technically were only supposed to go until nine, but I was determined to do well and she seemed happy to go over each principle multiple times.

"I'm beat," I said, closing my book. "I need to get some rest."

"Okay." She started packing up her things. "Will I see you Friday afternoon or will you be getting ready for the game?"

"The games this weekend are out of town, so the team is leaving around noon."

"Oh." She bit her lip. "Where are you going?"

"Upstate New York. Clarkson and St. Lawrence."

"How far is that?"

"About three hours."

"Maybe I could drive up for Saturday's game and spend the night, if the weather isn't crazy."

"Why don't you see if Naomi wants to go and then you wouldn't be alone?"

"I'll do that." She nodded.

"All right. I have to go." I got up and helped her get her coat on. "You want to meet for dinner tomorrow night?"

"Sure."

We walked outside and I lightly kissed her. "I'll see you tomorrow."

"See you tomorrow."

Saturday night's game was rough and I took a stick to the eye in the second period, which sent me back to the locker room for stitches. The penalty on the other team had earned us a goal but my face was throbbing and I couldn't wait to get back to the hotel and down a fistful of Tylenol. Except Ellie and Naomi were here, probably waiting to go get some food or something, and I didn't know how to tell Ellie I wasn't in the mood for anything but sleep.

"How's the face?" Paxton asked me once we were on the bus headed to the hotel.

I shrugged. "It's okay."

"Liar."

I smiled. "It's not bad. I just need some Tylenol and a good night's sleep."

He arched a brow. "You invited your girl to an away game and now you're gonna blow her off?"

"Of course not. She'll understand."

"Naomi and I were thinking we could split up... She could stay with me in our room and you could go with Ellie to theirs."

"Sounds good."

My head was killing me so I didn't care what we did, and by the time Ellie and Naomi met up with us at the hotel, I could barely keep my eyes open.

"Patrick?" Ellie's eyes filled with concern the moment she saw me. She glanced at Paxton. "How hard did he get hit?"

"Pretty hard," Paxton acknowledged, "but the team's medical staff didn't seem to think it was hard enough for concussion protocol." Special steps were taken if there was even a chance there might be a concussion, but they hadn't thought so for this. Now I was beginning to wonder.

Ellie ran gentle fingers along my brow, around the area where the stitches were, without actually touching them. Her fingers felt cool against my sore skin and I closed my eyes.

"Maybe you should stay here," she whispered after a moment. "Close to your trainers and stuff. Just in case."

I met her gaze and then glanced at my brother. "You guys mind?"

"Why don't we all stay here?" Naomi suggested lightly. "It's not like Pax and I don't have time alone together. Watching over you is far more important. And this way, if you do have to call your trainers or whoever, Paxton will already be here so no one will wonder where he is." Technically, we weren't allowed to have guests or sleep anywhere but the team hotel, though most of us broke the rules more often than anyone liked to admit.

"I should go get my stuff then," Ellie said.

"Don't go alone," I murmured. "It's late."

"I'll go with her," Naomi said. "And we can pick up takeout on the way back because Pax said he's hungry. Do you want anything, Patrick?"

I shook my head. "Nah. I'm good. I just want to lie down."

"Room 1412," Paxton told them as he guided me back toward the elevator. "You want to call Coach?"

"No." I shook my head. "I'm okay. My face is throbbing but I'll pop some Tylenol and close my eyes for a bit."

"You're a fun date," Paxton quipped.

I would have rolled my eyes but it hurt too much.

ELLIE

Patrick was fast asleep when Naomi and I got back to their room. She, Paxton, and I ate the burgers we'd picked up and then they snuggled up on their bed, watching something on TV, and I crawled in beside Patrick. He hadn't moved since we'd gotten back, which worried me a little, but Paxton assured me he was okay. If the team's staff had thought there was anything wrong that a few stitches couldn't fix, they wouldn't have let him come back to his room.

I still didn't like it, so even after Paxton and Naomi turned out the lights and went to sleep, I watched him. I pulled out my laptop and searched everything I could on a correlation between concussions and eye injuries and there didn't appear to be any, but I worried anyway. Obviously, it was impossible to know exactly how hard he'd been hit, and he had professionals who'd checked him out afterward, so I didn't think he was in imminent danger. It was just my first time going through something like this with him and my scientific background probably made me more of a worrywart than I should have been. The part of me my mother would insist would make me a fantastic doctor. She didn't understand I was more likely to find the *cure* for concussions, rather than spend any time treating them.

I didn't want to think about her tonight, because in addition to making sure Patrick was okay, there was also the added bonus of getting to watch him sleep. Even with stitches, a bandage and a bruise on one side of his face, he was still the most gorgeous guy I'd ever known. He was rugged and masculine, but also classically handsome, with straight features and full, well-formed lips. I could look at him for hours, drinking in every detail.

At some point, I must have fallen asleep because the next thing I knew, Patrick was gently shaking me.

"Babe?" His hand was warm on my arm. "Were you up all night?"

Those gorgeous blue eyes of his bore into mine and I blinked sleepily. "Mmm, most of the night. I wanted to make sure you were okay. Concussions are serious, you know?"

"But I don't have one."

"But you were showing some vague symptoms and I didn't want to take a chance." We were both whispering since Paxton and Naomi were still asleep, but Patrick lifted the covers and motioned for me to get in. I slid beneath them and he pulled me up against him.

"You're incredible, Ellie." He kissed the side of my face. "You didn't have to, but it means the world to me that you did. Thank you."

"I was *worried*."

"I know." He reached out to run his knuckles along my cheek. "But I'm fine. I took a shot on the side of my eye and it was so sore it gave me a headache. That's all it was. I slept it off and now I feel great. And really fucking hungry."

I giggled. "You're always hungry."

"I'm a growing boy."

"Uh-huh." I nestled against his chest.

"I can't believe you sat up all night watching me sleep."

I wasn't sure if I answered, because I fell asleep.

The guys had to drive back on the bus with the rest of the team, so when we got up again a couple of hours later, Naomi and I made the three-hour drive home. The bus was about an hour behind us so I took a long shower and was just about to turn on my computer when my mother's name flashed on the screen of my phone. I chewed my lip while I debated answering, but finally picked it up because the last thing I wanted was for her to call once Patrick got here.

"Hi, Mom."

"Ellie, you lied to me."

I grimaced. There were probably a dozen things I'd lied to her about lately, so who knows which one she'd caught me in.

"What did I do now?" I asked, sinking onto my bed and staring at the ceiling.

"You never applied to Johns Hopkins."

Nope. I sure hadn't. I hadn't applied to Harvard or Columbia or NYU either.

"Ellie, I'm waiting."

"For what?" This wasn't going to go well, but I was in too deep to put it off any longer.

"What in the world is going on with you? Why would you jeopardize your entire future by not doing the things you're supposed to do?"

"I'm not jeopardizing anything," I said calmly. "I'm already in a Ph.D. program here at Moo U. The only question now is whether I want to move into biotechnology or—"

"That is *not* what we discussed!" The increasing volume of her voice told me she was getting mad, but it was time we got this over with.

"Mom, I don't want to go to medical school. I don't know how many ways I can tell you and show you that, but you're not listening. I'm not going to spend the next dozen years studying something I'm not even remotely interested in."

"You don't know what you're talking about. This is your

future. All the testing we had done pointed specifically to medicine and—"

"No, it didn't." This time I interrupted her. "It pointed specifically to *science*. Which is exactly what I'm doing." My parents had some ridiculous psychological testing done to find out exactly what career I was most suited for. The results had been stupid, but essentially pointed to things like medicine, science, and research. My mother had immediately zoned in on the medical aspect. But they weren't the same damn thing.

"I didn't spend the last five years supporting you for you to become a goddamn teacher!" she yelled.

"Supporting me?" I asked quietly. "If this is what you call support, I'd hate to see what no support is. You haven't supported a single thing I've wanted to do since I was twelve. Starting with playing the flute or letting me dye my hair blue."

"What are you talking about? You had no time to play the flute and why the hell would you want your hair blue?"

"Because that's what teenagers do," I said softly.

"Elizabeth, this isn't acceptable. I spoke to my friend at Harvard and based on your background, they could pull a few strings. You'd have to send in your records and—"

"Mom!" I spoke a little more sharply than I'd intended. "Listen to me. I. Don't. Want. To. Be. A. Doctor." I enunciated slowly, with as much conviction as I could muster. My mom kind of scared me most of the time, but this was too big, too important, for me to let her walk all over me.

"You're *going* to be a doctor!" she hissed.

"I'm not."

There was a long silence before she said, "You have to trust I know what's best for you."

"And you have to trust that I'm an adult and the one who has to actually do the work. Forcing me to do something I'm not interested in isn't going to end well for any of us, and in the end, I'm going to be hundreds of thousands of dollars in debt for a career I don't want."

"I can't let you destroy your life because you're too young to understand what's best for your future."

"Mom, please don't do this."

"I could say the same to you."

"I don't want to be a doctor. Why is that so hard to understand? And what's wrong with being a scientist?"

"You were born for something special!"

"And maybe I'll find it in my research."

"This isn't debatable. I want to be copied on the emails you send to Harvard putting everything in motion. If it's not done, I'll be coming for the car on Friday."

"Well, then please bring all of my things with you when you come, because I won't be coming home. Ever again." I disconnected and burst into tears.

I was still crying when Patrick got there forty-five minutes later. He took one look at my red, blotchy face and pulled me into his arms, holding me tightly.

"What happened?" he asked as he held me. "Why are you crying?"

"M-my…M-mom." I burst into tears all over again and he stroked my hair as I managed to choke out what had happened.

"Oh, baby, I'm sorry." We'd collapsed on my bed with him still holding me.

I was equal parts hurt and furious. My mother was overbearing and manipulative, and though my father usually played mediator between us, he wanted me to go to medical school too, so I probably wasn't going to get any help this time.

"What can I do?" he whispered as I finally stopped crying.

"Just hold me," I whispered back.

We lay there for a long time, his warm hands moving up and down my back, over my arms, occasionally stroking my hair. With him holding me like this, nothing else mattered and I could forget everything. My mother, the future, and all the indecision surrounding me both academically and professionally.

"I need to wash my face," I said, sitting up and rubbing my eyes.

"Go on. I'll be right here."

I went into the bathroom and washed up, lamenting how puffy my eyes were and how red my face was. I looked terrible, but I felt even worse, so there was no help for it. I didn't think Patrick minded, though, because he'd been a huge support to me today. He hadn't tried to tell me everything would be okay or that she'd get over it, he'd simply let me cry and get everything off my chest.

He was waiting when I came out, and simply opened his arms again. I fell into them as if it was the most natural thing in the world, and I nestled against his chest.

"How's your eye?" I asked after a few minutes.

"It's a lot better. Sore but manageable now."

"Good."

"So she's taking the car on Friday?"

I nodded miserably.

"It's okay. I've never had a car and it's not that bad."

"I've done everything they've ever asked of me except this. I graduated with honors. My two bachelor's degrees were in biology and computer science, and there has never been any doubt I was going to do something that at least involved technology, even though my passion is bio. And dammit, they gave me that car for my eighteenth birthday! You don't take back a fucking birthday present!" I was rambling but too miserable to care.

"I know. It's pretty shitty. Will your dad take your side at all?"

"I don't know. Probably not on this. They're both completely enamored with the idea of me becoming a doctor."

"Are you going to stay here to finish your Ph.D.?"

"I don't know anything anymore. I was also thinking about taking a semester off to do some different things, but I can't do anything without money."

"Can you teach?"

"Yes, but what they pay for teaching just a few classes wouldn't be enough for me to get an apartment and stuff. I'd have to take out student loans for at least part of it and I don't even know what my scholarships would cover."

"It's doable, though, right? You could figure it out."

I nodded.

"And I've got your back. We'll work on it together and I'll do anything I can to help."

"I know." I dipped my head, fighting off a fresh bout of tears.

"Come on." He gently lifted my chin. "Don't be sad. You're not alone, Ellie. I'm here for you."

I wanted to remind him that he probably *wouldn't* be here more than a few more months, but I buried my face in his chest instead. We'd only been together about ten days, but I couldn't imagine Patrick not being in my life six months from now. And that scared me far more than my mother.

12

PATRICK

I did my best to distract Ellie but she wasn't herself. Between recuperating from my injury on Saturday night and dealing with her situation with her mom, we'd spent most of Sunday cuddled on her bed watching Netflix. We didn't talk much, didn't make out at all, and I had to coax her to do an hour of studying. I hadn't planned to sleep over, but there was no way I could leave her alone with how she was feeling, so I'd texted Paxton, told him what was up, and asked him to bring me my stuff for tomorrow. After hearing Ellie's situation, he and Naomi had come over with my backpack and clothes for me, along with a couple of pizzas from Tito's, which Ellie at least nibbled on.

Their visit cheered her up a little, but we were asleep early again. I was showered and out of there by eight and we agreed to meet up for coffee later. Mondays were busy for both of us and I felt a little bad that I wouldn't be able to check on her until after practice, but she'd been in a better mood this morning.

"How's Ellie?" Paxton asked when we were changing to get ready for practice.

"She was better when we got up, but I think Friday is going to be rough."

"That's the day her mom is supposedly taking the car?"

I nodded.

"Well, if it's during the day, before the game, I say we stick close to her so she has support."

"That's what I was thinking too."

"So, not to piss on your Monday, but I talked to Dad last night."

I made a face. "Oh, boy, can't wait to hear this."

"I got the whole lecture about convincing you to go pro at the end of the year."

"And?"

He hesitated and met my gaze almost guiltily. "You could do it. You're close enough to graduation that you'd still have your degree and get Dad off your back simultaneously."

"I need three more classes after this semester. Even if I can take one or two over the summer, I can't take all three, and I'm afraid if I leave in May, I'll never finish."

"I'll help you," he said quietly.

"You'll be in Seattle," I pointed out. "You're going to be thousands of miles away, playing pro hockey and starting your life with Naomi."

"Yeah, but I'm never more than a phone call away."

I didn't say anything.

"But it's not the same." He knew me well enough to voice what I'd mostly been thinking. "Look, I get it. But if you take two this summer, you can take the last one next summer. It's a long time and you probably won't get to walk across the stage, but does that part of it matter to you?"

I shook my head. "No. It would be nice, but it's not the end-all. Maybe I just haven't wrapped my head around the idea of this being it, that after this semester, I'll be done with college and be a fully functioning adult. Moving to Vegas and playing pro hockey still seems like it's something in the way distant future."

"Well, just because Dad wants you to doesn't mean you have to do it," Paxton said. "With me in Seattle, he'll be distracted and won't nag you as much. Even though I'm not his superstar child."

"Gross. Trade you." Our father had always favored me because I was the better hockey player but that wasn't necessarily true anymore. Paxton was great—he wouldn't have been drafted if he wasn't—and while I had a slight edge when it came to leadership, that wasn't a big deal in my opinion.

"I guess." I locked up my things. This was no time to think about anything that deep. "Anyway, let's get out there." I turned and made my way toward the ice. There were too many things to focus on during practice, so I tried to turn off everything but hockey. Usually when I was in the zone, everything else became white noise, but today I couldn't quiet it. I was worried about Ellie, my father, my grades, my future—and it was a lot. Even for a tough guy like me.

Luckily, my body knew what to do on autopilot, especially during practice, so I got through it without being too much of a fuck-up. I was distracted as hell, though, and all I could think about was getting back to Ellie. Both because I knew she needed me but also because, in a way that was hard to articulate, I needed her. The way she'd sat up all night on Saturday had touched me. I'd had a headache and had been kind of cranky, but it hadn't been serious. Ellie hadn't been willing to take anyone's word for it, though, watching me most of the night until she'd felt comfortable that I wasn't having a seizure or whatever crazy thing she'd thought. Concussions were serious, of course, but if there had been any chance of that, the team wouldn't have let me finish the game, much less go back to my room without supervision.

Still, it was one of many things I loved about Ellie. She hadn't been upset that she'd driven three hours to see me play and I'd gone to sleep on her. She hadn't cared that we'd decided to share the room with Paxton and Naomi in the interest of my safety instead of us having some privacy. And mostly, she'd been relieved the next morning when I told her I felt fine. The only thing she'd thought about that night was me. And aside from my twin, I couldn't remember the last time someone had put me first.

It was a nice feeling, knowing that someone cared about me

beyond Patrick-the-hockey-player. I hadn't known Ellie long, but she was spectacularly transparent and there was no doubt in my mind she would like me whether I played hockey, was a fellow science geek, or something else altogether. The way she looked at me sometimes, as if I'd personally hung the moon just for her, made me uncomfortable, but for different reasons than I would have expected. I couldn't put my finger on it, but it was like an addiction. I practically held my breath the whole way back from the rink, as I waited for her to buzz me in, and until she opened the door and I could touch her.

Then I kissed her like I hadn't seen her in weeks instead of hours.

"Hi," she breathed against my mouth. "I missed you too."

Damn, she was a mind reader on top of everything else.

I kicked the door shut with my boot and then backed her to her bed. We went over backwards, so I was on top of her, and she wrapped her arms around me.

"I didn't touch you nearly enough this weekend," I said, nibbling the skin under her jaw. "I need to make it up to you."

"So...second base?"

"Maybe." I grinned as I continued to kiss my way around her head. The sensitive points behind her ears, her temples, the line of her jaw... She was exquisite to explore and touch, and though it had been years since I'd kept my sexual progress stalled out at second base, it was somehow right with Ellie. I liked knowing I was the only guy she'd ever done these things with. It was exciting because while she was completely inexperienced with the sex, she was the smartest, most well-spoken and mature girl I'd ever been with. She was also direct to a fault, had no designs on my future paychecks—a lot of the girls I'd hooked up with did—and was a genuinely sweet, caring person. I liked everything about her and if the trade-off was going slow in the bedroom, I was okay with it. Despite jerking off in the shower at least once a day.

I pulled away long enough to tug at her hoodie. I knew she

had on a T-shirt or tank beneath it, and the fabric of the hoodie was too much of a barrier to her skin right now. She pulled it over her head and I sighed at the sight she made in a tight T-shirt that clung to her lithe body and showed me every detail of her hard little nipples. As I'd suspected, her breasts were small but perfectly round and perky, sitting up high on her chest, even without a bra. I longed to see them completely bare, but we weren't there yet, so I settled for running my thumbs over the tight peaks through the light cotton of her shirt.

Her eyes fluttered closed and pale lashes settled on her cheeks. There was a slight flush to her skin as I circled her nipples, and her chest rose and fell more erratically the longer I did it. We rolled onto our sides and I slid my hands beneath her shirt, moving them around to her back. My hands were big enough to cover most of her lower back as I drew her closer to me and claimed her lips again.

Damn, she was too sweet for words. When her tongue tangled with mine, I almost lost my resolve to keep things moving slowly. It felt that good to have her body draped all over mine, and my cock was stiffer than granite. Would a hand job be too much?

I took her hand and led it to where my erection was tenting my sweats, urging her to touch me the way I was touching her. Her hand seemed small against my crotch but damn, it felt incredible, even through my clothes. She splayed her fingers over my groin and then slowly squeezed. Not hard but just enough to make me moan. She jerked her hand away and I chuckled, reaching out to bring it back.

"It feels great when you do that," I whispered. "That sound I made was sheer pleasure."

"Oh." She looked down, worrying her lower lip as she struggled with some internal decision about what to do next.

"I want to…feel more," she said after a while. "I want to touch your skin."

"Okay." I edged down my sweats and boxers, watching her face as she took in her first sight of me. Her eyes widened a little but then she closed her hand around my cock and rubbed her thumb along the head. Her gaze was intense, focused, and I wanted to tell her to relax, but I let her do her own thing until I couldn't stand it anymore. It was heavenly torture that I gladly endured until I felt she was a little more comfortable touching me, and then I closed my hand around hers, guiding her into a rhythm I liked.

Maybe it was because it had been weeks since I'd gotten laid, or because Ellie was that good, or even maybe because of the way things heated up the moment we were in the same room together, but it didn't take long for me to lose control. I shot off after just a few strokes, squeezing her hand harder until I was done.

"Oh, wow." Her eyes were filled with the sexiest combination of desire and surprise and I watched her lick her lips.

"Are you ready for more?" I asked, reaching for a tissue to clean up.

"Yes, please." She shimmied out of her sweats before I could say anything, and my dick instantly got hard again. Her long legs were covered in pale, silky skin and her rounded hips were made for fucking.

"God, you're killing me." I buried my face in her abdomen, inhaling the scent of her arousal and using my hands to cup her ass.

"Show me, Patrick."

ELLIE

My first hand job had been totally different than what I'd been expecting. I'd thought an erect penis would be *hard*, and while it technically was, I hadn't been prepared for the skin itself to be so soft. Watching him ejaculate had been way better than anything I'd seen in porn, and the sound he'd made as he'd gotten off had made all my girlie parts damp. I loved knowing it was because of me, and now I was a thousand percent ready to feel what it was like to have that kind of pleasure myself.

I'd taken off my sweats before I had a chance to chicken out, and having his hands all over me, touching and kissing, made me squirm with need. I hadn't done any of this but I'd read about it and talked about it with my friends, so I had an idea what to expect. Except it was so much better. Patrick was gentle, his touch soft, but my body ached for more.

His fingers trailed along the hem of my panties and anticipation shot through me. No one had ever touched me there and Patrick was every virginal genius girl's fantasy. Just better. And hotter. And oh sweet hell, what was he doing now? One finger had traveled between my legs, toying with me, lightly tracing lines along my labia, my pubic bone, up and down my slit. Featherlight flicks of his finger made me squirm and then he touched the place that nearly made me vault up off the bed.

"Easy…" His voice was raspy, as if he was enjoying this as much as I was, though I couldn't imagine how that was possible. "Does it feel good?"

"Soooo good."

"It's going to feel better."

He circled the little nub of pleasure I hadn't even been sure existed until now, and then gently pinched it between two fingers.

"You're so wet," he said. "And I'm already hard again."

Our mouths locked together and he slowly pushed a finger inside of me. I moaned, arching into his hand. My body came alive as he finger-fucked me, my legs fell open, inviting him to do more, and his tongue dueled deliciously with mine. Sensations were starting to overwhelm me, the heat of his mouth matching the growing heat between my legs. He added a second finger and something inside of me began coiling up tightly. His fingers traveled back up to my clit, circling and teasing, taking me to the brink and then holding back. I panted against his mouth, anxious for more, and when he gave it to me, everything crashed white.

I'd been too shy and inexperienced to make myself come, so having an orgasm against Patrick's hand was the most amazing feeling ever. My whole body shook and I might have cried out, but I never wanted it to stop, riding each wave as it crested over the last.

"Fuck, that's hot," Patrick murmured against my ear. "I'm going to make you come at least twice a day from now on."

"Holy shit." I collapsed against the pillows now, my body like jelly as tiny aftershocks shot through me. He still had a finger inside of me and I clenched around him, unwilling to let go of the pleasure.

"We were only supposed to explore second base," he said with a wry grin. "And I'm pretty sure I just slid into third."

"Uh-huh." That was all the vocabulary I could muster up because my heart was still pounding and that damn finger was still inside of me. I whimpered as he pulled it out and tugged me against his chest.

"You're so fucking gorgeous," he said, kissing the top of my head.

"No one's ever said that to me before," I whispered, suddenly a little emotional. It wasn't about the sex itself, but the feelings it aroused. No one had ever told me I was beautiful or sexy, much less made me feel that way. If I was being honest, no one had ever made me feel loved either. At least not in a long time. And Patrick did it all.

"Are you crying?" he asked, reaching out to tilt up my chin and force me to look at him.

I shook my head. "No." But I was. A little. Tears blurred my vision and I wiggled free, burying my face in his chest, embarrassed and overwhelmed.

"Oh, geez, Ellie, why didn't you tell me to stop? I thought you wanted—"

"I did!" I looked up quickly, swiping at my eyes. "This isn't about third base or whatever. This is about me realizing how lonely I've been. How *alone* I truly am. I've been on my own, for lack of a better word, since I was twelve. The general parenting continued, but the smarter they realized I was, the less love and affection I got. All anyone cares about is what amazing thing the genius teenager is going to do next. No one has ever paid any attention to the things I want and need beyond food and shelter. I have a couple of friends but Harley doesn't understand me and Chastity is busy with her own life, her boyfriend…" I swallowed, feeling a little foolish.

"Babe, you're not alone. Not anymore." His eyes were filled with sincerity and I longed to ask him to take me with him when he went to Las Vegas, but even I knew better than to go there at this stage of our relationship.

"You're leaving soon," I whispered instead. "You'll be going to Vegas and I'll be here."

"I don't know if I'm going," he said, surprising me. "I'm

thinking about it, but I really, really want my degree. My dad never got his and he struggled to find decent jobs after he blew out his knee. He and my mom always had to work two jobs each, get seasonal work, things like that, to supplement their income because my dad never thought beyond hockey. All it takes is one injury—and I don't want to be that guy."

"You only have three classes left," I said gently. "You'd be able to finish, even if it takes a few extra years."

"Yeah, but I hadn't planned to go just yet, and maybe this is fate's way of telling me I need to stay."

"If you need to go, you can't stay because of me," I said firmly, even though it nearly killed me. "I'd never forgive myself if you ruined your career because my parents don't love me." I chuckled at how ridiculous that sounded.

"There's a lot more going on here than you and your mom," he said. "But honestly, I haven't made any decisions yet."

I nestled deeper into his arms and closed my eyes. I didn't want to talk about this anymore because I would have done almost anything to keep him around another year.

My father texted me on Friday morning and I scowled as I read his message.

> DAD: *Your mom and I will be there in about fifteen minutes. Can you go get the car and meet us at Tito's? It's easier than trying to find it in the student lots.*
> ELLIE: *Sorry, I'm in class.*

That was a lie, but screw this. If they wanted the car, they could damn well search for it.

> DAD: *What if we ate lunch first? Could you meet us around one?*

ELLIE: Tutoring. Also, can you leave my things in front of my dorm?
DAD: What things?
ELLIE: I told Mom to please bring my things because if you take the car, then I'm not coming home anymore. I'm officially moving out.
DAD: You and your mother need to talk.
ELLIE: I'm all talked out. Sorry, I have to go.

I closed the texting app and tried to focus on my paper. I was in the library waiting for Patrick. He'd insisted he'd stay with me while my parents picked up my car, even though it wasn't necessary since I didn't plan on seeing them. My mother obviously hadn't told my father I wanted my things or that I wasn't going home anymore. He was probably talking to her now, trying to find a way to smooth things over. That was the thing that pissed me off the most. He always sided with her, but he tried to play peacemaker so I wouldn't fight with him the way I did my mom.

They'd forgotten who I was, though. With my high IQ and the way my teachers and advisors liked me around here, it had only taken a couple of phone calls to make sure I could stay in the program here next year. I'd get an additional job this summer to save up for incidentals and hopefully a phone, since I had a feeling that would be the next thing my mother took away.

Said phone was ringing now but I ignored it as Patrick came in, dropping his backpack on the floor next to mine.

"Hi." He kissed me and met my eyes. "Did you hear from them?"

I nodded. "They're here now, searching for the car." I made a face. "They actually asked me to drive it over to Tito's to meet them so they wouldn't have to search all the parking lots."

He grinned. "And you said no? That's awesome."

I shrugged. "I'm in class and then I have a tutoring job."

He sank into the chair next to mine. "Yes, you do. And, on a positive note, guess what I got on my stat quiz?"

"A hundred?"

"A hundred and five—I got the bonus question!"

I held up my palm and he high-fived me. "I'm so proud of you," I told him.

"I have a great tutor."

"Have you shown your coach your first progress report with all A's on it?"

"I'll show him when I get to the arena."

My phone started ringing again and I sighed.

"Answer it," he said gently. "They'll just keep calling."

"Hello?" I snatched up my phone in irritation.

"Ellie." My father sounded out of breath. "Will you please tell us where the car is?"

"I'm not sure," I said lightly. "You see, I don't actually own a car since it wasn't actually a gift. So how would someone who doesn't own a car know where it is?"

"Ellie, I know you're hurt, but this is for your own good."

"My own good?" I demanded, forgetting all about the fact I was in the library and probably should have kept my voice down. "Your child is a straight A student who hasn't cost you a dime in college tuition. I got two degrees without a penny in loans, and yet, you're punishing me for not studying what you want me to study, by taking away the car you bought me for my eighteenth birthday. What part of that is for *me*?"

"You and your mother need to talk."

"She knows my number."

"The two of you are both so damn stubborn."

"And you always take her side." The bitterness in my voice was impossible to disguise and I heard his slight intake of breath.

"I'm sorry you feel that way."

"Did you bring my things?"

"Of course not. We'd just have to move them all back to Brattleboro in the spring."

"As usual, you're not listening." I was more resigned than

angry at this point. "I'm not coming home. I've officially moved out. I've got a job lined up and a place to live, so I'm good."

"You've done what?" I heard the surprise in his voice and the annoyance as he repeated to my mother what I'd said.

"I have to go," I said after a moment. "I love you, but I don't want to go to medical school. If that's the price for you to love me back, then we have nothing else to say." I disconnected and looked over at Patrick. "They drove it until it was almost out of gas, right?" I'd lent my car to Paxton and Naomi, who'd gone out to dinner last night, and I'd told them to leave the gas tank on empty.

He nodded. "He said it's on fumes."

"Good." It was childish and I knew it, but I was hurt. It wasn't about the car—I usually only used it once a week on the weekends to go stock up on snacks or make a drugstore run—but the principle of the whole thing really bothered me. Why would they take the car? They paid for the insurance but I was only nineteen and in college. I hadn't *asked* for the car. It had been a surprise for my birthday and mostly it had been for their convenience, so they didn't have to make the round trip twice every time I wanted to go home for a weekend or break.

Now they were punishing me like I'd done something wrong. I wasn't even twenty years old and they wanted to map out the next decade of my life, which was wholly unfair. I'd barely had a chance to figure out what I wanted short-term, much less long-term, so how could I make these decisions? Most people had another three years until they graduated college, and at twenty-two were a lot more likely to know what they wanted. My parents made the decision for me to go to medical school when I was fourteen. It hadn't sat right with me then and it hurt a lot more now.

"Babe?" Patrick had been watching my face the whole time.

"How long until you have to leave for the arena?" I asked him. "Can we go for a walk? I need to clear my head but I don't want to be alone."

"I have time. Let's go."

ELLIE

I had a lot on my plate because of the situation with my parents, but if I was honest, the only thing I'd been thinking about the last two days was that damn orgasm I'd had. I was so ready to lose my virginity but Patrick was being a perfect gentleman and I wasn't sure how to just blurt out that I wanted him to fuck me.

I giggled a little at the idea of saying it like that. Patrick would laugh, but I didn't want our first time to follow something so crude. I'd had a taste of what was to come and I was ready, but I knew myself well enough to recognize a need for romance and tenderness. I'd been hoping to pick Harley's brain about how to approach the whole thing, but she'd ghosted me lately.

Impulsively, I picked up the phone and called my friend Chastity. She'd been a twenty-one-year-old freshman two years ago and I'd tutored her in algebra for a while. She and her boyfriend, Dylan, lived in a house near campus with a few friends, so I didn't see her very often anymore, but we were still close.

"Hey!" She sounded happy to hear from me when she answered the phone.

"Can you meet for coffee?" I asked her. "It's been a long time and I have a lot to tell you."

"Oh?" Her voice was laced with amusement. "It wouldn't happen to have to do with a hunky hockey player, would it?"

I froze. "How would you know that?"

She laughed. "The hottest hockey player at Moo U is potentially off the market—hearts have been breaking all over. You're probably the most hated woman on campus right now."

I was so shocked, I didn't know how to respond for a few seconds.

"I can meet you right now," Chastity continued when I didn't say anything. "I have forty-five minutes until my next class."

"I'm supposed to be in class, but I'll email my professor and tell him I'm working on my final project."

"See you at the coffee shop in ten?"

"See you there."

I grabbed my things and pulled on my coat. It was snowing again, so I flipped up the hood on my coat and trudged outside. It took almost ten minutes to walk to the opposite side of the campus to the coffee shop, and Chastity was arriving at the same time.

"Hi!" I reached out and hugged her.

"Hi!" We walked inside and ordered before sitting in a booth in the back. It wasn't very busy since most kids were in class right now, and it was nice to be able to catch up.

"So tell me everything," she said when we'd picked up our orders.

"He's amazing," I said softly. "Gorgeous, athletic, sweet, and oh my god, the way he kisses…"

Chastity laughed. "I'm familiar with that sentiment."

"You and Dylan still fucking like bunnies?"

"Bunnies on steroids," she said, nodding.

"So, um, I wanted to pick your brain about that."

"About sex?" She cocked her head curiously.

"About how to get Patrick to do it. I could tell him I'm ready, but I'm not sure how. Like, just blurt it out? Plan a romantic evening in my dorm and pray he'll get the hint? Wait until we're fooling around and just whisper something like, 'Don't stop'? I want it to happen organically but he's being a gentleman so I'm afraid it never will."

"Then give him an abridged version of what you just told me, without the questions. That you're ready and he doesn't have to be a gentleman anymore. Does he know you have an IUD?" Chastity knew my mother had forced me to get one "just to be safe," even though, at the time, I'd thought it was dumb.

I shook my head. "It hasn't come up."

"Then that's your perfect segue into a conversation about going all the way." She met my eyes. "Are you sure, Ellie? I was already head over heels for Dylan before we had sex."

I sighed. "I'm already head over heels for Patrick. It's only been a couple of weeks, so I'm probably dumb for letting myself get this involved this quickly, but I can't help the way I feel. He's the whole damn package, Chastity. It's way too late for me to slow down the feelings."

"Then follow your heart," she said softly. "If he makes you happy, what more is there?"

"Him breaking said heart into a zillion pieces."

"But that's bound to happen in life anyway. You're going to get hurt so you might as well enjoy this. Let yourself go, Ellie. You're usually wound up so tight, always thinking about grades and medical school, what's next for you academically and professionally… It's time for you to enjoy life a little too."

"I'm trying," I whispered. "Did I tell you my parents took the car?"

"They took the car?" Her eyes rounded. "*Seriously?*"

I told her everything that had been going on the last few weeks and she caught me up on what she and Dylan had been up to. By the time we hugged goodbye, I felt rejuvenated and couldn't wait to see Patrick. He was in class and then had practice, so it wouldn't be until later. It was Wednesday, though, so I'd see him for tutoring tonight.

I sent him a text as I walked toward my dorm. I didn't have

anything else to do until it was time for tutoring, so I'd work on my final project for a while.

ELLIE: *Wanna get dinner and then have our tutoring date in my room? I don't feel like hanging out in the library.*
PATRICK: *We don't get a lot of studying done when we're at your place.*
ELLIE: *That's not a bad thing, is it?*
PATRICK: *Who are you and where's Ellie? MY Ellie loves to study.*
ELLIE: *YOUR Ellie also loves the idea of getting naked with a hunky hockey player she knows.*
I bit my lip as I waited for his response.
PATRICK: *Are you trying to tell me something?*
ELLIE: *I don't know what you mean... I was talking about YOUR Ellie.*
PATRICK: *LOL. So I should make a drugstore run before I come over?*
ELLIE: *I'll see you when you get to my place.*

I didn't own anything that even vaguely resembled lingerie but Harley did. I showed up at her dorm room unannounced and though she was surprised, she obligingly helped me sort through her things until we found a sexy, see-through black nightie. It was completely sheer and lacy with spaghetti straps, and so short it wouldn't even cover my bottom.

"No panties," Harley yelled after me as I was leaving.

I laughed, trying to decide if I was brave enough for that. Probably not. But I did have a sexy black thong in my drawer somewhere. That would be a nice compromise, and if I answered the door that way, Patrick would know I hadn't been kidding in our texts earlier. I was nervous but my body practically hummed with excitement and anticipation. I wasn't overly worried about this being my first time since my mother had insisted I get an IUD when I turned eighteen. She'd made it clear an unplanned pregnancy would derail my future, so she'd made sure I was protected, even though there had been zero sexual prospects at the time.

I spent too much time getting ready. Between shaving my legs, curling my hair, and at least three layers of mascara, I hoped Patrick would like what he saw. I slipped on the nightie and the thong and stared at myself in the mirror. I looked pretty, and though I rarely thought of myself that way, my gut told me Patrick would love my attempt at seduction.

When he buzzed from downstairs, I took a moment to fluff my hair and take off my robe. By the time he knocked, I'd talked myself off the ledge of nervousness and reminded myself that I wanted this. Wanted him. And my first sexual experience was going to be entirely on my terms. Unlike most things in my life.

I opened the door a crack to make sure he was alone and took a moment to smile at how ruggedly handsome he was.

He quirked a brow. "Is there a password or something to get in tonight?"

"Nope." I opened the door but stood behind it so anyone who might be passing by in the hall wouldn't see me.

"So, hey, I was thinking…" His voice trailed off as I shut the door and leaned against it. I had no idea what went through his mind in that moment, but his eyes darkened and he kicked his backpack out of the way. "Jesus, Ellie."

I didn't say anything, mostly because I was frozen in place watching him watch me. The look in his eyes was one I'd never forget, full of passion and admiration and desire. He wanted me as much as I wanted him and my nipples hardened just thinking about what was to come.

He peeled off his coat, gloves and hat, his eyes never leaving mine. Then he pulled his Henley over his head and kicked off his boots. Seeing him standing there in nothing but low-slung jeans made my mouth water and I drank in the sight of him. I'd seen him without a shirt lots of times, but this was different. He was already getting hard behind the denim fabric and he slowly crooked a finger at me.

I took a few tentative steps in his direction and he reached out a hand. I put mine in it and let him pull me the rest of the way forward. He circled my waist with one arm and stared down at me.

"You're fucking gorgeous," he whispered in a raspy voice.

"Thank you." I swallowed and looked up into those beautiful blue eyes of his.

"I want to kiss you, but I also just want to stare at how sexy you are. I don't know what to do first."

"K-kiss me," I said softly. "I need you as close as possible."

"I'm not just going to kiss you… I'm going to strip that nightie off and kiss every inch of you."

15

PATRICK

Ellie's texts from earlier in the day had been intriguing, and I'd had a feeling she was up to something, but I hadn't been expecting this. Seeing her in the sheer nightgown thing was almost as good as seeing her naked, and my dick was already so hard, I had to unzip my jeans to get a little relief. She was leaning her face up, though, her mouth parted expectantly and I had a hard time thinking about anything but kissing her. I lifted her off the ground and she wound those silky legs around my waist. I drove my tongue into her mouth and kissed her the way I'd wanted to since the first time I'd seen her at that party.

I walked us to the bed and fell back on it with her on top of me. Our mouths fused together and she was grinding against me. Normally, she only did that when I had a finger inside of her, but this was next-level stuff with her. She was so ready for me to fuck her, it was practically written all over her face, but I wanted to make it good. First times tended not to be, from what I remembered, and that's not what I wanted for Ellie.

I dragged my mouth from her luscious lips and gently nudged her onto her back.

"Can I undress you?" I asked.

She nodded and I yanked the nightgown up and over her

head. I let it fall to the floor as I looked at her in nothing but that sexy little thong, and my brain momentarily shorted out.

"Fuckkk…" I drew out the word because I wanted to burn this memory into my subconscious, so I'd never, ever forget what she looked like as she gave herself to me. I'd been telling myself to go slow because there was so much at stake in both our lives, but it was impossible at this point. I'd wanted her from the first time I saw her, but having her like this was so much better than anything I'd fantasized about that first night on the dance floor.

"We should, um, talk about—" I tried to focus on safety and protection, but Ellie, as always, was a step ahead of me.

"You have condoms, yes?" Her bright blue eyes burned up into mine.

"Yes."

She reached up and wound her arms around my neck. "Then shut up and kiss me."

She didn't have to ask me twice. I drove my tongue into her mouth and forgot all about the other things I'd wanted to do first. Like sucking on those pert little nipples or sliding my tongue inside her slick pussy. There was no time for any of it, though, because she was pushing at my jeans and I somehow managed to get them down and off, taking my boxers with them.

Now there was nothing between us but that little triangle of silk from her thong, and I reached down, flicking the strip along her hip until the fabric gave way. My mouth never left hers, our tongues brushing insistently as she tangled her fingers in my hair.

"Do it," she whispered. "I can't wait to see what it's like."

"I don't want to hurt you."

"You won't."

"Fu-uckkkk…" That seemed to be one of the only words I was capable of tonight. I reached for my jeans, fumbling to find the condom I'd stuffed in my pocket, and moved away from her long enough to slide it down my aching shaft. Then I was between her legs, the tender skin of her thighs brushing the outside of my legs. God, she was beautiful, and never more so than right now.

I lined myself up at her slick entrance and paused again, looking down into her pretty face. Then I pressed forward with one slow but firm thrust. And slid all the way in. She clenched around me and I nearly lost my mind. It was so tight, she was practically strangling my cock, and I squeezed my eyes shut, hoping to last longer. This was the very best kind of torture and I pulled back enough to give me room to move.

"You okay?" I rasped, managing to open my eyes long enough to look into hers.

"Yesss…" She leaned her head up for a soul-bending kiss that scorched me from the inside out. "More." That last word was a breath against my mouth but that's all it took.

I picked up speed and angled my hips, going harder and deeper each time I bottomed out. Her legs wound around my back and her nails dug into my skin.

"Oh god, Patrick, more!"

There was no stopping now and I let go of all my inhibitions. She was tight and wet and arching up to meet my every thrust. She took greedy pulls from my tongue, matching the rhythm of my cock, and my body took over. I slid my hands under her ass to lift it for maximum penetration and within a few more strokes, I felt fire shooting down my spine, my balls starting to tingle. I was so damn close but I needed her to get off first because her pleasure was more important than mine.

"Patrick!" Her shriek caught me off guard, but the look on her face told me she was close. I barely noticed the pain of her nails digging into my forearms as I shifted, looking for the spot that would set her off, and out of nowhere, her body tensed and arched up. "Yes-yes-yes-yes!" She bucked beneath me, her orgasm bringing on mine, and I rode her like a fucking bronco. She was tight and hot and convulsing around me, each ripple setting off another round of spasms that had us both gasping for air.

"Holy shitballs," she whispered, her face nestled in the hollow of my shoulder as I collapsed on top of her. "Is it always like that?"

"Mostly." I kissed her shoulder. "But I have to say that was pretty fucking amazing for your first time. Did I hurt you?"

She shook her head. "I have an IUD, so my hymen probably was broken when they put it in."

"You have an IUD?" I frowned. "But you weren't sexually active?"

"My mother is nothing if not prepared," she muttered. "She wanted to make sure I didn't do anything stupid that might derail my future as a doctor."

"Like getting pregnant."

She nodded, her arms still tightly wound around me.

"Your mom is something." I shifted, slowly pulling out. "Let me go clean up. I'll be right back."

"Okay."

I padded into the bathroom and just as I was about to take it off, I noticed the condom had a tear in it.

Shit!

It took a second for me to remember Ellie had an IUD, and I breathed a sigh of relief. I'd never had a condom break before, which was probably a testament to how hard I'd gone at Ellie. I should have been gentler, but she'd begged for me and it had been fucking awesome.

"So another first, babe," I called out to her as I finished up.

"Hmm?" She looked up and I couldn't help but lean down and kiss her before crawling under the covers with her.

"We broke the condom. That's never happened to me before."

She grimaced. "Well, thank god for my mom then, I guess."

"First time for everything," I chortled.

She burrowed into my arms and wound her legs through mine. Our bodies fit together perfectly and I had zero urge to move. Usually after sex, I either fell asleep or got antsy, and I didn't feel either of those things right now. Ellie's warm, curvy body was pressed against mine, her silky hair draped over one arm, and there didn't seem to be any rush to do anything but languish in postcoital comfort.

We must have dropped off to sleep because the next time I opened my eyes, it was five in the morning. My stomach was rumbling since we'd skipped both dinner and tutoring, but looking at Ellie's beautiful body made me forget all about food. Last night I'd planned to kiss every inch of her soft skin but she'd derailed that plan, so I would make it up to her—and myself—now.

I dipped my head beneath the covers and moved between her legs. I hadn't had a chance to see much last night so I took my time now, touching her most intimate places with gentle fingers since she was still asleep. Her pussy was pink and inviting, like the petals of a flower opening for the first time in spring. I dipped my head and used the tip of my tongue to get my first taste.

Oh, yeah, this was going to be epic. She tasted like bourbon and salt water and sex, which were three of my favorite fucking things in the world. I scooted down as far as I could and then dove in, starting with light kisses on her mound while I traced a line up her slit with one finger. She shifted, a soft sigh coming from her, and I smiled to myself. I stroked her clit with my tongue, circling and teasing until she arched up into my face.

"Patrick…" Her voice was breathy, sleepy, but full of wonder.

I slid a finger inside of her as I continued to focus my attention on her clit, and she was already soaked. Her lips quivered prettily as I licked them, and when I slid my tongue inside of her, the moan that escaped her chest was long and low. She was going to come any second now, so I slowed down and went back to her clit.

"Patrick, please… Oh shit, please!"

I picked up the pace again, unable to refuse her, and pushed two fingers inside of her. She was small and tight but clenched around me like a little vise, her hips rising and falling as I finger-fucked her. When I flattened my tongue against her clit, she clasped her hands over her mouth to cover her scream, her lower body bucking against me, soaking my face with her arousal.

"Fuckkkk…" She mimicked my use of the word last night, drawing it out as she dropped an arm over her face. "What was that? Is that how you wake someone up? By giving them an orgasmic heart attack?"

I chuckled, wiping my mouth with the back of my hand. "If you want."

"God, yes. Yes, every damn day." She tugged me up to her face and kissed me, sucking on my tongue and pressing those sweet tits against my chest. "Fuck me, Patrick."

"Yes." I fumbled on the floor to find my bag and grab another condom, and then I was inside of her for the second time in I didn't know how many hours. I rolled onto my back, taking her with me, and settled her on top. "Ride me, baby. The pressure is different in this position."

"Oh, wow." Her eyes rounded a little as she sank down all the way. "It feels so good."

"Uh-huh." I put my hands on her hips and gently lifted her. "Just like that. Find your rhythm."

She was as quick a learner in bed as she was everywhere else and didn't hesitate to start gyrating on my lap. I ran my thumbs back and forth over her nipples, watching as they hardened and peaked, pinching them until she gasped. But her pussy clenched around me tighter than ever, so I knew she liked it. She was stretched around my cock tightly and I felt every miniscule movement, how she clenched when I hit certain spots. She was so damn responsive and I let her have her way with me because watching her discover her sexuality was fucking amazing. She lifted and lowered, circling a little as she explored what felt good. Watching my cock disappear inside of her over and over was more than I could stand, though. It was truly the most erotic thing I'd ever seen.

Color exploded behind my eyelids as my orgasm raced down my spine unexpectedly. I growled, pumping harder inside of her even as I pinched her clit. And then there was nothing but lightning, shooting between us, around us, all over us. It was all but electrocuting me as she exploded over me.

When she finally dropped down to rest her chest against mine, I squeezed her tighter, holding on to the feeling of being buried to the hilt, her warmth enveloping me.

"This is way more fun than statistics," she whispered.

ELLIE

With Patrick away with the team the following weekend, I distracted myself from how horny I was by studying and then hanging out with Chastity on Saturday afternoon. I'd been thinking about putting a few streaks of hot pink in my hair, so we went to the drugstore to see if we could find some. She opened a bottle of prosecco once we got back to her place so I told her all about my sexcapades with Patrick, and by the time we finished it, I was tipsy enough to pull out the bottle of pink dye. I didn't drink very often, but Chastity and I had gotten drunk together on a few occasions and she'd taught me to love both prosecco and the buzz I got from it.

We opened a second bottle and examined the instructions on the package of dye.

"Looks easy enough," she said.

"Let's do it."

It took about an hour, but when we were done, I loved it. I stared in the mirror, taking in the two streaks. I'd done one in the front, so it fell over my face, and the second on the left side. Both were thick and chunky, and the color stood out against my honey-colored hair.

"You think Patrick will like it?" she asked, twirling a hot pink lock around her finger.

"As long as we're naked, I don't think he'll care."

"It's not just sex, is it?"

"No." I smiled. "There's a lot more than sex going on between us, but since my experience is limited to just him, it's possible I'm wrong."

"He adores you," she said, smiling back at me. "And my only experience with boyfriends is Dylan, but I know he loves me."

"You and Dylan were friends for a long time first. Patrick and I have barely known each other a month." I picked up the second bottle and poured what was left into our glasses. "And no one's used the L-word or anything crazy like that."

"But do you?"

"Love him?" I flung myself onto the couch and let my head fall back against the cushions. "My analytical mind says no, that it's way too soon. My heart, on the other hand, says I'm an idiot and repeatedly tells my mind to shut the fuck up."

Chastity laughed, sitting on the other end of the couch. "Does your mom know you have a boyfriend?"

"My mom and I haven't spoken since the night she told me she was taking the car."

"If you ever need to go anywhere, I can take you in Dylan's truck."

"I've been okay so far, but thanks." I drank some more prosecco. "I don't think she believes I'm never going home."

"Never? Holidays? Nothing?"

"I'm tired of the pressure, Chastity. It's all I've ever known and just once, I want to feel not just happy, but free."

"Does Patrick make you feel free?"

"God, yes." I stared up at the ceiling. "Can I tell you a secret?"

"Of course."

"I hate computer science."

Her eyes met mine and she blinked. "You, um, what?"

"I chose it just to piss off my mom. I mean, there's aspects of it that are great, but I miss science. Sitting at my desk coding all day is boring *as fuck*."

"So…what are you going to do?"

"I don't know. I'm already in the program and I'm pretty sure what I have now would translate to a master's degree by the end of the semester, but I don't know if any of it would transfer over to biology, which is what I want. I really fucked up with the direction I went."

"So stop pussyfooting around and go into biotechnology, which is what you want." She knew me well and I sighed.

"I know. I've just made a mess of things because I was so determined to thwart my parents' efforts to get me into medical school. Now I'm doing something that I like but don't love, and it's time for me to make some hard decisions."

"What does Patrick say?"

"I haven't told him this part of it. I mean, he knows I'm bored with coding all day, but not why I chose it or that I want to switch majors. Again."

"The school will work with you," Chastity said firmly. "Dr. Lancet loves you. Why haven't you talked to him?"

I shrugged. "Maybe a little afraid he would be mad at me for leaving the biology department and defecting over to computers."

She shook her head. "He's spent the last thirty years in academia, watching young minds grow and mature—I'm willing to bet you're not the first shining star to stray off a path and then go back."

I yawned and downed the rest of my glass of prosecco. "You're probably right."

With both bottles empty, we dozed off on opposite ends of the couch, which was how Dylan found us when he got back from wherever he'd been.

"You two obviously cannot be left unsupervised," he said, his eyes twinkling. "Lucky for you, dinner's cooking and you two are awake."

"Hi." Chastity smiled up at him and he leaned down to kiss her.

They were so cute together, I loved watching them. It made me miss Patrick, though, and I couldn't wait until he got home tomorrow afternoon.

I met Patrick at the dining hall for dinner the next night since the team's flight from Minnesota had been delayed and he didn't get back to campus until almost five. He scooped me up for a kiss and then grinned.

"Pink hair. I like it."

"Do you?" I asked, biting my lip. "Or is it too much?"

"Too much what? Color? It's hot." He looped an arm around my shoulders as we walked inside.

"I've wanted to do it for a long time, but my mom always said no and then I kind of didn't have the nerve... Like, what would people think?"

"Well, you don't have to worry about what I think. You're hot no matter what color your hair is."

"So...Mohawk would be okay?"

He shrugged. "Sure. We could do it so your pubes match too."

I snickered. "Let's leave my pubes alone."

"Like I said, that's all up to you. I don't care one way or the other."

"I knew there was a reason I liked you."

We got our food and sat in a booth in the back. I toyed with mine, distracted by a lot of different things, so I hadn't realized Patrick was watching me.

"Something going on with you?" he asked after a moment, his eyes meeting mine.

I smiled. "Yeah. Kinda. School stuff."

"Still hating the project you're working on?"

"I hate sitting there coding all day," I said after a moment. "I miss the lab. The biology department."

"So go back to it."

"It's not that simple."

"How come? Can't you switch majors?"

"I'm in a graduate program. You can't just say, okay, I'm bored now, let's try something else. Especially when you're on a scholarship."

"Well, there have to be options. Is there an advisor you can talk to?"

"You sound like Chastity. And yes, there is. I'm going to stop by his office tomorrow. Dr. Lancet was my favorite undergrad professor and my advisor while I was a biology major."

"You should definitely talk to him and get some options."

"I just don't know what I want, so it's hard to talk about options."

"Sounds to me like you know exactly what you want, you just don't want to tell your mom because she'll say I told you so."

"Oh, no!" I said quickly. "I have zero interest in medical school. I want to work in a lab, and maybe teach on the side, but I don't want to be any form of medical doctor. I want a Ph.D., not an M.D."

"Straight biology or biotech?"

I sighed. "And that's the problem. I don't know. I haven't narrowed down my focus, so I didn't want to go to Dr. Lancet until I could tell him exactly what I wanted."

"Isn't that the purpose of college, to help you figure that out?"

"Not once you're in a graduate program."

"Will you lose credit for everything you've done so far?"

"Not everything, I don't think. All of my projects have had an element of biology to them since that's what I love, but I don't know how the course work will translate if I move over to biotech."

"The best person to help you sort through all that is Dr. Lancet."

"For sure."

He reached across the table and put his hands over mine. "Don't worry so much. You're brilliant and hard-working, with a good head on your shoulders. I think you know what you want, but you've been pulled in so many directions, for so long, you haven't been able to focus on what you'll need going forward."

"Sometimes it feels like I'm never going to get there, like I'm just spinning my wheels so I can make everyone else happy and my own needs are way down on the list."

"I think I take care of lots of your needs," he said under his breath, his blue eyes darkening.

I swallowed. I loved when he looked at me like he was going to throw me against the wall and rip my clothes off. Speaking of which, he hadn't done anything like that yet, and I made a mental note to add it to the sexual bucket list I'd started.

"Something is going on your special bucket list," he said knowingly. I'd told him about the list, though I hadn't let him see it yet.

I grinned, wiggling my eyebrows. "Mayyyybe."

"Can't you at least give me a hint?"

I opened my mouth to answer just as his phone rang and I clearly saw the word "Dad" flashing on the screen. He made a face, hesitating.

"Go on," I told him. "When was the last time you talked to him?"

"Not long enough."

"Get it over with or he'll probably call back a dozen times."

"Shit." He grabbed the phone and put it to his ear. "Hi, Dad."

17

PATRICK

"It's about time." My father's voice held that same hard-edge tone it always had when he called me. It was one of a dozen reasons I rarely answered when he did.

"How's it going?" I asked him, gazing across the table at Ellie and she just squeezed my hand since I was still holding one of hers with my free one.

"What's going on with the Sidewinders?" he asked automatically.

"I don't know. I don't play for them yet."

"Don't be a smartass."

"We have this same conversation every time you call. Nothing has changed. I'm still in college."

"Dammit, son, you're on fire right now! You need to ride this momentum into the pros. This year! Maybe even now, if they get into the playoffs."

"Even if I decide to go pro early, it's not going to be before the end of the semester," I said quietly.

"Listen to me," he continued, "there's no reason to wait. That degree isn't going to do anything for you but—"

"The *degree* isn't going to do anything for me?" I demanded.

"You mean the one you wished you'd gotten a thousand times after you got hurt?"

There was silence on the other end and I knew he was gearing up to explode. He hated when I threw that in his face, so I did it whenever I wanted him to stop whatever he was doing to aggravate me. Like trying to force me to make a decision I wasn't sure I was ready to make.

"You've been using that lame-ass excuse your whole goddamn life," Dad growled. "You think I'm a loser because I got hurt in my first season and didn't make a lot of money? That what's bugging you? You don't want to be a loser like me if you get hurt?"

"You're not a loser," I snapped. "But right now, you're being an asshole and I'm tired of it. You don't yell at Paxton, you yell at me. You don't mind if he gets his degree, but you don't want me to get mine. You're—"

"Because you're better than he is!"

"That's not true." It might have been true when we were younger, but not anymore. I was one of the best college players anywhere but Paxton was up there too. It was why we'd both been drafted in the first round. His skill was also a big part of the reason why Paxton was going to the pros now, instead of waiting another year; he was hot and on their radar. He didn't want to take the chance someone hotter would catch their eye and he'd wind up down in the minors. The fact that he had enough credits to graduate factored into his decision as well, of course, but there was a little fear that I didn't have because I'd never worried about my skill or my game.

Dad was still talking, trying to explain about my god-given athleticism and wasted opportunities, but I'd tuned him out. I was staring into Ellie's pretty face, which was etched with concern at the moment, her eyes never leaving mine, both of her hands clasped around my one.

"It's okay," she mouthed. "I'm here."

"I know," I mouthed back.

We smiled at each other and I realized she'd become the calm in my storm. I hoped I'd become hers as well, but right now she was the entire reason I could tune out my dad and hang on to my temper. Her sweet face. Her firm grip on my hand. The bright blue eyes watching me worriedly.

"Patrick, are you listening?"

"I'm listening," I said after a moment. "I just don't know what to say. Not now and not the other five hundred times we've had some version of this conversation. I want to get my degree and since I've spent most of my time focused on hockey, instead of school, I don't have the credits to graduate. It's that simple."

"There's about a million dollars that says it's not simple at all."

"That's really all it boils down to for you, isn't it?" I asked. "You're so focused on the money, you can't see the big picture. Well, I do, and I'm not ready yet. I wish I could make you understand. Anyway, sorry, Dad, but I have to get to class." I disconnected and hung my head, closing my eyes and breathing in and out slowly.

I felt movement behind me and then Ellie wrapped her arms around me from the back. She rested her chin on my shoulder and pressed the side of her face against mine. "We've got this," she whispered. "You have me and I have you. We're going to be okay because we have each other. You'll see."

"I can honestly say you're the best thing that's ever happened to me," I said, leaning into her warmth.

We sat like that for a little while, despite the weird looks we got since we were in the middle of the dining hall. I didn't care, though, and Ellie held on to me as if she was holding me up instead of the other way around.

"So…I'm guessing you don't feel like studying," she said as we cleaned up and headed out.

"Actually, I feel like giving you your first hockey lesson."

She arched her brows. "At *night*?"

"Sure. Come on." I took her hand and we walked across campus to the hockey house. I walked in and was glad to see Lex on the couch, watching a movie.

"Hey." He looked up in surprise. "What's up?"

"You have a couple of sticks and a puck we could borrow?"

"You don't have a stick?" he asked, laughing. "There are about four hundred in the garage. Help yourself."

"Thanks." I went in that direction and found two sticks I thought would work. Ellie was right-handed so I found a couple of right-handed sticks for us. Pucks were scattered all over the place and I picked up a few before leading Ellie out back.

The guys had a makeshift rink set up, without the ice. There were red and blue lines spray-painted on the ground and two goalie nets, only partially covered by snow at the moment. There obviously wasn't anywhere near the room needed for a real setup, but a lot of drunken floor hockey had been played here the last few years.

"Your first lesson will be stickhandling," I told Ellie, who was watching me in amusement. "Now, this is how you hold a stick properly." I stood behind her, putting the stick in her hand and bending her body into the right position. "It's actually easier on skates because of balance, but you get the idea... That's right, just like that. Now, when you shoot—" I covered her arms and hands with mine, rotating both our bodies as we wound up the shot. I swung our arms, flicked my wrist and sent the puck sailing into the dead grass about ten feet away.

"Can we do it again?" She was concentrating on every little thing I did.

"Sure."

We shot a few more times with me guiding her arms and hands. She watched intently and then went to collect all the pucks.

"I think I get it," she said. "Can I try now?"

"Absolutely." I stood a few feet behind her, watching her get herself in position. Then she wound up and sent the first puck flying up, over the fence, and out of the yard. She turned, biting back a laugh.

"Too much?"

"Actually, that was perfect." I put another puck down in front of her. "If we were in a real arena. Here in the backyard, let's try something a little shorter."

We had a blast as I taught her how to shoot and stickhandle. Doing it on the grass was different than on ice, of course, but there were no ice rinks open to the public right now anyway. Besides, she didn't care. She just wanted to learn something new. She got off on trying different things, which was making life really fun in the bedroom, but it was a lot more than that.

She was a hundred-and-ten-pound bundle of sexy fun and every damn day was a new adventure. I was completely addicted to Ellie McGinn and there wasn't anything I could do about it.

I played my ass off that weekend. We'd been up against a huge rival, Boston College, and we kicked ass and took names. They were a great team but no match for our energy Friday night and I racked up two goals and an assist. Paxton scored too, so we were in a good mood as we headed out to meet Ellie and Naomi.

"You and Ellie have been inseparable these last few weeks," Paxton said to me as we walked.

"She's amazing," I said, nodding.

"Well, damn. Now I owe Naomi ten bucks," he muttered.

"You guys bet on whether or not I was going to dump her?" I demanded.

He shook his head. "Not exactly. She said this was the real deal; I said it would burn itself out in two weeks."

"I don't know what it is," I admitted, "but it's definitely not burning itself out. Ellie's..." My voice trailed off because I couldn't think of the right word to describe her.

"Special?"

"Yeah. Smart, sweet, and sexy. The freakin' trifecta of special."

"You're right about that. Make sure you don't fuck it up."

"She makes it easy to be with her. Even with her parents messing with her head and how hard she works, she's so relaxed and casual about everything. I think about her all day long." I cut a glance at him. "I'm falling hard, aren't I?"

He shrugged, lifting his hands, palms up. "Who am I to say?"

I elbowed him. "You're a big help."

"I fell hard not that long ago, and I definitely see some of the same signs."

"And you're happy?" I asked him. "I mean, I know you love her, but you're genuinely happy and like living together? You're comfortable with the idea of taking her to Seattle? No doubts? Nothing?"

"Nope. She's amazing and we're good together. Why?"

"Ellie and I are way too new for that kind of conversation, but man, I can't imagine leaving her now that I've found her."

"So stay another year. College is paid for, the Sidewinders aren't going anywhere… Stay and fall in love and do what makes you happy. Don't let Dad manipulate you out of the future you want. If Ellie is that important, you're either going to take her with you, or stay around another year to figure it out. And anyway, it's only February. You have time for all that."

"It feels serious," I blurted out. "And it scares the shit out of me."

"I think it's supposed to. I can't speak for anyone else, of course, but it's pretty scary when it's the real thing with the right woman."

"Even at our age? I mean, she's only nineteen."

"I don't think that matters. Age is just a number."

"I know. And thinking about being without her in the fall makes me want to puke."

"Holy fuck, you're in love." He stared at me for a second

before starting to walk again. "Been a long time coming. Better not tell Dad, though."

"Believe me, he's the last person I'd tell."

ELLIE

I met with Dr. Lancet that week, dropping by during his office hours. I'd stopped by another time but he hadn't been there and now I fidgeted outside his door nervously. Finally, I lifted my hand and knocked.

"Elizabeth." He smiled at me. "Come on, come in!"

"Thank you." I walked in and set my backpack down. "Do you have a few minutes?"

"For you?" His eyes twinkled. "Always."

I sank into the chair by his desk, but now that I was here, I wasn't sure what to say.

"Whatever it is, just spit it out. You look like a young woman with a lot on your mind."

"I..." I blew out a breath. "I hate coding all day."

He smiled. "I figured you would."

"Why didn't you say anything?"

"Would you have listened?"

"Probably not."

"And that's why I didn't say anything." He leaned forward. "Tell me what's on your mind. Do you want to drop out of the program?"

"There are so many issues at this point, it's hard to know

where to start." I looked away, almost embarrassed.

He didn't say anything, waiting for me, and I finally found the words. "Science has always been my thing, but the idea of medical school makes me a little twitchy. I don't want to be that kind of doctor. I want to be a scientist. I want to study everything at this point; I can't even narrow down what field of biology I love the most, because I truly love it all. But my mother won't let up about med school, so I went the other way completely, just to piss her off. And now I'm in a program I hate, doing the parts of coding I dislike, and moving further away from anything that remotely makes me happy."

"Ellie, it's always been biotech," he said gently. "You know it and I know it."

"How do you know it when I don't even know it?"

"The same way I knew you'd hate computer science." He smiled faintly. "I've been around the block a few times, mentored a few students in my day."

I sighed.

"You don't have to take my word for it, but what are you going to do?"

"My mother is cutting me off," I admitted. "She took my car and I think the only reason she keeps paying for my phone is because she can track me that way."

"You and your mother are both as stubborn as they come." He shook his head.

Tears stung my eyelids even though I was trying to be mature and responsible about all of this. I'd been so busy with Patrick, I hadn't allowed myself time to think about what it would mean to be on my own as soon as this summer, and talking about it now, made it real.

"What can I do?" he asked. "Do you want me to talk to my colleagues in the biology department? See if we can move you over? It'll be a bit like starting over, but you're only nineteen, and with your work ethic, you'll probably breeze through any program you get into."

"I'd like to find out what my options are," I admitted. "There's someone important in my life right now, so before I do anything, I want to run them by him first, but I need options."

"Of course. Let me make some calls, talk to some colleagues and see what there is to see. Stop by next week and maybe I'll have news by then."

I smiled. "You've made my whole day. Thank you."

"Any time." He paused, narrowing his eyes a little. "I know she's been hard on you, but maybe reach out to your mother. She loves you, Ellie, and doesn't want you to make the same mistakes she made." He knew my mother well since she'd taught here for a long time before retiring to write books. However, I wasn't sure what he was alluding to.

I arched my brows. "Mistakes?"

He busied himself with papers on his desk. "I've another meeting, I'm afraid. We'll talk next week."

"Thanks again." I picked up my backpack and walked out, wondering what he'd meant about my mom, but not curious enough to actually call her. Taking the car had hurt and every time I thought about it, I wanted to cry. My father had left me a message a few days ago, but I'd ignored it. I was probably being childish, but so were they, and I was a lot closer to being a child than they were.

Patrick and I were walking back to my dorm that night after classes when I spotted a familiar figure standing in front of the building. I slowed down and groaned under my breath.

"What's wrong?" he asked, following my gaze.

"It's my dad," I said.

"You want me to leave?" he asked.

"No. I don't have anything to hide. Come on." We went the rest of the way at our regular pace and I watched my father's face as he realized I was holding hands with a big, sexy hunk of a guy.

"Ellie." He had his hands in his pockets as we approached.

"Hi, Dad."

"Who's your friend?" He met Patrick's gaze directly.

"Patrick Graham, sir." Patrick held out his hand and they shook.

"You're on the hockey team."

"Yes, sir. Team captain."

I couldn't be sure but I thought my father's lips were twitching, though he tried hard to hide it. What the hell was that about? Did he find it funny that I had a boyfriend or that he was a hockey player?

"What are you doing here?" I asked abruptly.

He dangled familiar keys in front of me. "I've brought you back your car."

I didn't reach for them. "You can keep it if the trade-off is me going to medical school."

He sighed. "There's no price, Ellie. It was a birthday present and it was wrong of your mom to threaten you with it."

"But you're the one that's here, not her."

"She's waiting in the van. She's hurt."

"*She's* hurt?" I stared at him. "What is there for her to be hurt about? That I won't follow her dreams or because I might repeat her mistakes?" I hadn't planned to say that last part but it slipped out anyway.

His eyes narrowed as he looked at me. "How did you find out about that?"

"She worked here for a long time. People talk."

"She was pregnant. She had no choice but to marry that guy. Him leaving her was a blessing. If he hadn't, I never would have met her and you wouldn't be here, so all the scandal was worth it."

Scandal? Yikes. I didn't know what to say to that because I had so many questions. "What happened to…the baby?"

"She lost it. The gossipmongers didn't tell you that part?"

"They didn't say anything about a baby." At least that much was true.

"There was damage after the miscarriage. We didn't think she could have children at all, so you were a surprise. But it was her only viable pregnancy and that's why she's so protective of you, Ellie."

"So instead of building a relationship with her only child, she goes out of her way to push me away?"

"As I've said repeatedly, you two need to talk. I wish you'd reach out."

"She's the adult. I'm the kid. And I didn't do anything wrong." I don't know why I was being stubborn about this, but the wounds caused by the rift between us ran deep and just this once, I needed her to make some sort of apologetic overture.

"Will you come home this weekend?"

"The team is playing Dartmouth," I said automatically. "It's a big rivalry I can't miss. But they'll be on the road in two weeks, so maybe I can come home then."

"All right." He nodded, turning to Patrick. "You're welcome to come with her at some point, Patrick. We'd like to get to know you better if you're someone important to Ellie."

"Thank you, sir, I'd like that too." They shook hands again, Dad hugged me and handed me the keys, and then started heading away.

"Where did you park the car?" I called after him.

He shrugged as he kept walking. "It's not my car—how am I supposed to know where it's parked?"

I laughed in spite of my annoyance.

"That's cold," Patrick said, laughing. "Funny, but cold."

I elbowed him.

"Two minutes, elbowing!" he yelled.

"Are you putting me in the penalty box?" I asked, wiggling my eyebrows.

"Maybeee…"

"Sounds like fun!" I made a run for the door.

19

PATRICK

Between hockey, studying, and spending every spare second I had with Ellie, I didn't have time to think about the Sidewinders or the growing pressure my dad was putting on me. He was calling every few days now, and if I didn't answer, he'd call Paxton to find out where I was and what I was doing. Luckily, my twin was adept at putting him off, but it irritated me.

On the plus side, I was having the best season of my hockey career so far, my grades were all A's, and my sex life, well, Ellie and I spent a lot more time naked than I'd ever imagined we would. In general, my life was pretty fucking great and I'd unofficially made the decision to stay in school next year, so I was caught off guard when my phone rang and I saw a Las Vegas exchange flash on the screen. That had to be something related to the Sidewinders and I quickly answered.

"Hello?"

"Patrick? This is Anatoli Petrov from the Las Vegas Sidewinders."

I almost shit myself. Toli Petrov was one of the leading scorers in the league and a veteran both on the Sidewinders and in hockey, so it took a second to find my voice and get over the shock that one of my heroes was on the phone with me.

"Uh, hi. Yes. Hello."

He chuckled. "You had a hell of a game Saturday night," he said, referring to our game against Dartmouth.

"Thank you."

"Management is definitely looking forward to having you on the team here and so am I—hopefully before I retire!"

"I'm working on it," I said slowly. "I have another year here but I've been waffling on whether or not to go pro before I graduate."

"Well, we'd like to entice you. The reason I'm calling is to invite you to Montreal the first weekend in March. It's a Sunday game and my understanding is that you're off, so if you'd like to come, hang out with us a little afterward, it'll be a good chance for you to ask all your questions and get a feel for the vibe in the locker room."

"I'd love that."

"If you have a significant other, he or she is welcome to come along."

"She'd love it," I replied automatically. "Thank you. It sounds great."

"Someone from the team will call in a couple of days to give you flight info. You'll fly in that morning and fly back late that night."

"Oh, wow, thank you. I'm excited to meet all of you."

"We're excited to bring you on board." He paused. "Is there anything you want to ask me now or would you rather wait?"

"Honestly, the biggest question on my mind is whether or not to play in college another year or to go pro at the end of the school year. I've done the pros and cons on paper and the only con is that I'm afraid if I leave now, I'll never go back to finish my degree. It's only three classes, though, so Ellie, my girlfriend, keeps telling me I can do it virtually."

"You have a lot to consider," Toli said thoughtfully. "But let me see if I can help at all. From the perspective of hockey, the team is going to wait for you whether you come next season or the season after, assuming you continue playing at the level you've been playing. You have to make this decision based on what's best for you in the long run."

"But if it was you," I said carefully, "would you leave college and go pro now?"

"I never went to college but my younger brother did. We've both had long, successful careers in hockey, even though we took different paths in getting here. Me, personally, yes, I would go now. But I'm not you. Nate Calloway came to us from college—talk with him when we meet up in Montreal. He might have better perspective for you since he's already been through it."

"Thank you," I said. "I will."

"All right, well, take it easy and we'll see you in a few weeks."

"Thanks again, Toli." I hung up and immediately texted Ellie.

PATRICK: Want to go see the Sidewinders play in Montreal in a few weeks? All expenses paid!

ELLIE: Hell, yes! Did they invite you?

PATRICK: Toli Petrov, who's a pretty big deal in hockey, called me personally.

ELLIE: OMG, that's amazing! This means they're watching you, right? And are, like, seriously interested?

PATRICK: They drafted me… I think they're pretty serious about me! LOL.

ELLIE: And they invited me to go to Montreal, too?

PATRICK: Yup. My significant other was specifically invited.

ELLIE: I feel very special.

PATRICK: You were special long before this, babe.

ELLIE: And you might get a very special gift tonight to celebrate…

PATRICK: Will you be naked?

ELLIE: Maybeeeee…

PATRICK: I'm intrigued.

ELLIE: LOL. See you later.

Ellie met me at the door of her room wearing a robe. I almost laughed when she dropped it the moment I shut the door behind me, but her naked body was nothing to laugh at. I yanked off my own clothes in record time, but before I could grab her, she'd pushed me onto the bed on my back and then crawled over me. Her eyes were glittering with desire as she stroked my cock.

"How come you haven't asked me to do this before?" she murmured, dipping her head and pressing a chaste kiss on the tip.

"Because...uh...I wanted to...uh...wait until you were...uh... comfortable." It was really hard to concentrate when the most beautiful girl in the world was kissing your dick.

"I'm comfortable." She opened her mouth and licked a line along the length of my shaft, and I moaned. "I've been dying to try this."

"Well, don't let me stop you." My head fell back as she sucked me partway into her mouth. Jesus, if this was her first blow job, I was a very lucky man because it didn't get much better than this. Deep-throating was overrated; I far preferred being balls-deep in her pussy over her mouth. But magic happened any time we were together. Our sex life just kept getting better and I didn't understand it. I'd had a lot of sex over the years, but it all faded to nothing now that I was with Ellie. Her body, her mouth, her soulful eyes, they all kept me completely mesmerized, both in bed and out.

She sucked a little harder and I dug my fingers into her hair, moving her head with a steadier rhythm until she got the hang of it. And then she was off and running, using her hands and mouth to work me into a frenzy. Grazing my balls, scraping her teeth lightly along the sensitive skin, she had my number from the get-go. My staying power was always at risk when we made love because her touch was literally magic. For me anyway. A few strokes here, a kiss there, and—bam! I shot off into her mouth like a freakin' freight train and I didn't know whether to be embarrassed I couldn't hold out more than a couple of minutes or proud that she'd learned how to read me so quickly.

"Mmm," she said, licking her lips as she sat up. "What are you going to teach me next?"

"What do you want me to teach you?" I asked, pulling her up so she was resting across my torso, her mouth close to mine. "A little ass play, maybe? Sixty-nine? Orgasm denial? What about—"

"*Orgasm denial?!* What the hell is that? Nobody's denying me any damn orgasms, mister!"

I laughed at her indignance, kissing her pouty lips. "I'm kidding."

"On the other hand, sixty-nine sounds fun…"

"Next time," I said, flipping her on her back. "I need to reciprocate what you just did."

"Now that *definitely* sounds like fun." Her legs fell open and I dove between them. Going down on her never got old and I did it almost every day we were together. Which was every day unless I was on the road with the team. We essentially lived together now, so I had access to her day and night, and her waiting for me naked was always fun. Waking her up by going down on her was my favorite, though I enjoyed it any time.

Sometimes I took it slow, getting her all worked up until she was begging me to let her come. Other times, it was a race to see how quick I could get her off. And that's what I was doing now. I had a trick up my sleeve that my gut told me would make that happen even faster tonight, and I swirled a finger in her juices in preparation.

I circled her clit with my tongue as I slid my finger back to her ass. She was completely caught up in what I was doing, so she didn't notice at first. I kept my touch light, skimming her asshole before attempting anything more. Then I captured her sweet little pleasure bud between my lips while simultaneously pressing the tip of my finger into the tight, puckered hole.

"Patrick!" Her breath left her in a rush and I pressed my finger in a little deeper before she clenched in protest.

"Easy," I whispered. "Just the tip of my finger. Let me in and then I'm going to make you come so hard you won't care how I do it."

The word no wasn't in Ellie's vocabulary when it came to sex and this was no different. She took a deep breath and I distracted her by sucking on her clit some more. She was squirming, alternately arching into my face and bearing down on my finger, so I got her right on the edge of orgasm and then slid my finger all the way in. She gasped as I bit down, and then she exploded around my face. I could barely breathe as she clenched her thighs around my head, but damn, it was pretty watching her lose control like that.

"Holy fucking shit, did you just finger my ass?" she demanded, laughing.

"I did. And you fucking came like a lunatic. I thought you were going to snap my neck with those thighs of yours."

"Sorry."

"You don't sound sorry."

"Nope."

"Let me wash up. Be right back."

A minute later, we were snuggled up together under her heavy down comforter and she moved right into her favorite position against my chest, her legs twined with mine.

"I don't know what I'm going to do when you leave me," she whispered in the darkness.

"I'm not going anywhere," I whispered back as we dropped off to sleep.

ELLIE

Valentine's Day was tomorrow and I had no idea what to do for Patrick. He was with me almost every night now, but my room was small and my twin-size bed was cramped for a guy his size. He never complained but I wondered if he missed the bigger bed at his apartment and if it was bad for an athlete like him to sleep with a girl draped all over him. It probably wasn't a big deal, but I worried about him because he worked his body so hard with hockey. I was often amazed at how much it took for him to stay in shape. He practiced and played games with the team but there were also workouts in his free time that blew me away. I'd gone on a run with him once and thought I might die trying to keep up.

I wanted to do something nice for him, like a professional massage or something, but it really wasn't in my budget. With my future more uncertain than ever, I was trying to be frugal, but I hated not doing something special for him on our first Valentine's Day together.

"Kissing games," Harley said when we ran into each other in the coffee shop.

"Kissing games?"

"Yeah, like watching an episode of *Friends* and every time Joey does something stupid, you have to kiss. I mean, you can get creative, but that could be a fun way to spend Valentine's Day."

"That does sound kind of fun."

"You could cater it to hockey, too. Put on a game and every time the team he's not rooting for ices the puck, you kiss. Every time his team gets a power play, you kiss."

"I could probably make a list," I said thoughtfully.

"And then you'll end up getting naked anyway."

We laughed.

"So where have you been hiding?" I asked her.

She shrugged. "Here and there. That guy I was hooking up with ghosted me, so I'm kind of doing my own thing these days. Guys are too much of a headache."

"They're not all like that," I said gently.

"Yeah, you got lucky." She paid the cashier and took a sip of her drink.

"Patrick is pretty special," I admitted. "I don't know how I found him, but I'm so glad I did."

"You deserve a nice guy," Harley said, smiling over at me. "Just keep your options open, you know? He's going to be going off to the pros, whether it's next year or the year after, and your Ph.D. is going to take longer than that."

"Shit!" I suddenly remembered I'd never checked back with Dr. Lancet. "I have to go see my advisor. I'll call you later!" I grabbed my coat and coffee and ran out the door. I hurried across campus and into the building where his office was.

I'd forgotten all about checking in with him and I wanted to have my ducks in a row before I saw my parents again. I didn't know exactly what I was going to say to my mom, but I wasn't as mad now that I had my car back and I just wanted them to understand me. To let me follow my dreams and find out who and what I was going to be on my own. They couldn't do that for me, and while I now understood that my mother had dropped out of medical school because she'd been pregnant and gotten married, that wasn't me. I wasn't completely sure where I was going professionally, but I knew that wasn't it. Maybe with Dr. Lancet's help I could shift my focus, and if I presented them with something more concrete than computer science, they'd understand that I could figure out my future on my own.

"Ellie!" Dr. Lancet was just leaving the building as I arrived and I fell into step beside him.

"I'm sorry I haven't come by before now but I've been so busy."

"It's all right, my dear. I do have some news for you, though."

"Oh, tell me."

"First of all, I believe there's a professor needed for the Intro to Biology course during both summer sessions. They're both hybrid classes, so you'd only have to physically be in the classroom for the labs, not the lecture portion. Second, Dr. Phillips in the biotech department would like to talk with you before you do anything else. So, while I don't know what you'll discuss with Dr. Phillips, I have a feeling he'll work with you to move over some of your credits while helping you come up with a game plan for going forward. Everyone here wants to see you succeed. You're a very special student, Ellie."

"Thank you," I said gratefully. "I'll go over there now and make an appointment."

"Very good. Well, I'm late for a class of my own. Stop by any time, dear."

"Thank you!" I waved and headed in the opposite direction. I couldn't wait to tell Patrick the news.

Patrick had a team meeting that night so I worked on the kissing game idea. I picked up some colored cardstock at the bookstore and printed cards with it. Each one would go into a bag of some kind and he could pull one out every so often and we had to do whatever it said on the card.

I'd also picked up his favorite candy—strawberry Twizzlers—

and a card. I hid everything at the bottom of my laundry basket and then tried to focus on my project. With everything going on, I wasn't sure if I needed to finish it or not, and the indecision was messing with my mojo. Dr. Lancet had given me hope that I could switch over to biotechnology, which was what I truly loved, but it felt like I'd wasted a lot of time and energy on something for no reason other than to spite my mother.

I felt kind of ridiculous now, like I'd wasted everyone's time, and I had no solution. I was working on one, but nothing felt a hundred percent right. Mostly, I wanted to run away to an island in the South Pacific and lie on the beach for a few months. Was the drinking age eighteen there? If so, I could be one of those beach-side bartenders, talking and laughing with people a few nights a week and learning how to surf and perfecting my tan the rest of the time. I'd have time to read trashy novels, watch all the movies I'd never had time for, and find a cute guy to make love with all day.

I grimaced.

That last part sounded gross.

The only person I wanted to make love with was Patrick. And no matter what he decided, he definitely wasn't going with me to the South Pacific.

Dammit.

I was so confused and stressed but I couldn't really talk to him about it because he was confused and stressed too. He wanted to stay in school so he could get his degree, but watching him on the ice, I sensed he was ready to go pro. He wanted to be out there with the Sidewinders, doing what he did. Because that's who he was. Just like I eventually wanted to be in a lab doing what I did: science. Why was everything so fucking complicated? And how were we going to be together if he went to Vegas and I either stayed here or applied to another science program somewhere that wasn't Vegas?

Maybe we weren't.

Which was why my mother had worked so hard to keep me

from being distracted. Because I was definitely distracted now and it scared me a little. Not because I cared so much about my studies short-term, but because my whole outlook on life had changed since meeting Patrick and I had no clue what to do. And if there was anything I hated, it was not knowing how to do something.

I woke up on Valentine's Day to Patrick's dark head buried between my thighs and his warm, wicked tongue doing all the things I loved. He made me come once and then went at me a second time, not letting up until I'd done it again, which had never happened before. By the time he was done with me, I was limp and sweaty, completely spent, but he wasn't finished yet. He pulled me on top of him and slid inside of me, letting me ride him to a third orgasm, and then we just lay there in the aftermath. I'd assumed that after a while, the sex would be pleasant, but no longer mind-blowing, like I'd somehow get used to it or something.

Yeah, that wasn't accurate at all.

He found new ways to get me off all the time and it was incredible.

"Happy Valentine's Day," he whispered as I snuggled into his side.

"Happy Valentine's Day," I said, using one hand to toy with the light smattering of hair on his chest. "If that was my present, I approve."

"That was one of your presents," he said.

"I don't need presents. I just need you."

"You've already got me, so that wouldn't count as a present."

"We agreed not to spend money on stuff," I protested.

"I didn't spend a lot," he said. "Promise."

"Okay." I reluctantly pulled free. "I do have a class I can't miss this morning."

"Yeah, me too." He leaned over and kissed my cheek. "But I'll be done early and we don't have practice today because Coach figured everyone would be distracted and antsy, so I'll be done around one."

"I'm not done until after three," I told him, padding into the bathroom with him on my heels. "Is there a plan for tonight or is it a surprise?"

"Well, parts of it are a surprise, but the first part is you and me alone at my place. Paxton and Naomi got a hotel room, so we'll have the apartment to ourselves and it'll be awesome having sex in a king-size bed."

"Oooohhh," I said playfully. "Sounds like fun."

"So pack what you'll need for the morning and we'll do a sleepover at my place for once."

"Wow, I actually get to sleep in the big-boy bed?" I teased.

He laughed. "You probably won't do much sleeping, but sure, let's go with that."

I stepped into the shower and wrapped my hand around his cock. "How fast can you get it up again?"

He got under the warm spray and hooked an arm around my waist, yanking me against him.

"This fast."

21

PATRICK

Starting the day with sex was always good, but starting Valentine's Day with multiple orgasms and a shower session that nearly made us miss class was the best. I had an excellent libido but we might have broken a record this morning and I was still grinning about it when I met up with Paxton at lunchtime. Ellie had a class and normally I was at practice by now, but since we had the day off, Paxton and I agreed to have lunch.

We barely saw each other outside of hockey these days, and though we texted daily and kept in touch, the new dynamic between us was a little odd. It wasn't necessarily bad, just different, and I wanted to find out what his plans were for the summer since he was moving to Seattle.

"I don't know the timing yet," he said when I brought it up. "I think we're going home to Minnesota so I can show her where I grew up, but I don't have any of the logistics from the team yet. They're going to help me find an apartment and get settled but there's a lot up in the air for now. What about you? You make any decisions yet?"

I shook my head. "Every time I weigh the pros and cons, it comes up even. Staying in school is good, going pro is good. Staying in school means I stay with Ellie, but what if she doesn't stay? She's going through a kind of midlife crisis related to her degrees and I'm nervous she's going to wind up somewhere else altogether, just to get away from her mom."

"Have you talked to her about it?"

"Not in so many words. She has so much pressure from everyone else about her future, I don't want to add to it or make her think I want her to go a certain direction for me."

"But if things are going so well, wouldn't you want to move in a direction together?"

"It's been six weeks," I said quietly.

"When you know, you know." He paused. "Do you know?"

"I don't know." I realized how ridiculous that sounded the second I said it and we both chuckled. "I mean, I think things could be serious, but we have a lot to sort out first."

"Things don't get sorted out until you discuss them. It doesn't happen by osmosis."

"Shut up." I rolled my eyes at him and got in line for a burger.

I'd had one of my friends give me a ride to the store yesterday so I could pick up flowers, dessert, and the ingredients to cook dinner for Ellie. I wasn't much of a cook but I'd found a pasta recipe that looked simple enough and hoped she'd like it. I'd practiced one night last week when she'd been in class, and Paxton and Naomi loved it, so I wasn't overly worried tonight.

I did all the prep work, chopping garlic ahead of time and getting all the ingredients ready to go. Then I set up the flowers in the middle of our kitchen table, which I'd covered with a pretty tablecloth I'd borrowed from one of my friends, who'd borrowed it from his mother. I got out the package of fake rose petals I'd ordered online and spread them all over the bedroom. I'd made my bed for the first time in ages and lit as many candles as I could get my hands on. Paxton and I owned a few, Naomi gave me a couple of hers, and I'd bought a few as well. Hopefully, I wouldn't set the place on fire between the candles and me cooking.

Just before Ellie was supposed to arrive, I put on dress pants and a button-down shirt. We'd never gotten dressed up since we'd been together, usually opting for jeans and sweats, and I wanted to make tonight a little more special than usual. It was our first Valentine's Day together, and really, our first holiday of any kind, so I wanted it to be memorable.

Things had gotten serious between us much more quickly than I'd imagined they would and it had really all been studying, hanging out, and sex. I felt a little guilty that I hadn't taken her out on real dates, beyond a few times at Tito's and the coffee shop, but there was really no time and I couldn't afford it. My savings was dwindling and there were four long months until I could get any kind of paycheck.

Money wouldn't be a problem anymore if I went to the Sidewinders, though. Hell, even the entry-level salary was almost a million dollars a year, so that would change everything. Both for me and for Ellie, if we could find a way to be together. Like I'd told Paxton, I didn't want to put any more pressure on her. She got enough of that from her family and professors, so the last thing she needed was a boyfriend pushing her in one direction or another. Everything would be so much simpler if she would just come to Vegas with me and we could figure out school from there, but that wouldn't be fair.

She could probably go anywhere, to Harvard and beyond, so why would she want to be stuck at UNLV? It was a decent school, but it wasn't Ivy League. Neither was Moo U, but this was different because her mother was both an alumna and a former professor, so Ellie had gotten a full ride. As a fifteen-year-old going away to school, it made sense her mother had wanted her somewhere she could keep an eye on her, but she could have gone anywhere. So it didn't seem realistic to assume she'd drop everything and move to Vegas for a guy she'd only known six weeks.

I was so lost in thought I didn't realize how late it was. I'd told

Ellie to come over around five but it was almost six and she still wasn't here. That wasn't like her, so I went into the kitchen to see if she'd called or texted and there was nothing. I called her but it went straight to voicemail and that was kind of weird. Ellie was as attached to her phone as I was and she was enough of a technology geek to always have portable chargers and such with her.

I was contemplating going to look for her when there was a knock on the door. I opened it and had to stare for a minute. Ellie looked…incredible. Not just her usual pretty self, but like a supermodel or something. Her hair was curled and hung in perfect waves around her face and over her shoulders, and her face, well, it was always pretty but tonight it was flawless.

"Aren't you going to invite me in?" she asked, giving me a seductive little smile.

"Yes. Hi." I stepped aside and shut the door behind her. I turned as she was unbuttoning her coat, and froze. She was wearing a dress. A short, tight, sexy little black number I'd never seen before. Well, I'd never seen her in anything but jeans and sweats, so this was a spectacular surprise and I was doubly glad I'd opted to dress up.

"You look…amazing." I leaned down to brush my lips across hers.

"So do you." She put a hand on my chest, blatantly checking me out from top to bottom. "I have to say, I like you in grown-up clothes."

"And I really like you in a dress." I reached for her hand. "I was getting worried, though."

"Sorry. I got caught in traffic. I went to the mall and wound up spending more time than I planned to and then it was rush hour."

"You went to the mall?"

"I didn't own any dresses appropriate for a Valentine's Day date with the hottest hockey player in the world. The mall was a necessary sacrifice."

"And one that's greatly appreciated." I took her hand. "Now, I'm starving so I'm going to start dinner."

"You're cooking?" She looked at me in confusion.

"Yup."

We went into the kitchen and I started melting butter in the skillet.

"What are we having?" she asked, standing beside me.

"Garlic-Parmesan linguine."

"Wow." She looked around. "What can I do to help?"

"Can you open that bottle of wine over there?"

"Sure." She picked up the corkscrew while I sauteed chopped garlic and added the remaining ingredients. She poured us each a glass and I paused in my cooking to clink mine against hers.

"To the first of many holidays together."

Something strange flickered in her eyes but then it was gone and she took a sip. "I've never tried Chianti before—it's good."

"I thought it went well with Italian food." I put the lid on the skillet and let it simmer. "Everything should be done in about twenty minutes. You want to go out to the living room?"

"Sure." She followed me into the other room and we sat on the couch.

"You look extra beautiful tonight, Ellie."

"Thank you. I went and had a makeover, got my hair done... I wanted tonight to be special."

"How come?"

"I don't know." She looked a little embarrassed. "I've never had a boyfriend on Valentine's Day before and..."

"And?" This didn't sound good. Her voice was a little funny.

"Chances are you'll be in Vegas next year and who knows where I'll be."

"I haven't made any decisions about next year," I said slowly. "But what do you mean you don't know where you'll be? Aren't you staying here?"

"I can't prove it, but I think maybe my mother had a talk with Dr. Phillips in the biology department. He told me he didn't think anything I've worked on in my computer studies will transfer over to the bio track, and that it's too late for me to apply for the

Ph.D. program for next year anyway. It's complete bullshit, since I'm already a student and a teaching assistant, but that's why I think my mother got to him."

"Did you ask him straight up?"

"I decided not to be confrontational until I talk to Dr. Lancet again. He usually has the best advice and I don't think having the equivalent of a temper tantrum helps my case."

"Well, if they don't want you here, can you apply at other schools? There have to be biotechnology programs in other schools, right?"

"There are, and I'll get on that first thing tomorrow, but tonight I don't want to talk about any of that."

"What would you like to talk about?" I asked, tugging her onto my lap.

"Why I've never seen you all dressed up before." She pressed a soft kiss on the side of my mouth. "Why I didn't know you could cook." She ran her lips along my jawline. "Why you've never cooked for me before…" She started kissing my neck.

"Because I'm a terrible boyfriend who never takes you out on dates," I grumbled, though gooseflesh had broken out on my skin.

"You're not a terrible boyfriend." She ran her hand over the bulge starting to tent my slacks. "You're a wonderful boyfriend. We're just broke all the time."

I caught her hand with mine. "We're going to need to put this on hold until the pasta's done."

She chuckled. "Okay."

"Speaking of which…I better check on everything." I got up and headed back into the kitchen.

I wasn't upset with her, but it bugged me when she talked about us being broke. I had a contract worth almost a million dollars a year. All I had to do was make a fucking decision. But every time I thought about not finishing my degree, I got a little sick to my stomach. I'd watched my father struggle with his inability to get a well-paying job and I never wanted to be that kind of man. Whether it was with Ellie or someone else, I hoped to be married and have a family someday, and I never wanted them to suffer because I was greedy and impatient.

"It smells so good." Ellie had trailed in behind me, refilling our wine glasses.

"Looks like it's just about done." I switched off the stove and got some platter thing down from the shelf. Naomi had pointed it out to me and said it was more elegant to serve the food on a platter instead of just out of the skillet, so I transferred it over and had to admit it looked incredible. Hopefully, it tasted good too.

"Oh my god, there is no way I'm taking my clothes off after we eat food this rich," Ellie said, laughing as I added a basket of bread to the table.

"Don't worry—I'll work all those extra calories off you."

"I'll be too full to participate."

"I seriously doubt that. Especially not with what I have planned tonight." I wiggled my eyebrows.

"I like the sound of that."

"You will." I put a good helping of the pasta on her plate. "But now, dig in."

She took a bite and slowly closed her eyes as she chewed. "Holy shit... I might have just had a foodgasm."

"And my dick got hard watching you do it."

ELLIE

Every time I thought I knew Patrick, he did something new to surprise me. Cooking for me tonight was amazing. The pasta was as good as anything I'd ever had at a restaurant, the bread was fresh and warm, and the Chianti rich and flavorful. He'd bought me a beautiful bouquet of flowers and we ate by candlelight. Every time our eyes met across the table, my insides clenched in anticipation of what was to come and my heart did that stupid thing where it skipped a beat because I was so damn close to falling in love with him.

Maybe I already was, but I hadn't let myself acknowledge it yet, so my heart did its best to make me think about it. I wanted to love him. More than almost anything, but the more complicated our lives became, the more afraid I was that there was no way for us to be together. I kept telling myself it was way too soon to think in terms of forever, but my heart and soul told me this wasn't something you found every day. There was something much more important going on here. We'd shared a special connection right from the start, before I'd even become his tutor or known his name, and now that we'd been together a month and a half, he was quickly becoming the most important thing in my life. Even more so than science and my degrees and every other thing I'd thought was important.

"Let me do the dishes," I said when we finished eating. "You cooked, so I can clean up."

"Negative." He shook his head. "This is my Valentine's Day gift to you, so it's all on me. But we have a dishwasher, so it's no biggie."

He started rinsing dishes and putting them in the dishwasher while I put away the leftovers and wiped down the table.

"I have presents for you too," I said. "I'll get them out while you finish up."

"Okay."

I went into the living room and got out the gift bag I'd bought. It had the card, the Twizzlers, and the kissing cards I'd made, so while it felt a little lame compared to the romantic evening he'd planned, I figured the kissing would make up for it.

"What's this?" he asked, joining me in the living room.

"Your present." I handed him the bag.

"Thank you." He opened it slowly and pulled out the card first. He read it to himself and then smiled. "That's sweet. Thank you." He leaned over and kissed me. "Now what's this?" He reached in and took out the massive package of Twizzlers and grinned. "See? This is fifty percent of the reason you're my girlfriend."

"What's the other fifty percent?" I asked, laughing.

He arched a brow. "You have to ask?"

I rolled my eyes, pretending to be annoyed, though I really wasn't. "There's one more thing in the bag."

He reached back in and a look of confusion crossed his face as he found the Ziploc bag I'd put the cards in. "Okay, I truly have no idea what this is."

"It's a kissing game," I said, trying not to laugh at the look on his face. "Pull a card and we have to kiss in whatever way it says on the card."

"Yeah?" He looked intrigued and immediately reached in,

digging around until he'd picked one from the middle of the stack. "Kiss using a timer—fifteen seconds to start, or thirty if you think you can last that long without getting naked." He paused and then reached for his phone. "Oh, baby, you know I love a challenge." He opened the clock feature on his phone and set up the timer. "You ready?"

I licked my lips. "I was born ready for you to kiss me."

"You up for thirty seconds?"

"Oh, yes."

I closed my eyes as he pushed the button to start the timer and then his lips were grazing mine. He was taking his time, pressing light, caressing kisses on my lips before slowly sliding his tongue against mine. Our mouths opened and then locked together, familiar need and passion and sensuality morphing into one as we raced against the clock. We'd make it, of course, but the website hadn't been kidding about how hard it would be to kiss for thirty full seconds without wanting more. I always wanted more but never more so than when he kissed me like this. He was being a perfect gentleman, though, keeping his hands to himself, even as my breath caught and my heart rate kicked into high gear.

By the time the buzzer went off, I was flushed and damp in all the right places, and the erection poking through his slacks told me he was equally turned on.

"That was harder—and longer—than I thought," he said, glancing down at his erection. "But I'm not quite ready to take our evening's activities into the bedroom."

"How come?" I asked.

He shrugged. "You'll see." He went back into the bag of cards. "What's next?"

"Pick another card."

"Re-create the kiss from a famous movie." He frowned as he read it. "Hmmm."

"Need help?" I teased.

He slowly shook his head. "Actually, no." He got up and

looked around. "I have an idea, I just need to figure out how to execute it so I don't kill myself."

I had no idea what he was talking about but he got up and looked around. "Okay, it's too cold for us to go outside, so you're going to have to use your imagination here."

"Okay."

He reached for my hand and led me around to the back of the couch. "You sit here, on the floor, with your back against the back of the couch."

"O-kayyy…" I sat down and looked up at him curiously. "Now what?"

"Please hold." He left my field of vision and then he was looming over me, hanging over the back of the couch. "Ready?"

"Hmm?" His face was upside down, but poised right in front of me, and he slowly leaned forward until his mouth found mine. I still didn't know what movie scene we were recreating, but damn, this was hot.

"Put your hands on either side of my face," he whispered.

I did it and then it clicked. *Spider-Man*. The upside-down kiss between Spider-Man and Mary Jane. Oh, damn, this was beyond hot. He was so romantic. *Fuck*. I couldn't deny it anymore. I was in love with him. There were no two ways about it.

We were breathing hard again as we pulled apart, and I sighed, torn between wanting to rip his clothes off and wanting to play this game a little longer. "*Spider-Man*," I whispered.

He grinned. "*Spider-Man 2*, to be precise. But now it's time for dessert." He disappeared into the kitchen and I got to my feet. This kissing game was turning out to be even sexier than I'd expected.

I was about to follow him to the kitchen when he came back with a small square box. "Happy Valentine's Day again," he said. "I didn't get you a card because I wasn't sure what to say, and words aren't my thing, but I hope my actions tonight speak louder than any six-dollar words in a Hallmark card."

I opened the box and stared at the most elegant—and delicious-looking—red velvet cupcake I'd ever seen. The cream cheese frosting swirled at least four inches above the top and was covered in sparkly confetti. There was a set of intertwined hearts drawn in red icing, with our initials inside of them.

P.G. + E.M.

"This is incredible," I said. "I have to take a picture of this because I want to remember it always." I reached for my phone and took the picture and then lifted the massive cupcake out of the box. Torn between being seductive and playful, I opted for playful and stuck my face in the frosting, licking a big glob of it and then sticking out my tongue, proffering it to him. He took me up on my offer and soon we forgot all about the cupcake. His mouth was fused to mine and those big, strong hands of his were circling my waist.

"Damn, you taste like sex," he said, all signs of playfulness gone now. His eyes blazed with intensity and he looked like he was going to take me right here and now.

"One more kissing game," I whispered. "I have a very specific one in mind."

"Oh?"

"Getting undressed while kissing," I said.

"How would we do that?"

"Anything that has to go over your head comes off before you start, then you close your eyes and kiss while getting undressed. You can't open your eyes or stop kissing until we're both naked."

"Like I said." He used a napkin to wipe some frosting off my chin. "I love a challenge."

"My dress has a zipper," I said, "so it'll definitely be a challenge, but I think we're up to the task."

"I don't have anything that needs to go over my head." He smirked.

"Then you're ready?"

"Fuck yeah." He pulled me against him and we started to kiss. He undid his belt and the button at the top of his slacks while I stepped out of my heels. I had panties on but it would be hard to get to them until my dress was off, so I worked on the buttons of his shirt, though it was harder than it sounded. And took a lot longer. A few times, we almost broke apart but managed to keep going, despite laughing a little.

It was awkward and sexy and fun, both of us struggling to focus on kissing while simultaneously trying to shed our clothes. Patrick unzipped my dress and brought it forward over my shoulders while I shimmied out of it. Then he slid my panties down and I managed to step out of them while holding on to him for balance.

When we were finally naked, we were both a little breathless and he was hard as stone.

"I don't know what I like better," I said, running a hand over his hip. "Your six-pack abs or that sexy little tattoo on your hip."

"My abs," he said drolly. "All the chicks like the abs."

"Then I might have to be different." I dropped to my knees so I could kiss it. He'd had his jersey number, fifty-one, drawn ornately within crossed hockey sticks, on the inside of one hip bone and he moaned as I ran my tongue along it.

"Time for the rest of your present," he murmured, reaching down to help me up.

We went down the hall and he opened the door, letting me walk in ahead of him. My breath caught in my throat as I took in the scene. The room was filled with candles and rose petals, with a small box of chocolate in the middle of the bed. It was the sweetest, most romantic thing I'd ever seen and I turned to him with tears in my eyes.

"Patrick...this is amazing. I love it."

"I wish I could have afforded to take you out somewhere fancy and wine and dine you like a lady."

I laughed. "I'm not old enough to drink in public so this actually works out better for me." I wrapped my arms around his neck. "Now why don't you go back to kissing me?"

"I've been waiting for instructions," he deadpanned. "I don't know how to kiss if there isn't a goal..."

"The goal," I whispered, wrapping my hand around his cock and squeezing, "is for you to make me come."

"Oh, well, that works for me." He dipped his head and found my lips again. It felt like we'd been kissing all night but I truly never got tired of it. It was a weird combination of new and familiar, our bodies knowing exactly what the other needed but always manifesting in different ways.

Patrick stretched out on the bed, moving the box of chocolate to his nightstand. "Come here, beautiful."

I crawled onto the bed after him but he nudged me so that I was facing away from his head. "Straddle my face," he said softly. "And I'll do you while you do me."

"Ohhh…" Sixty-nine. I'd been wanting to try this and I hurried to get into position.

It was harder than it looked, though, because he was so much taller than me and the moment he put his tongue inside of me, I couldn't remember what I was supposed to do. He didn't seem to mind, doing his thing with his mouth while I tried to focus on the fabulous cock in front of me. I managed to lick the tip and suck a little, but he was nibbling my clit and my whole world was flashing bright colors behind my eyes. I moaned, moving against him, and he chuckled.

"Put my cock in your mouth and hum," he said softly. "It feels really good for me and takes less concentration for you. Moaning works too."

I hurried to comply and he seemed to like it. I assumed it had something to do with the sound vibration, but even my overly analytical mind couldn't concentrate on science with his tongue buried inside of me. He was fingering my ass again too, which was my new favorite thing. Of course, everything he did was my favorite, so it was hard to choose just one.

"It's hard to time our orgasms in this position," he murmured. "I know how to get you off this way…so your challenge, should you choose to accept it, is to figure it out for me."

"I accept," I said, sucking him deeper and reaching down to

cup his balls. They were even more sensitive than his dick, so contrary to what he thought, I'd already figured that out about him. I squeezed them lightly at first, taking as much of him into my mouth as I could, and then squeezed harder. He jerked a little, but I knew I hadn't hurt him, and continued to alternate sucking and squeezing, until he was fucking my mouth hard and fast.

I probably would have gotten him off first but he cheated and pressed his finger deeper into my ass. It was better than my G-spot because it triggered an orgasm every damn time and this was no exception. I did my best to hold it off but it was no use and I came harder than ever before, my body stiffening and then shuddering repeatedly.

"Suck me, baby," he growled, pushing deeper into my mouth.

I could barely focus but I tried my best and then everything spiraled into an atomic bomb of pleasure because I was coming again and he was coming and it was next-level sex to the nth degree.

"God damn," I whispered, resting my head on his thigh. "How do you do that to me every time?"

"Same way you do it to me," he replied, patting my bottom.

I rolled off him and turned so I could put my head on his chest.

"Happy Valentine's Day, sweetheart."

"It was amazing. You're amazing. I can't believe you're mine."

"Believe it."

23

PATRICK

The next couple of weeks were busy. Ellie had been applying to every biotechnology Ph.D. program in the country while simultaneously finishing her current project. Instead of a doctoral thesis, she'd changed her focus to make it a master's thesis so she would end with a master's degree if Dr. Phillips agreed to work with her on moving into biotechnology. Beyond that, she was struggling to come up with a plan, and while I felt bad for her, I wasn't sure what I could do. I didn't understand how it all worked and she was frustrated and cranky. I could usually distract her with sex but I was busy too. We were gearing up for the NCAA championships and the team was on fire. We were undefeated since the first of the year and I was on a ten-game scoring streak.

I was getting a lot of attention from the sports journalists too, which was both exciting and frustrating. I was truly at the top of my game right now and it was the perfect time to go pro. There were just so many issues to work through, and the most important to me was Ellie. Deep down, I knew if I left her now, so early in our relationship, it would be almost impossible to stay together. I'd be in Vegas and on the road, and she'd be here—or at one of the other schools she'd applied to—for at least three or four more years.

She might be able to get through a doctoral program in two years, but that was a long shot and even if she did, two years was a long time to be apart. I'd been trying not to think about it, but she updated me daily on her progress and which schools she'd been applying to, so it was in the forefront of my mind. Part of me wished she'd stop talking about it because I was starting to fall in love with her and it was hard to imagine losing her after what we'd shared the last two months.

She'd blossomed since we'd been together, coming out of her shell and beginning to find herself, for lack of a better phrase. There had been a party at the hockey house last weekend and I'd seen a couple of my teammates checking her out, asking who she was and then high-fiving me for finding her before anyone else had a chance. I'd thought it might embarrass her, but she'd just laughed and kissed me. As if showing the whole world I was hers. And she was mine.

Mine.

The word echoed through my subconscious a lot lately. I was crazy about this girl but hadn't had the nerve to tell her how I felt. I sensed she was being cautious too and I wasn't sure how to change any of it. We were dancing around huge issues and they would be coming to a head in about eight weeks. I had to get through the championships first, though, and needed to make sure my head was in the game since I was meeting up with the Sidewinders this coming weekend. I wanted to make sure I was prepared both professionally and emotionally for the type of conversation I hoped to have with them.

I was leaning toward staying in college for my senior year, but I didn't know if I could afford it. Without Paxton, I couldn't stay in the apartment, and though I had the option of living with Ellie, I couldn't sleep in that twin size bed with her much longer. It had been fun and exciting at first because we were always all over each other, but now that we'd settled into a form of domestic bliss, I needed to stretch out and rest. We'd spent a few nights at my place this past week because I needed the room, but

I didn't think she could afford to pay half the rent and utilities. Especially when she had a free room in the dorms. She'd suggested me becoming an R.A. in a different dorm, which would get me a free room, but that meant we couldn't sleep together very often.

I had to go to a team meeting tonight to talk about strategy and watch some video as a way of preparing for the championships. It was nice to hang out with the guys outside of practice and I realized I hadn't done much of anything with my friends since meeting Ellie. In a way, I'd started pulling away from the guys on the team, and part of me wondered if it was because I was ready to leave school.

Guilt ate at me every time I thought about not getting my degree, but it was only three classes. I could get them done in two summers if I put my mind to it. But that still left Ellie. I didn't want to leave her and—

"Are you even paying attention?" Tate nudged me, a playful look on his face.

"I'm paying attention," I muttered, shifting my gaze to the screen at the front of the room. Coach Keller was going on and on about a mistake one of the rookies had made, trying to pound it into our heads that those types of mistakes would cost us the championship.

I zoned out again because I knew all that. I wasn't a rookie. I was ready for the pros, and more and more, it was beginning to feel like college was holding me back. Which brought me right back to feeling guilty.

I absently took a bite of the pizza that had been provided, glancing over at Paxton. He looked bored too and we exchanged a knowing look. We'd had a heart-to-heart the other night and he knew I was struggling. His advice had been to wait until I met the guys from the Sidewinders and had a chance to pick their brains. He was right, but I was impatient and it was messing with my focus.

PAXTON: Breathe. Focus. You're about to jump out of your skin. One day at a time.

His text made me smile. That was one of the best things about having a twin—he read my body language like a book.

PATRICK: I can't get out of my own head today.
PAXTON: We have the games tomorrow and Saturday, and then you'll go to Montreal on Sunday. Until then, there's nothing you can do, so stressing about it is a waste of time.

I hated when he was right so I sent him back an emoji of someone flipping a bird and grinned as he bit back a laugh when he saw it.

Luckily, the games that weekend were intense and I had no time to breathe. Both games went to overtime, I kept up my scoring streak, and I scored the game-winning goal on Saturday night. I'd been wound up afterward and had a hard time sleeping but then was up at the crack of dawn, showering and getting ready for the car service that was picking up Ellie and me, to take us to the airport. The Sidewinders were going all out for us and I kind of hoped it gave Ellie a taste of what it would be like if we moved to Vegas together.

Together.

Holy shit, I hadn't allowed myself to think like that because I knew she couldn't, but I wanted her to. More than I wanted to admit. Going without her felt wrong, but asking her to give up her dreams to follow me around with mine was never going to happen. She was too smart and too important to me. Too bad I was too fucking chickenshit to have a frank conversation with her about all of the things that had been going on in my head.

"Are you nervous?" I asked her when we were settled on the plane.

She glanced at me. "Not really. You?"

"I'm excited to meet the guys and hang out, but it's unnerving, knowing they've been watching me all season."

"Probably a lot longer than that."

"I guess so."

"You're badass," she whispered, squeezing my hand. "Everyone knows it. So relax and enjoy this. You deserve it."

"You're not nervous at all?" I asked after a moment. "I mean, you're going to meet some of the wives and girlfriends, not to mention my future teammates and coaches."

"I'm a little nervous about that," she admitted. "I think I can hold my own, but I always kind of wince when anyone asks me how old I am."

"None of anyone's business," I said firmly. "Just be yourself. You're smart, educated and accomplished. Age is just a number."

"I know. I'm probably letting my mom get in my head. She gave me the whole lecture when I went home last weekend, about us rushing things and you not buying the cow when you're getting the milk for free... You know what I mean." She'd finally given in and gone home while I'd been on a road trip last weekend, but it hadn't gone well.

"I really hate that she does this to you," I muttered. "I understand that she wants to protect you, but I'm never going to hurt you. That stuff about not buying the cow is stupid. Putting our specific relationship aside, I don't know that I could marry a woman I hadn't already slept with. I don't know if that makes me a jerk, but I think it's important to be sexually compatible. And I know from experience that not everyone is."

"I wouldn't know," she chuckled. "My only experience thus far has been quite compatible. At least I think so."

"Oh, we're definitely compatible. And I can't wait to remind you just how compatible as soon as we get home tonight."

"Horndog."

"Last time I checked, you had no problem with this."

"I don't."

"Speaking of which." I remembered something I'd wanted to

mention to her. "We broke another condom last night. This is like the fourth time. I've never broken condoms before, ever, and I thought maybe the box I bought was defective so I bought a different box and it still happened."

She frowned. "What could that mean?"

"I don't know a lot about IUDs, but is it possible the strings or whatever they're called are hanging lower than expected or something like that?"

"I don't feel anything, but I can call my ob-gyn and get an appointment, just to be sure."

"I'm happy to get tested, to show you it's safe for us to go without condoms at all, but I want you to be comfortable with that."

"I'm comfortable with it," she said. "Let me schedule something with my doctor first to make sure the IUD isn't to blame and we'll go from there. I can get bloodwork done as well."

"Cool." I twined my fingers with hers and hoped this would take our relationship in the right direction. I didn't know what was next for us as a couple, but going without condoms felt like we were moving toward something even more serious than we had now, which was what I wanted.

The only question was whether or not she cared enough about me to try to find some sort of compromise where we could be together. Otherwise, I didn't know what the hell we were going to do.

ELLIE

The game that afternoon in Montreal was exciting and it was hard for me to imagine Patrick as one of the guys out there on the ice six months from now. Wearing a Sidewinders jersey and making a huge salary. I tried not to think about it because it made me more nervous than I wanted to admit. I didn't know what I would do if Patrick left me to go to Las Vegas in just over two months. By the same token, how could I go with him? I wanted to, but it was so damn complicated, and anyway, he hadn't asked. We'd talked about the future in general, but it was always in terms of him staying in college another year.

"Ready?" he asked me, taking my hand as we rode the elevators down to the main concourse. Someone from the team was supposed to meet us there and take us to say hello to everyone.

"Patrick?" A tall, attractive redhead approached us with a smile, holding out her hand. "I'm Lana Carmichael, Head of Media Relations for the Sidewinders."

"Nice to meet you." Patrick shook her hand. "This is my girlfriend, Ellie."

"Hi, Ellie."

"The guys are looking forward to meeting you," Lana said to

Patrick as we walked toward an elevator bank. "And some of the WAGs came on this trip specifically to meet Ellie."

"They did?" That surprised me.

"Of course. Everyone wants you both to feel welcome."

"We appreciate it," Patrick said. "We were excited to come up for the day."

"Well, you'll meet the bulk of the team and coaches now," Lana said as we stepped out of the elevator. "And then a few of the guys said they're happy to hang out at the bar of the hotel for a little while, answer any questions you might have, or just shoot the shit for a while until you have to leave for the airport."

"Great. Thank you."

We followed her into a small, private room where a group of women were gathered, chatting casually. They looked up when we came in and a blond woman of about thirty-five called out a greeting to Lana.

Lana turned. "This is Ellie, you guys. Ellie, this is Tessa Petrov, Chelsea Calloway, Renee Wylde, and Everly Campbell."

"Hi." I smiled, hoping they couldn't tell how nervous I was.

"You'll be in good hands here," Lana said, "so I'm going to take Patrick into the locker room."

"See you later." Patrick gave me a quick kiss before following Lana out of the room.

"Did you enjoy the game?" Tessa asked me.

"It was wonderful," I replied. "I can't imagine Patrick being out there with them six or seven months from now."

"It's an exciting time," Chelsea said. "I didn't know Nate his rookie season, but I still get excited when he's on the ice."

"I'm the head coach's wife," the woman named Renee said. "I didn't even know him when he played—he's been retired a while —but I love seeing him behind the bench."

"I think we're spectacularly enamored with our husbands," Tessa said, grinning.

"So have you and Patrick been together long?" Renee asked.

I shook my head. "Just two months. It's been kind of a whirlwind."

"Are you graduating this year?" Chelsea asked.

I wrinkled my nose. "I have a complicated situation. I'm currently in a Ph.D. program in computer science but I hate it and want to switch so there are issues. I won't bore you with the details, but I'm at a bit of a crossroads."

"Sounds difficult," Renee said sympathetically.

"But exciting," Tessa said. "That's incredible to be getting your doctorate—you look so young!"

I hesitated. "Well, I'm only nineteen but I've been in college since I was fifteen."

"So you did what typically takes six years in four," Chelsea said. "Color me super impressed."

I flushed. They hadn't even batted an eyelash at my age, which made me feel better about a lot of things. "I'd been toying with the idea of medical school, but that's not the direction I want to go, so I'm trying to find a program that's going to be the right fit."

"Are you staying in Vermont?" Tessa asked.

"Well, Patrick hasn't decided what he's doing yet," I admitted. "Whether he's going pro at the end of this school year or staying for his senior year. He'll only need three classes after this semester, and I think he can handle two over the summer, but he was looking forward to talking with the guys tonight, maybe getting some perspective from them."

Chelsea nodded. "I imagine it's a tough decision, to delay going pro another full year just to take three classes."

"And it's probably hard on you as well," Renee said gently. "I have a daughter who's just a little older than you and she still has no idea what she wants to be when she grows up. And with you already in a graduate program, you're ahead of the game."

"I bet you could teach for a year or two," Chelsea suggested.

I nodded. "I'm already student teaching, so that's one of many things I'm considering."

"We went through a little bit of this with Toli's son Anton,"

Tessa said. "He plays for the Sidewinders now, but he wanted to leave college early and we fought hard to keep him there."

"Was it better for him?" I asked quietly.

"Anton wanted to leave when he was nineteen, after his sophomore year—he started college at seventeen—and the team didn't think he'd matured enough as a player, so it was different. I don't think that's an issue with Patrick. From what I've heard, he's ready, and the guys are going to do their best to talk him into joining them in the fall."

"Oh. Wow." I wasn't sure what I'd been expecting, but that wasn't it.

"It's a little overwhelming, huh?" Renee asked gently. She had a motherly vibe to her, something my own mother rarely showed me, and I couldn't explain the sudden urge to throw myself in her arms and ask her to tell me everything was going to be okay.

"So overwhelming," I whispered. "We're both being pulled in a lot of directions by outside forces, and it leaves us very little time to work out what we want together."

"If you love each other," Renee said, "and it's meant to be, it's going to work out. I know that sounds like bullshit grown-ups tell kids to make them feel better, but it's not. I just lived through something similar with Jared. We were at two different places in life and it didn't look like there would be any way to make it work going forward. Until we broke up and subsequently realized how miserable we were without each other. So we found a compromise and I've never been happier."

"That's good to hear," I said.

"Come on, let's talk about something else," Tessa suggested. "Ask us questions. Do you have any?"

"I have a million," I said. "Mostly about the lifestyle. What's it like to be married to a professional athlete? They're gone a lot, right? So you're alone?"

Chelsea nodded. "They're gone a lot, but then they're home a lot during the off-season. They've done well the last few years, but realistically, they're not going all the way to the finals every year, so you can figure he'll be home from mid-May to mid-September. That's a nice stretch, you know? By the time hockey season is starting, I'm ready for him to go back because I have my own stuff to do." She smiled. "I love my husband, but I have a career, friends, other things, so it's not like when he's gone I'm bereft."

"Agreed," Renee said. "I have a busy career of my own, and it's a lot harder to get anything done in the off-season, though I adore my husband."

"I, on the other hand," Tessa said, "can't wait for Toli to retire. We have four kids under the age of ten and I could use the help."

We all laughed.

"Wait," I said, thinking back to what she'd said earlier. "So you have five kids? Because Anton isn't under ten…"

She smiled. "Anton is my stepson, and my eight-year-old daughter, Raina, is from my first marriage, but yes, together we have five. And he's forty-two, so I'm ready for him to retire."

I was a little taken aback. If Patrick went pro, some of his teammates would literally be old enough to be our parents. I'd never thought of that, somehow assuming everyone would be somewhere between twenty and thirty, with a few exceptions. I wondered if it was on Patrick's radar at all. How hard would he have to work to keep up with veterans like that, with a lifetime of experience? And how did I fit into the mix? Were there any WAGs who were anywhere near my age?

I had questions to things these kind ladies couldn't answer. Things that maybe even Patrick couldn't answer. For the millionth time, I wished I had a mother to talk to, confide in, and ask for advice.

"If you'd like to talk sometime," Renee said softly, putting a hand on my arm. "I'll give you my number. You look a little conflicted and I'm happy to give you my perspective, both as a WAG and as a mom."

"Thank you," I whispered, fighting the emotion welling up behind my eyes. "I'd love that."

"Adulting is hard," Tessa said softly. "You're at such an important time in your life while simultaneously under so much pressure. Remember to take a few minutes to focus on yourself—mentally, physically and emotionally. Whether it's lunch with a girlfriend, an afternoon of shopping, even a yoga class. You need to step away from everything, including Patrick, every so often to just focus on yourself. It's much more important than you might think."

"I rarely take time for myself," I admitted. "I don't have it. I used to study all the time and I've cut back on that a little so I can spend time with Patrick. I do have a couple of girlfriends but we're all busy with school, boyfriends, whatever, so I don't see them much."

"I rely on my girlfriends more than I'd like to admit," Chelsea said. "I love Nate, and he's wonderful, but when he's focused on hockey, I need to have my own thing going on. I'm a journalist, so I do have a career, but he can't always be there for me and my girlfriends can. When you get to Vegas, you'll find the WAGs are an invaluable source of support."

"That's good to know," I said quietly. My thoughts were reeling, though. She'd said *when* I get to Vegas, as if it was a foregone conclusion. The truth, unfortunately, it was anything but.

25

PATRICK

The minute I stepped into the locker room, it was like I'd been transported to another realm. I was no longer some twenty-one-year-old college kid; I was now about to become a Sidewinder. I was introduced and everyone greeted me like I was already one of them. It was heady stuff to feel like one of the guys even before I'd made any decisions about leaving school, but if I'd needed a push to go pro, this was more like a shove.

Being around them, these professional athletes that would be my contemporaries in the near future, felt natural. I wasn't nervous or uneasy anymore, and as we talked about the game they'd just won, I could imagine myself on the ice with them, in the locker room, hanging out both on and off the ice. These guys were consummate professionals and I wanted to be like them. I wanted to be one of them. The realization hit me like a bucket of ice water being dumped on my head, and it was all so clear, I almost had a physical reaction to it.

Coach Wylde came over and introduced himself, shaking my hand.

"Have you decided what you're going to do next year?" he asked. "Training camp will be here before you know it."

"I really wanted to get my degree," I told him, "but I'll be three classes short. I've waffled over leaving school without the degree because I'm itching to get to Vegas too. Especially now."

"You look good out there," Coach Wylde said. "We've been watching and I'm excited to get you on the team, but you do what's right for you. I understand the importance of a degree more than most. After my career-ending injury, it took me a while to find my way and it wasn't easy. On the flip side of that, it's just three classes. You could go back and finish, even if you never played another day, you know? And if you took one this summer, that leaves you with two."

"I was thinking of taking two this summer, but it depends on availability. There's even a chance I could take one online, so there are a lot of options."

"You have a couple of months to decide, so there's no rush. Is there anything you want to ask me specifically or should I leave you in the capable hands of the team?"

I grinned. "I think I'm good, Coach."

He shook my hand again and disappeared, leaving me to talk to the guys.

I didn't know who to approach first but I started with Toli since he'd been the one to reach out on the phone.

"That goal last night," he said, shaking his head. "Fucking epic. You make shit happen out there. You're exactly the type of player we need right now. With me retiring and—"

"You're retiring?" I asked, my eyes widening.

"I've been playing professionally since I was eighteen. That's twenty-four years of my life on the road, missing out on my kids growing up, not being there for my wife… It's time. I got to play with my oldest son, which was a big goal for me, and now I think it's time to do something else. I may move to a back office position, but I'm going to take a year to figure it out. It's a big decision, which I'm sure you know something about." His eyes twinkled.

"Yeah. The degree is important but I feel like the time is now. I can't explain it."

"You have to follow your gut. Your brain and your heart will tell you different things, but your gut is the one you really need to listen to. That pull is strong for a reason and if it's getting stronger, that might be your answer."

"That's what I'm afraid of."

Our eyes met. "It sounds like you've already made up your mind."

The car service the team had hired for us took us to the hotel and we sat in the bar, waiting for a few guys from the team to get there. Ellie was drinking a soda and I ordered a beer, but I was only going to have one. I had so much going on in my head, the last thing I needed was alcohol. Plus, I felt bad for Ellie and didn't want her to feel awkward being the only one who couldn't drink.

A few of the WAGs showed up and Ellie went over to join them at a table just as Nate, Toli, and his son Anton got to the bar. We settled at a high-top table and I kept an eye on Ellie as they ordered drinks. She'd been quiet on the ride over, but I'd been so busy telling her about my conversations with the guys in the locker room, I hadn't really noticed until now.

"Everything okay?" Toli asked me, following my gaze.

"Just worried about her," I admitted. "This has been a lot to take in and she has some stuff going on at school, so I'm being overprotective. She can hold her own but I'm assuming the ladies are also looking out for her."

"They are," Toli nodded. "And the goal here is to get you to want to come to Vegas, not to scare you or your girlfriend off."

"Good to know."

We bullshitted for a few minutes and then Nate turned to me. "So I hear you're waffling about leaving school."

"Yeah." I blew out a breath. "My dad never went to college and he had a career-ending injury his rookie season, so we struggled financially because he didn't know how to do anything but hockey."

"Well, there are two sides to that," Nate said. "Obviously, I didn't go pro until after I got my degree—for a lot of the same reasons. Staying in college also allows us to grow both physically and emotionally. If you were going to be coming to Vegas just to get sent down to the minors, I'd suggest you stay in school, but from what I've seen and heard, that won't be the case with you."

"So you think it's time for me to leave school." It was more of a statement than a question and Nate didn't hesitate to nod.

"Here's the thing," he said quietly. "Once you start feeling the pull, that little voice in your subconscious urging you to do it, hockey will continue to gnaw at you until you feel like you can't breathe. And then you'll be mid-season and it's going to fuck with your head. Making a clean break now is really the best decision."

"I agree," Anton said. "In my case, I wanted to go pro after my sophomore year but I was only nineteen and wasn't ready. My game wasn't where it needed to be and I was nowhere near mature enough. Playing those extra two years in college made a huge difference. It doesn't sound like you need that extra time and, frankly, with guys retiring at the end of this season, this is the perfect year to fight for a spot."

"Multiple guys retiring?" I asked.

Toli grinned and elbowed his son. "Yes, there are a few of us going that route, but no one has announced anything officially, so Anton should keep his mouth shut."

Anton laughed. "Sorry."

I glanced over at Ellie and she was laughing with the WAGs—a really good sign—and seemed at ease with them, which would make a world of difference if I did manage to get her to go with me.

We talked for another hour until the car service told us it was time to go, and I called Ellie over so she could meet the guys.

"Nice to meet you, Ellie." Nate shook her hand and then put his arm around Chelsea.

"Hey, nice to meet you." Anton shook her hand too.

"Thank you for inviting us to come out," she said politely. "We were really excited to meet everyone."

"You two have a lot to talk about," Toli said gently. "And my best advice is to come up with your decisions together. Communication is key in life-changing decisions like this."

"Since Patrick is making the move to Vegas," Nate said to me, "you should definitely look into online classes, since it sounds like getting your degree is important to you."

I nearly groaned at the look on Ellie's face but she quickly masked it, smiling politely. "Oh, absolutely. We're going to discuss *everything*." Her emphasis on that last word told me I'd fucked up big-time, but I honestly hadn't made any decisions yet and Nate had jumped the gun. I hadn't told the guys I didn't want to leave my nineteen-year-old girlfriend behind because that wasn't the kind of thing you said to a group of professional athletes you'd just met, even though that was my only hesitation at this point.

I couldn't say anything in front of everyone, though, so we said our goodbyes, Ellie got a couple of phone numbers from the ladies, and then we were in the car on the way to the airport. She was quiet and I reached for her hand.

"You're mad at me."

"When did you make the official decision to leave school?" she asked, not looking at me.

"I haven't," I protested. "I mean, I'm definitely starting to feel the pull, especially after meeting everyone today, but I haven't decided anything."

"Why would Nate say that if you hadn't said something to let him believe you would?"

I sighed. "We talked about the pros and cons of me leaving school and there really aren't any cons."

"There aren't any cons?" she demanded, turning to stare at me.

"Well, leaving you is a con, but it's not like you can go with me! You've applied to Ph.D. programs all over the country but don't know what you're doing, so what am I supposed to do? Wait until you figure it out?"

"So leaving me didn't even make it onto your list of cons?"

"It did!" I said in frustration. "I just didn't tell the guys that."

"Why not?" The hurt in her eyes was unmistakable.

"I don't know. We were talking about degrees and whether or not there would be a spot for me after a few guys retire this year… It wasn't about personal stuff."

"I see that." She turned to stare out the window.

"Come on, Ellie. Talk to me. You heard what Toli said and—"

"Yes. How we have all these decisions to make, and that would be excellent advice, except you already *made* yours. Admit it, you're going to leave school and go to Vegas."

"I… Maybe?" Shit, I didn't want to lie to her but in my heart of hearts, she was right. I'd subconsciously made the decision the minute I'd walked into the locker room tonight. And asking her to go with me would be selfish as hell.

"Without giving a second thought to what I'm going to do."

"You don't *know* what you're going to do and even if you did, it's not in Vegas!"

"I guess we've already made the decision," she said, looking at me intently.

"No, it's not like that."

"Then what is it like?"

"You have to make your decisions based on what *you* need. You've already had your mom and your advisors and everyone else pulling you in the opposite direction of where you want to go. I don't need to add to that. I've been trying to do what's best for you, not for me."

"You were never going to ask me to go with you, were you?" Her eyes blazed with hurt and anger. "And you just let me find out from the guys on the team."

"Ellie, no." I was getting nowhere fast with this conversation and I didn't know how to fix it. "If you'd just let me explain…"

"Explain what? Deep down, I've known all along. I didn't

want to believe it, because you kept saying you were going to stay, but I knew. It was right there and I let myself get attached anyway. First boyfriend, first lover, all that bullshit. But I'm a big girl. And honestly, I think the best thing for us to do is break up now and get it over with."

ELLIE

The words came out of my mouth before I could stop them and we'd just pulled up to the airport. The driver had opened the door for us and I got out, walking straight into the building without waiting for Patrick. I didn't want to cry, not in front of him and definitely not in a freakin' airport, but my heart hurt as I walked away.

"Ellie!" He caught up to me in the security line and I sighed, wondering how the hell I was going to sit next to him the whole flight home and then in the car too.

"It's fine," I said quietly. "Let's not do this here. Okay? Please?"

"Ellie, I don't want to break up." He'd taken my hand and was looking into my eyes. There was sincerity in his, but I was so hurt and confused and, more than anything else, afraid. Afraid I would give up everything to be with him and even more afraid that I wouldn't.

"But that's where we are," I said after a moment. "You have to follow your dreams and I have to follow mine. Like you said, I can't go to Vegas anyway." That wasn't entirely true because UNLV had a biotech program, but I hadn't applied yet and now it didn't matter.

We showed our ID's to the TSA agent and then walked through the scanning machines. We didn't talk as we made our way to our gate and I sank into the nearest chair, with him beside me. Neither of us had anything to say and the silence had become deafening. Had we been alone, I probably would have broken down, but I wasn't going to make a scene in public.

"You said you don't want to talk about it here," he said as we boarded the plane. "But we're going to talk about this when we get home."

I nodded, even though I knew we wouldn't. There simply wasn't anything else to say.

By the time we'd landed, I was tired and sad, and didn't resist when he reached for my hand in the car. I rested my head on his shoulder, memorizing his scent, everything that made Patrick the man he was. Fuck, I was going to miss him. This hurt so much more than I'd thought it would.

"Listen, you think we could just go to bed and talk about this tomorrow?" he asked as the driver dropped us off in front of the path that led to my dorm.

"I think you should...go home," I said slowly. "To your place. My bed is too small for you anyway and we both need time to think."

"Ellie, don't do this." He pulled me close. "*Please* don't do this."

"I didn't," I whispered. "We did it together and you know as well as I do that this was inevitable."

"It wasn't."

"You weren't going to ask me to go with you and it's not like I could anyway. It's been fun but it's probably run its course."

I waited for a few seconds but he didn't deny it and that told me all I needed to know so I pulled away and moved toward the entrance.

"So, um, I'm gonna go to bed and you should too. I'll, uh, see you around."

"Ellie..." He reached for me again, but I moved out of his

grasp because I'd lose my resolve the second he touched me. And I had to be strong because that was the only way to hang on to my sanity. Another few seconds and I'd let him talk me into almost anything.

"Ellie?"

I stopped when he called my name the second time, though I didn't turn around.

"Let's take a couple of days to think, okay? I don't want to leave things like this."

"All right." There was nothing else to say so I put my key card into the reader, opened the door, and went inside without looking back.

The next day might have been the longest day of my life. I didn't go to class, didn't go to breakfast, didn't even get out of bed. Patrick had texted me a couple of times but nothing had changed, so I didn't respond. Harley had texted and asked if I wanted to meet for coffee and I made an excuse about being busy. Then I'd cried most of the day. I was hungry, though, so I'd waited until I knew for sure Patrick would be at practice and made my way to the dining hall.

I ran into Chastity on my way in and she immediately knew something was wrong.

"We broke up," I told her as she followed me inside.

"Do I need to kill him?" she demanded.

I managed a wan smile. "No. I broke up with him."

"What? Why?" She followed me as I got in line to get a burger. I didn't feel that great but I needed something in my stomach.

I told her what had happened and she didn't say anything until I was done.

"But if he said he didn't want to break up, why did you do it?"

"Because what's the point of dragging it out?" I demanded. "If we don't break up now, we'll break up in May."

"Are you sure?" She met my eyes curiously.

"Am I sure what? I can't go to Vegas with him, but even if I could, he didn't *ask* me to go and that's pretty telling."

"But he said he didn't ask because he knew you couldn't."

"I put him on the spot and he didn't deny it or even say it in anger. You know, like, 'So, do you want to go with me?!' Something like that. He could have but didn't."

"It's been two months. Guys take a little longer to come to terms with their feelings. Look how long it took Dylan…"

"Well, it doesn't matter because we don't have a future whether he loves me or not, whether he asked me to go or not."

"I think it matters because your heart is broken."

"It was bound to happen, right? I mean, no one marries their first love."

"I plan to," she said softly.

"You and Dylan are special. And he's a relatively simple guy who doesn't want to leave his family's farm or the state he grew up in. Patrick is going to be a big hockey star very soon, and he probably won't even think about me come September."

"I think you're telling yourself the things you want to hear so you feel better about what's happened. The two of you had that connection you told me about and that doesn't just go away."

"Oh, what do I know about love connections?" I mumbled, grabbing my burger and walking over to a table. "For all I know, you have the same connection every time you want to sleep with someone. I guess I'll find out as soon as I find someone else I want to sleep with."

She cocked her head, smiling softly. "You know damn well you have zero desire to sleep with anyone else."

I nodded. "I know. But all I can do is put one foot in front of the other and keep going forward."

"What can I do?" she asked. "You want to come over to the house and hang out?"

"I love you for offering, but I honestly just want to be alone. I might study for a little while, so I'm prepared for whatever happens next academically, and then I want to go to bed early. I cried all last night so I'm tired."

"Okay. But I'll sit with you while you eat."

"Thank you. You're a good friend."

I didn't sleep much the next couple of nights, and on Thursday morning, I felt like hell. I rarely got sick but I felt something coming on and took an extra dose of vitamin C. It was probably just the residual effect of my broken heart but regardless of the cause, I didn't feel good. I made it through my first class but I was starting to get cramps and they felt weird. I went to the bathroom and was surprised to find I was bleeding. Since getting the IUD, my periods were light and barely lasted two days, so this was not only unexpected, it wasn't the right time of month either.

My panties and sweats were a mess so I made my way back to my room to change and find a pad. By the time I got there, the toilet paper I'd stuffed in my underwear was soaked and I realized I didn't even have any pads, just tampons.

Crap. I got undressed and took a shower since I needed to clean up, and then used a tampon to help curtail any other surprises. They sold pads at the bookstore, which was more like a campus general store, so I'd stop by there and grab some on my way to class.

I sat on the bed to rest for a minute and decided to take a nap instead. I genuinely felt like crap and didn't have time to be sick. I sent my professor a quick text, as well as the guy I tutored on Thursdays, and then lay back, closing my eyes. Maybe a good nap would help and I'd be able to catch up on some sleep as well as homework tonight.

A sharp, stabbing pain in my abdomen woke me up with a jerk, and I gasped. What the hell was going on? If this was a stomach flu, on top of an unusually heavy period, this was going to suck. I stumbled into the bathroom to look for some Motrin and barely made it back to bed. I was practically doubled over with pain and didn't know what to do. Hoping the Motrin would kick in, I grabbed my phone to distract myself.

The first thing I saw on Instagram was a picture of Patrick, Paxton and Tate standing in front of the bus used to transport them to games. They were on their way to a weekend of games that signified the beginning of the NCAA championships. They normally didn't leave on a Thursday but the championships afforded them some leeway in their classes.

Seeing Patrick's face brought tears to my eyes and I stared at the picture for a few minutes before closing out the app. I missed him a little more every day, so getting sick on top of a broken heart seemed spectacularly unfair. I was lost without him, finding it hard to care about anything. I'd finally stopped crying but my heart hurt so much, it was sometimes hard to breathe. I made up a dozen different scenarios where I might run into him but there didn't seem to be a point in it.

He didn't love me and hadn't even suggested trying out a long-distance relationship for a while, and that spoke volumes about his feelings for me. Or lack thereof. It was as simple as that.

I dozed off again when the pain started to abate, but by midnight it was back and worse than ever. I was also bleeding heavier than before and now I was scared. I'd never experienced anything like this and didn't know what to do. Finally, I dialed Chastity's number.

"Hey…" She sounded sleepy.

"Chas, something's wrong," I whispered.

"Wrong how? Are you okay?"

"I've been bleeding and cramping all day, like really bad, and now I'm scared."

"Bleeding and cramping? Ellie, is it possible you're pregnant? Or miscarrying?"

Her words hit me like a physical blow and I couldn't breathe as I tried to wrap my head around the idea of being pregnant. We'd been so *careful*. How could this have happened?

All those condoms breaking.

I'd forgotten to call my ob-gyn.

"Ellie, I'm getting dressed and we're coming over, okay? Hang on, I'm on my way."

I managed to get up and unlock the door when Chastity and Dylan arrived, but I was in so much pain I couldn't see straight. I'd already bled through another outfit and the whole box of tampons, so I grabbed a hand towel instead, stuffing it between my legs as I changed into yet another clean pair of sweats.

"I think we should go to the E.R.," Chastity said when I'd curled back into the fetal position on my bed. "This isn't normal."

I wanted to say no, but I was in so much pain and if I was having a miscarriage, I was going to need medical care anyway. I longed for Patrick more than ever, but not only were we fighting and essentially broken up, he was out of town on a road trip. There was nothing he could do and worrying him served no purpose.

"You get her things," Dylan told Chastity. "I'll carry her down to my truck."

"No. I can walk…" I started to get up but the pain had me doubled over again and Dylan scooped me up in his strong arms. Chastity joked about his arms being one of her favorite things about him, and now I knew why, but I was in too much pain to even giggle about it.

———

The emergency room was empty and they took me back right away. Chastity stayed with me while we answered a million questions and filled out a bunch of forms. She'd had the presence of mind to get my purse with my ID and insurance card, along with my backpack, containing my laptop and chargers. I'd never been more grateful for her friendship than now, but I was having a hard time focusing on anything but the pain.

"Hi, Elizabeth." A smiling doctor came in. "I'm Dr. Marsh. I see you're having a bad night, huh?"

"It's Ellie," I whispered.

"Well, Ellie, we're going to give you something to take the edge off the pain while we wait for test results."

"Am I having a miscarriage?" I asked, meeting his eyes.

"I'm not sure," he replied gently. "Is that a possibility?"

"I have an IUD and we always used condoms too, so I wouldn't have thought so, but what else could this be?"

"Let's not get ahead of ourselves." He patted my shoulder. "Try to rest and we'll figure this out."

Whatever they gave me for pain helped me doze off for a little while, but the next thing I knew, Dr. Marsh was waking me up.

"Ellie?"

I focused bleary eyes on him, blinking awake.

"What is it?"

"It looks like you're about five weeks pregnant. We're going to do a few more tests, but I suspect it's ectopic."

ELLIE

"Ectopic..." It took a few seconds for his words to sink in. "Oh my god."

"Once we verify, we're going to have to remove it, Ellie. I suspect either the fallopian tube has burst or it's about to. Either way, it's not a viable pregnancy and your life could be in danger once the tube bursts."

I swallowed. "I need surgery?"

"Let me do a few more tests and we'll talk again, okay? I know it's scary, but don't worry—we're going to take good care of you."

"Should I call my parents?"

He hesitated but then nodded. "If you'd like them here with you, then yes. But I don't want to wait too long. The amount of bleeding suggests the tube is bursting or already has, and we want to stop that as quickly as possible."

A million things shot through my mind, but I fumbled for my phone to text my mom, operating on autopilot. None of this made sense.

We'd been so damn careful.

An IUD *and* condoms.

What more could anyone possibly do beyond abstaining, which was unnecessary in my opinion. I thought about calling

Patrick but again, there was no point in worrying him. I was going to lose this baby whether he knew about it now or not, so why potentially ruin the games this weekend? I had Chastity, and my parents were on the way.

Not that their presence would change anything.

A baby.

We'd made a baby.

Patrick and I had created a life together.

And in a little while it would be gone. Before I even had a chance to get used to the idea. Not that I wanted a baby any time soon, but there was one. For a few more minutes, I had a child growing inside of me. And it was the most terrifying thing that had ever happened to me.

I longed for Patrick so badly and couldn't reach out to him. I closed my eyes and swallowed a silent sob, my heart breaking all over again.

Everything happened in kind of a whirlwind after that. The surgeon had come to talk to me and then I was whisked off to surgery. I vaguely remembered waking up and seeing my parents, but then I'd gone back to sleep and now it was morning. I blinked at the bright sunlight streaming through the windows.

"Good morning." Mom's voice was soft and soothing and I looked up gratefully.

"Good morning," I croaked.

"Water?" she asked.

I nodded and she held a straw up to my mouth. I took a few sips and cleared my throat. "Thank you."

"How are you feeling?"

"Like I got run over by a truck."

She smiled. "It's normal. The doctor said everything is going to be fine. Apparently, your IUD had slipped out of place." She paused. "The doctor mentioned broken condoms, and although it's pretty rare, when the IUD dropped down, the strings may have been causing that."

"Oh." I didn't know what to say. I should have called my ob-gyn, but it hadn't seemed like a priority at the time.

"Does he know? Er, Patrick?"

"No." I shook my head. "He's away on a trip with the team. There's nothing he can do so what's the point of worrying him?"

"It's part of being in a relationship," she said gently. "You share the good times and the bad."

"We broke up a few days ago," I whispered. "So we're not in a relationship anymore."

"Because of the pregnancy?" she demanded, her eyes narrowing.

"No. Neither of us had any idea about that. He's leaving to go play professional hockey in Las Vegas and I'm stuck here, so there was no point in delaying the inevitable. I broke up with him."

She frowned. "So a preemptive strike? Why would you sabotage your relationship like that, Ellie?"

"I thought you didn't want me in a relationship at all?" I countered.

"I don't, but that's not what I asked. *You* wanted the relationship. And then you ended it."

"Maybe I'm not ready for…all of this." I made a mildly wild motion with my hands. "So far, adulting sucks."

She put a gentle hand on my cheek. "Yes, sometimes it does. But this, what happened to you with the IUD, is very rare. I'm so sorry it happened, but we're going to have a long talk with your OB-GYN once you're feeling better. I've used an IUD since you were born and never had a problem. And I'm proud of you for using condoms in addition to the IUD."

"I'm not a moron, Mom. When we started dating, we didn't know each other very well so that was a no-brainer."

"Well, you should rest. I'm going to text your father that you're awake and see if he'll bring us breakfast. It's almost eleven so you slept through the hospital's delivery."

"Okay."

I was kind of shocked at my mother's casual attitude, especially about my sexual relationship with Patrick, because she tended to get cranky about things like this. I wanted to ask what was up, but I liked having her this way, where she was actually my mom instead of my professional mentor. I had plenty of those at school so I didn't need it from my mother too.

I slept on and off all day and the doctors let me go home to Brattleboro the following morning. Chastity had brought me some clothes because most of my winter wardrobe was in my dorm, and I settled into my old room. It was kind of strange being home, but it was comforting during a time when I desperately needed it. The posters on my walls, the comforter on my bed, even my old desk helped me feel secure again. My life had spiraled out of control the last couple of weeks, between my academic worries, the breakup with Patrick, and of course, my short-lived pregnancy and surgery.

It had never crossed my mind that those broken condoms might lead to a baby. I'd been so secure in the knowledge I had an IUD, it hadn't occurred to me something could happen to make it move out of place. Though I had zero interest in sex at this point, when the time came, I was going to look into a birth control implant. Harley had one and hadn't had any issues, so I was definitely done with IUDs.

For the first time in a long time, I felt vulnerable. I was tired and sad and unsure what to do next. Studying was usually my escape from everything, but that had lost its luster now since I didn't want to major in computer science. I still loved everything about technology, but my academic future was on hold. Finishing the semester was kind of a waste since I wasn't going forward with computer science, but the idea of starting over in biology or biotechnology was daunting, and frankly, after everything I'd been through lately, I didn't care that much.

I was seriously considering the whole "bartending in Tahiti" scenario, but a quick internet search told me the drinking age was twenty-one, so that plan was a bust already. Which meant absolutely nothing in my life was going right. It was so disheartening, I stayed in bed for four days, only getting up to eat, use the bathroom, and shower on Monday since I felt gross. Mostly, I stared at the ceiling, feeling sorry for myself.

On Wednesday morning, I finally wandered downstairs and sat in the family room, staring out the window instead of at the ceiling of my room. I was depressed and had zero motivation. I didn't feel terrible physically, just sore and tired, so I figured I could go back to school soon even though my parents wanted me to stay home.

I'd debated texting Patrick a dozen times but had decided against it. I'd eventually tell him what had happened, but I wasn't up to a conversation like that right now. I was raw, both physically and emotionally, and nothing felt right. Not even being home. I wanted to get away as much as I wanted to stay, which made no sense. Intellectually, I understood the subconscious need to run away from myself, but since that wasn't possible, I had to deal with these disparate emotions and conflicting situations.

"Ellie?" Mom sat on the other side of the couch, looking at me intently. "Are you okay?"

"Just contemplating the meaning of life."

"As someone speaking from experience, I promise that never ends well."

"I'm beginning to see that."

"Do you want to talk?"

I shrugged. "I don't know."

"Honey, I know you've had a rough week, but it's going to get better. I promise."

"You don't understand."

"So tell me."

"You don't want to hear it."

"Maybe not, but I'm trying to be better. I was never so scared as I was when we got to the hospital and found out you were already in surgery. The idea of losing you, Ellie..." She shuddered. "You and I have butted heads since you were a baby, but I hope you know how much I love you."

"I do."

"You can talk to me. Really. Tell me what's going on."

"You mean beyond recovering from surgery, breaking up with the love of my life, and losing a baby I hadn't even known I was pregnant with? Not to mention no longer having a direction in school."

"Are you leaving the program you're in?"

I gave her a wry smile. "I have to. While technology is still my thing, sitting and coding all day isn't. I need the science part of it too. And now I'm almost two years into a program I don't want to continue with."

"I know you don't want to hear this, but the reason I've been pushing you toward medical school is because I truly believe it's your calling. You're going to do something magical in the future, Ellie, but it's hard to see that far ahead at your age. And you're probably right, that I've babied and micromanaged your life a little too much, so I'm trying to back off a little."

"This is backing off a little?" I asked, giving her a sad smile.

"I want you to be happy and you're obviously not, so what can it hurt to apply to Harvard? That way, you'll have a backup plan in case whatever else you're considering falls through. It's not written in stone until you accept, so what's the harm?"

I sighed. I didn't have the energy to argue with her, and if nothing else, she was right about having a backup plan. It couldn't hurt to apply and talk to someone over there, especially since I had absolutely nothing else going for me right now.

"I'll look into it after my nap," I said, getting to my feet. "But I'm going to go lie down now."

She reached for my hand. "It's going to be okay, Ellie. You'll see."

"How long did you grieve the baby you lost?" I asked quietly.

She hesitated. "A long time. But that was different. I knew I was pregnant. I wanted the baby. I was in love with my husband, even though it turned out he didn't love me, so it took me about a year to see the light in the world again. And honestly, it was meeting your father that finally helped me heal."

"Do you think it would help if I talked to Patrick about what happened?"

"I think you have to whether it helps or not."

Too bad that was the last thing I wanted to do.

28

PATRICK

Going on a three-day road trip in the aftermath of my breakup with Ellie had been hell. I didn't play well, I couldn't focus, and I was fucking miserable. I hadn't told anyone we'd broken up, not even my brother, while I worked on sorting out my feelings and figuring out how things had gone so wrong. I hadn't handled it well, but in retrospect, she'd caught me off guard. The last thing I'd been expecting was for her to suggest breaking up, and in the moment, I'd been both hurt and angry.

I'd shown her how I felt about her a thousand different ways, but she apparently had zero faith in me. Zero faith in *us*. And I didn't understand it. Yes, me going to Vegas this summer wasn't going to be easy, but she hadn't even wanted to discuss it. I'd been trying to put Ellie's needs before my own, letting her figure out where and what she wanted to study without me pushing her in any direction. Her mother did enough of that so I didn't want to add any more stress to her life.

Instead of recognizing how much I was willing to sacrifice for her, she'd gotten mad and made it sound like I didn't care about her. To be fair, I hadn't said or done anything to dispel those notions, and now we'd been apart for over a week. I'd tried texting and calling, but she hadn't responded, and I'd been stalking all of her classes the last few days in an attempt to find her. I'd just about given up when I saw her friend Harley walking out of the dining hall.

I grabbed my backpack and chased after her. "Harley! Harley, wait up."

She turned in confusion, her eyes narrowing when she saw me.

"Hey, do you know where Ellie is?"

She didn't say anything for a minute, watching me with a dour look on her face.

"Look, I know she's mad at me, but I've been trying to apologize, maybe make things right, and I can't do that if she doesn't pick up the phone. She hasn't been in class either, so I'm getting worried."

"You really don't know?"

"Know what?"

"She had a…medical emergency. I don't know the details but she's been up in Brattleboro recovering."

"A medical emergency?!" I stared at her. "*Fuck*. Is she okay?"

"I think so? She hasn't said much to me either, but I think she's coming back to campus tomorrow."

Of course. Tomorrow was Friday and Fridays were game days, when I had very little free time, and it would be hard for me to catch her.

"Thanks," I said quietly. "And if you talk to her, tell her to call me back, please."

She shrugged. "I think she's done with you, but I'll pass the message on."

Double fuck.

I was freaking out, wondering what was going on. Her friend Chastity would know, but I didn't know her class schedule or where she lived, so that was out. Dammit. I was really worried and there wasn't anything I could do about it. Why didn't we know more of each other's friends? If I ever got another chance with her, we'd have to fix that immediately.

In the meantime, I was left trying to wrap my head around what to do next. I understood that she'd probably been hurt when Nate had blurted out that I'd changed my mind about staying in school, but she hadn't even given me a chance to explain, which hurt me. I'd been planning to sit down and talk it all out with her, going over the pros and cons together, in the hopes that we could find a solution, a way to be together. I'd known it was more likely that it wouldn't work out, but I hadn't wanted it to go down that way.

The unfortunate truth was that in that moment, when she'd unexpectedly dumped me, I hadn't known what I wanted. I liked her. A lot. I was starting to have feelings I wasn't comfortable with and I was about to set off on the professional adventure of a lifetime. How could I do that with my nineteen-year-old girlfriend in tow? I didn't have any answers then, and while I still didn't have any now, the one thing that was different was that I missed her. More than I'd thought I would. Not just the sex or her sweet laugh or the fun we had together, but my life was empty without her. Even hockey didn't give me the rush it usually did, which was going to be a problem if I was going to Vegas next season.

I tossed and turned that night, determined to find her in the morning, talk to her, figure out what had gone wrong and try to fix it. It was a long shot, because our lives were going in two entirely different directions, but I had to try. More than that, I needed to make sure she was okay. I couldn't imagine what had happened that required her to go home to recover, but I hated that we were in a place where she hadn't felt comfortable reaching out.

I was up and out early, getting breakfast and then settling in front of her dorm. It was a two-hour drive from Brattleboro and she would have to go through the front of the dorm to get in. I didn't know what I'd do if she didn't show up, and I had to leave for the game tonight by three, but I'd sit here until the very last minute if I had to.

Luckily, I didn't. I spotted her immediately, walking with her friend Chastity and a guy I didn't know. The guy was carrying her stuff and Ellie was walking slower than usual. Definitely like someone who'd been sick.

I got up and approached her slowly. "Ellie."

Her step faltered but she looked up as if she'd been expecting me. "Hi."

"El?" The guy was eyeing me suspiciously.

"It's okay, Dylan. I'm fine."

"You want us to stay?" Chastity asked.

She shook her head. "I'm good, really."

"Let me carry your stuff upstairs," Dylan said.

"I've got it." I reached out a hand for the two bags.

Dylan hesitated but Ellie nodded and he grudgingly handed them over.

"Call if you need me, okay?" Chastity asked, hugging her.

"Thanks. Both of you."

Her friends walked away and she dug out her key card. "You want to come up?"

"Yeah, I do." I followed her to the door. "What happened, Ellie? Are you okay? Why didn't you call me?"

"There was no reason to worry you," she said, walking in and heading toward the elevator. You needed a special key card to use it as it was usually just for disabled students. Ellie had access as an R.A. but we always used the stairs, so she had to be hurting.

"Of course there was a reason," I muttered. "I would have been there for you."

"You were in Connecticut," she said. "So even if we hadn't been broken up, you still wouldn't have been here."

I grimaced because she was right. Short of a death in the family, there was no way I would have been able to leave Connecticut to be with her. And things like that would be even worse when I got to Vegas.

We got up to her room and I put her things down, watching as she sank onto the bed, wincing.

"Tell me what happened," I said, pulling the chair from her desk over to sit beside the bed.

"It's kind of a long story," she whispered, looking me in the eye for the first time today. She was tired, her face pale with dark circles under her eyes. God, I hated that she'd gone through whatever this was alone.

"I have plenty of time," I said, leaning forward and resting my forearms on my thighs.

"Well..." She took a breath. "Remember all the broken condoms?"

I frowned. "Yeah."

"My IUD slipped out of place and though the doctors aren't sure, it was probably in a position that you rubbed up against something when you were inside of me, tearing the condoms."

"Oh, Jesus." I had a feeling I knew what was coming and my stomach clenched painfully.

"On Thursday I started bleeding. Not some spotting like my usual periods, but full-on soak through all the layers of clothing type bleeding. And then the cramping started." She told me how she'd done her best to suffer through it, eventually calling Chastity and agreeing to go to the E.R.

"Oh, baby." I reached for her hand. "Was it a miscarriage?"

Tears filled her eyes. "It was *ectopic* and one of my fallopian tubes burst when I got to the hospital."

I blinked. I'd heard of ectopic pregnancies but didn't know what it was. "I'm sorry, I don't know what that means exactly."

"Ectopic pregnancy is when the fertilized egg implants in the fallopian tube, which is what carries eggs from the ovaries to the uterus. Sometimes it happens in other parts of the body, like the cervix, but mostly it's the fallopian tubes. Anyway, the baby can't survive there and the growing tissue, as the baby gets bigger, can cause life-threatening problems to the mother."

"To you." My heart squeezed painfully and I moved from the chair to the bed, holding out my arms.

She fell into them without hesitation. "We made a baby," she whispered. "And then it died before I even knew it existed. I'm sorry!" She burst into tears.

"Sorry?" I was on the verge of tears myself, the scratchy feeling behind my eyes intensifying as she cried. "What are you sorry for? We were so careful and there was no way to know your IUD had moved… Please don't cry. It wasn't your fault. Jesus, none of this was your fault." A million emotions whipped through me, running the gamut from sadness to relief to pain. Pain that she'd suffered alone. Relief that there wasn't going to be a baby in my life at this stage of the game. Guilt that I felt that way. And then more pain that our baby had died, almost killing Ellie too. So much fucking pain, but all I wanted to do was take some from her. Her sobs wracked her whole body, as if she'd been holding them in, and I would have done anything to ease her suffering, despite my own.

She cried for a long time and all I could do was hold her. I felt even worse than before that I'd been in Connecticut, playing hockey and oblivious to what she'd been going through. That we'd made a baby and subsequently lost it. That all of this had happened despite how careful we'd been. It was a lot to process, but I could do that later, when I was alone. Right now, Ellie needed me more than I needed to sort everything out.

I handed her a tissue and she blew her nose, but I was gratified that she moved back into my arms when she was done.

"So are you okay now?" I asked after a while. "Did the surgery fix everything?"

She nodded. "They removed the IUD and the fallopian tube that burst, and I've already stopped bleeding, so I'm on the mend."

"Is there any permanent damage?"

"No. If I want to have kids in the future, the other fallopian tube is perfectly healthy. But I'll never use an IUD again, that's for sure."

"I don't blame you." I stroked her hair and held her tightly. "I'm the one that's sorry," I said after a little while. "I should have been there for you. I hate that I wasn't."

"It's okay. Nothing you could have done would have changed the outcome, and hockey is more important."

"What? No, that's not true. It's important but not more important than your health. If you hadn't gone to the E.R., you could have died."

"I didn't let it go that far," she said. "I called Chastity when I realized something was very wrong."

"I still hate that I wasn't there. It was my baby too. I would have wanted to be there with you, had I known."

"Honestly, I just wanted the pain to stop," she said softly. "I didn't give much thought to anything else. And I was so scared…"

"I know." I kissed the top of her head.

We sat like that for a long time, her small body engulfed in mine, and I never wanted to let her go. The chaos in my brain calmed the moment I wrapped my arms around her and I didn't know how to move forward without her. I didn't want to either.

"I wanted to tell you," she said after a while, "but I didn't know how."

"I'm sorry we've gotten to a place where you don't feel like you can talk to me anymore, but Ellie, I miss you. I want to fix this."

"We can't," she said sadly, lifting those big blue eyes to gaze into mine. "If nothing else, this whole thing has shown me that I'm not ready for…this. *Us*."

"Not ready?" I wasn't sure what she meant.

"I've been trying to play catch-up, so my maturity and life experience is at least a little closer to my book smarts, but right now the gap is too much. I'm beyond overwhelmed. School, careers, a serious, sexual relationship, unplanned pregnancy, surgery… It's too much too soon. I wanted to be a normal teenager and have a little fun, but I got way more than I bargained for. And I'm mentally exhausted."

I pulled her close again, unable to respond because she'd just broken my heart into a zillion pieces. I hated that she was going through this and that I'd inadvertently added to her pain, but I didn't know how to fix it.

"I don't want to add any more stress to your life," I said. "I'd do almost anything to try and work things out, but not if it's going to cause you pain."

"I wish I was stronger," she whispered. "I wish I was older, more mature, so I could be the woman you need in your life, but I can't, Patrick. I'm so sorry, but I can't."

"It's okay." It wasn't, but I cared for her enough to pretend it was, to hide my broken heart from her because she didn't need me adding anything else to her already overflowing emotional plate. There was so much I wanted to say, feelings I wanted to explore, but not now. Not if it was going to hurt her or confuse her. I loved her too much for that.

I squeezed my eyes shut as reality dawned.

When the fuck had I fallen in love with her?

29

PATRICK

The game that night was probably the worst I'd played since I'd gotten to college. I couldn't do anything right, got several penalties, and broke my scoring streak. I was fucked in the head after my emotional morning with Ellie, and it took all of my self-control not to start throwing punches at anyone and everyone. Everyone noticed, and Paxton tried to talk me down like he usually did, but it didn't help. Nothing was going to soothe my broken heart. Not yet anyway.

I'd never had one before. I'd never had a relationship like the one I'd had with Ellie before either. Most of my relationships had been sex-only or friends-with-benefits, so Ellie had broken all the emotional barriers I'd put up over the years. I'd been laser-focused on hockey and getting a degree, and there hadn't been time or energy for anything serious. Then Ellie had caught my eye across the room and I'd been a goner. I couldn't explain it, but I'd known something was different about her the minute I laid eyes on her.

How we'd gotten from there to here was beyond me and while I hadn't said as much to her, I felt guilty as hell about the ectopic pregnancy. I had all the sexual experience. I should have known it wasn't normal to break that many condoms. It probably wouldn't have changed anything, but I should have pushed her to have it checked out. Maybe if she'd gone to her doctor right away, they would have discovered the pregnancy and taken care of it before she started bleeding.

"You okay, man?" My friend and teammate J.D.—Jonah Daniels—fell into step beside me as we headed out. We'd won the game so there had been journalists all over the place as we geared up for the championship games coming up, but I'd hidden from them, unwilling to answer questions about why I'd sucked so hard tonight.

"Yeah." I gave him a half-hearted smile. "Just some personal shit going on. I'll shake it off by tomorrow."

He frowned a little. "You and Ellie hit a rough patch?"

I sighed. Everyone knew about Ellie and now I was going to have to say it was over. "Something like that," I said vaguely. "I don't wanna talk about it yet. It's kind of new."

"Hey, no problem. If you want to go tie one on, I'm happy to."

"Tomorrow night," I said. "I can't be hungover for tomorrow's game."

"You got it." He strolled off, leaving me even lonelier than before. That was probably the least masculine thought I'd ever had, but it was accurate. I didn't think about it much, but my mother was gone and my father was an emotionally abusive asshole, so the only person I'd ever been able to rely on was Paxton. Now that he had Naomi, I'd lost a little bit of the closeness we'd shared too, and with him going to Seattle soon, I realized I had no one. Not really.

I had a handful of friends, like J.D., Tate, and Lex, but it wasn't like what I had with Paxton or what I'd shared with Ellie. And dealing with everything I was going through right now on my own was harder than I'd thought it would be.

I'd hoped to talk to Paxton tonight but he and Naomi had gone out after the game, so I sat on the couch, opened a beer and turned on the TV. I wasn't really watching, though, mostly staring at nothing as I sucked down one beer and then another. I was in a bad place, my heart heavy and my stomach churning. I'd had no idea a broken heart would feel this way, and coupled with the guilt of Ellie's pregnancy, I'd never been as down as I was tonight.

I heard the key turn in the lock and Paxton and Naomi came in, laughing.

"Hey, what are you doing?" Paxton asked curiously, eyeing me.

I shrugged.

"You okay?" He came around the couch to frown down at me.

"Not really." I met his gaze warily, unsure whether he was going to make fun of me or if he would instinctively understand how much I was hurting. I didn't have it in me to spar with my twin tonight and thankfully, he must have sensed this was different.

He murmured something to Naomi and she nodded and left the room. He sank down next to me and gave me a gentle nudge with his elbow. "What's going on with you? You've been out of sorts for a week. Something happen with Ellie?"

"So much." I closed my eyes and let my head fall back.

"You break up?"

"Yeah, but that's not the worst of it."

"Uh-oh."

"She was pregnant, Pax."

"*Was?*"

I told him the latest, starting with our trip to Montreal to breaking up to finding out about the pregnancy and her subsequent surgery.

"Oh god, I'm sorry." He shook his head. "Is she okay now?"

"Physically, she's going to be okay, but she's dealing with a lot."

"So why aren't you there with her?"

"She's overwhelmed and instead of helping, my presence just adds to her stress." I told him the rest, how Ellie was second-guessing everything about her life and future, how she didn't see a way for us to go forward with our relationship, and how the events of the last few months had been more than she was ready for.

"She found out she was pregnant and then immediately had to have surgery to remove it," he said sadly. "All on her own?"

I nodded miserably. "Jesus, Pax, we made a baby… a *baby*!" That weird scratchy feeling behind my eyes came back and I pressed my thumb and forefinger over them to hide my tears.

"I'm so sorry." He reached out and wrapped an arm around my shoulder. "What can I do? Are you okay?"

"I'm fucking miserable without her. And I can't fix it. I can't put her in a position where she has something else to juggle on top of all the other shit in her life."

"But did you tell her you love her?" he asked quietly.

"No." I swallowed hard. "How could I? I didn't realize it until we were broken up and then when she told me how much of the stress in her life was because of me—both directly and indirectly—I couldn't. I don't want to hurt her any more and she's already hurting so much."

"I wish I had words of wisdom," he said quietly. "I can't imagine how you're feeling knowing she went through that whole pregnancy thing alone."

"So much guilt," I admitted. "Guilt that I got her pregnant, guilt that the baby had to die and I wasn't there with her… Fuck, man." My eyes felt wet again and I turned away, unused to showing so much emotion. We were close, but I didn't think either of us had cried since our mom had died more than a decade ago.

"You can't feel guilty about getting her pregnant," he said. "She had an IUD *and* you were using condoms. This wasn't about carelessness or heat of the moment. There was almost zero chance of her getting pregnant."

"I should have made a bigger deal about the broken condoms.

I'm the experienced one—I was her first and only. She wouldn't know that breaking so many wasn't normal."

"The doctor couldn't verify one way or the other if the IUD caused that. It could be coincidence, but either way, focusing on that is a waste of energy. It happened and it's over. Yeah, it sucks that you weren't with her, but even if things were hunky-dory and she was going to Vegas with you, you still wouldn't have been with her. Any woman you get serious with is going to have to get used to you being gone and missing a lot of important things. It's part of life with a professional athlete. And maybe Ellie realizes it's not for her."

"Yeah." Fuck, that was the last thing I wanted to hear. "And that's why I didn't tell her how I feel."

"Maybe you did the right thing."

"Sure doesn't feel like it."

"I know." He paused. "You want to watch a movie and get drunk?"

I managed a half-hearted smile. "I don't want to be hungover tomorrow."

"Well, I'm here for you. You know that."

"You don't know how much I appreciate it."

"I kinda do."

I'd forgotten all about my stat test that week and grimaced when I walked into the classroom. I hadn't cracked a book in more than a week and it was probably going to show in my grades. I'd had straight A's all semester and hated that I was going to blow it now, but without Ellie's help, and her in my life in general, studying was nothing but a nuisance. At this point, having decided to go pro, I almost didn't care whether I graduated or not.

That wasn't entirely true but in my current state of mind, I didn't have it in me to give a shit. In fact, I barely gave a shit about hockey, and it showed in the games that weekend. My head and heart just weren't in it and I didn't know how to fix it. I couldn't make myself forget Ellie or the baby we'd lost or anything else, and after another pair of terrible games, I did something I never thought I'd do: I reached out for help.

Toli Petrov had given me his cell phone number and told me to call any time, for any reason, and with my future on the line, I did it.

"Patrick!" He answered on the first ring, his voice as friendly and jovial as ever.

"Hey, Toli. Do you have a few minutes?"

"Of course. What's going on?"

I took a breath. "A lot. Too much."

"You had a rough couple of games, eh?"

"You watched?" I nearly winced at the thought.

"Of course. We're all so excited to have you joining us this fall, we watch either the games or the highlights once we're at the hotel for the night when we're on the road."

"Man, my life is a shitshow right now," I admitted. Then I told him everything, leaving out some of the more personal aspects of what was going on in Ellie's life, though I did tell him about the baby.

"That's a lot," he said when I was done. "No wonder you're off your game."

"I've got so much on the line and it's all blowing up in my face. I don't know how to compartmentalize something this serious."

"If it was just a breakup, I'd tell you to knock it off and get your head back in the game, but this is different. The breakup, the baby, your grades, it's all piling up and I don't know many men who could handle it all without losing a step or two. My wife went into labor with our youngest while I was stuck in Chicago during a blizzard. I couldn't get home no matter what, and it was hard. It made me realize there's more to life than hockey, but at the same time, my wife doesn't hold it against me."

"That's just it—she *didn't* hold it against me. *I'm* holding it against me. I'm the one who can't stay focused, who's about to lose everything I've worked for because my life is a goddamn hot mess."

"Listen, you get nothing by letting this consume you. I know you don't want to hear that, but you have to. So here's my advice: Make a deal with yourself. For the next week, until regionals are over, you focus on nothing but hockey. No Ellie, no baby, no nothing. And then, when it's done, you're allowed to wallow in self-pity, get shit-faced, whatever it is you need to do to get through it for a few days. But then you need to get back on track until you get past the Frozen Four, assuming you do what you have to do at regionals. You think about hockey and hockey alone, knowing that after the championships, you'll have all the time you need to grieve and work out the things you're feeling. That's the only way to get through this."

I took a breath. "You think that'll work?"

"You make it work. And as an added incentive, you give yourself permission to try once more with Ellie. Whether it's one last heart-to-heart conversation or a grand plan to win her back, whatever you need to do to satisfy yourself that you tried everything. But not until hockey season is completely over."

"You're right," I said, warming to that idea. "You're absolutely right."

"Of course I am. Now get out there and kick some ass."

I didn't know how I was going to do it, but I had to try.

ELLIE

My first few days back at school were quiet. It was the weekend and I used that time to catch up on studying even though I had zero interest in what I was working on. I was still sore and moving a lot slower than usual, but I had to pick up the pieces of my broken heart and find a way out of the darkness that had enveloped me. I was so damn depressed and as I walked to class on Monday, it felt like the weight of the world was on my shoulders.

"Ellie!" Someone was calling to me and I nearly groaned as I turned to see Dr. Lancet hurrying in my direction.

"Hello, Dr. Lancet."

"My dear, I heard you had emergency surgery. Are you okay?" There was nothing but genuine concern on his face and I managed a smile.

"I'm getting there. Still sore, but I'll be okay."

"Should you be carrying a backpack?"

"I emptied out everything but my laptop, charger, and wallet. I'm being careful."

"Very good. How are you doing with your quest for a suitable graduate program?"

I swallowed. "I, um, I guess I'm not. I applied to Harvard Medical School."

I saw the surprise that flickered in his eyes and it was quickly replaced with concern. "Is that what you want?"

"I don't know what I want," I whispered. "I just know I have to have a plan and that was the only one that's something of a sure thing. It's late in the year to be applying to other doctoral programs so…" I let my voice trail off because I was struggling with it too.

"You always have options," he said gently. "With your background, most schools are going to jump at the chance to have you. And I'll write any recommendations you need. All you have to do is ask."

"Thank you." I nodded. "I appreciate it, and I'll take you up on it if the time comes. But I have to get to class. Thanks for checking up on me."

"Any time."

I continued toward my class, feeling even worse than I had before. The pain in my soul was far worse than that of my healing abdomen and I hadn't been sleeping for shit since I'd been back at school. Coupling my emotional heartache with the indecision regarding my future, made everything that much worse, to the point I thought of little else. My brain was like a computer's hard drive that never stopped spinning. I thought about Patrick, medical school, my current computer science program, and Patrick some more, on a loop.

I'd been so sure I'd done the right thing in breaking up with him, but instead of relief, all I felt was indecision and an ache so strong it literally kept me awake at night. In the days since we'd broken up, I'd gone from desperation to depression to sheer misery. I couldn't articulate how awful this was and while I knew, intellectually at least, that this was normal for a broken heart, my gut told me there was more to it. I might not have had a boyfriend before, but this wasn't puppy love. What Patrick and I shared was intense, so much more than a college fling, and now it was gone.

The worst part was that I'd watched the game Saturday night and Patrick didn't look like himself at all. He'd been almost clumsy out on the ice, as if he hadn't been focused on what he was doing, and I knew it was because of me. I knew him better than almost anyone, and I'd spent a lot of time watching him play hockey—both in person and in videos online—so I knew when something was off. And the Patrick Graham I'd seen the other night had been more than off.

My phone rang and my mother's name flashed on the screen. I grabbed it because she'd been checking in multiple times a day and I didn't need her driving up here because she was worried.

"I'm about to go to class, Mom," I said by way of greeting.

"I'm sorry, love, but guess what?" Her voice was laced with excitement.

"What?"

"I spoke to my friend at Harvard and she said you're a shoo-in for medical school and that you'll be getting a welcoming letter any day now. I pulled a few strings, obviously, but—"

"Mom, I asked you not to," I said quietly.

"I know, but I was so excited for you. And anyway, time was of the essence. So now you're all set for the fall and don't have to worry anymore!"

I wanted to cry but it wasn't her fault. I'd agreed to apply, after all, and though she'd said I didn't have to do it if I didn't want to, it was hard to go back to arguing all the time now that we'd been getting along. It was the first time since I was little that we weren't at each other's throats and I desperately needed a mom right now.

"Mom, I'm sorry, I'm going to be late, but I'll call you later, okay?"

"Okay, honey. And remember, don't overdo it today!"

"I won't. Love you." I disconnected and paused to lean against the wall of the building. Both to catch my breath because I was tired and to get hold of my emotions before walking into a class-room. I'd promised myself I was done crying, but my heart seemed to have other ideas. Damn, this was hard. And I had no one to talk to. Chastity thought my mother was manipulating me, my dad just wanted us all to get along, and Patrick wasn't in my life anymore.

A stray tear leaked out anyway and I clenched my fist, trying to get my emotions under control. I absolutely couldn't go to class like this.

"Ellie?"

The soft voice beside me made me jump and I quickly swiped at my eyes before turning.

"Naomi, hi."

"Oh, sweetie." She took one look at my face and opened her arms.

I barely knew her but a hug sounded pretty good right about now.

"I was going to ask how you were, but it's written all over your face that things aren't good."

"I'm hanging in there," I said, pulling away and offering a lame smile.

"You could pack a month's worth of clothes in those bags under your eyes," she said, "and it looks like you've lost weight, which you didn't have to lose."

"I'm okay," I reiterated, more for my own benefit than hers.

"Liar. You're as miserable as he is." Her eyes gleamed with intensity.

"Is he?" I whispered. "Miserable, I mean."

"He got so drunk Saturday night, Tate and Paxton had to carry him home… He was literally out cold."

I dipped my head, sad for both of us but unsure how to respond to that.

"I have to get to class," she said, "but give some thought to what you really want. From where I stand on the outside looking in, you're both so much better together than apart. Oh, and he failed his stat test last Thursday. Just thought you'd want to know." She turned and walked in the other direction, leaving me staring after her dejectedly.

He'd failed his stat test after we'd worked so hard to stay on top of his grades. I was disappointed in him, but also felt a familiar twinge of guilt, because it was my fault too. I wasn't going to get all righteous and take the stance that he was responsible for his own actions, his grades, and everything else. That was true in general, but there were extenuating circumstances, most of which were my fault. Not the pregnancy or resulting loss, but the breakup and me pushing him out of my life just before the Frozen Four tournament, which was the penultimate college hockey tournament.

Was I a terrible human being or what?

I sat through my classes trying desperately to concentrate but failing miserably. I needed a nap but I was already so behind. And I still had to call my mom back.

Ugh.

The thought of going to medical school turned my stomach but I didn't know what to do. There were no other options at the moment and I'd always had a plan. *Always*. At twelve I'd known I would graduate high school by the time I was fifteen, finish my undergraduate degree by the time I turned eighteen, and move right into a doctoral program. And I'd done all that. Except I'd chosen a graduate program solely to spite my mother, I'd unexpectedly found my soul mate, and absolutely nothing was going according to plan.

I'd just gotten to the dining hall for dinner when an unfamiliar number flashed on the screen of my phone. It said it was from Las Vegas and I frowned, wondering who it might be. I cautiously lifted it to my ear.

"Hello?"

"Ellie? This is Renee Wylde."

"Renee…hello." I sank into a chair even though I didn't have any food yet.

"I heard you've had a rough couple of weeks."

"Yes." I put my chin in my hand, resting my elbow on the table and holding the phone with my other hand. "H-how did you hear?" It was a little disconcerting to think the members of a professional hockey team were talking about me.

"Toli spoke to Patrick and then told Tessa, who of course told me. She thought I might want to reach out."

"Patrick and I aren't together anymore." My voice caught; it was so hard to say those words aloud.

"I know that, silly, but that doesn't mean I can't reach out to make sure you're okay. Losing a baby is never easy, but especially not at your age and under those circumstances. How are you doing? Both physically and emotionally."

"I'm doing okay physically. Everything is healing and though I'm still a little sore, it's better every day. Emotionally, well, I'm a wreck."

"Which part of it is the hardest for you?"

"It's not about the baby so much as...everything." I got up and walked back outside. I couldn't have this conversation in the dining hall where people might hear me.

"I'm here if you need an unbiased shoulder to cry on. I promise not to say all the bad things about Patrick, which some of your friends and family are probably doing."

"Not really," I said, sitting on a bench outside even though it was freezing. "Everyone's been pretty respectful, especially since I was the one who broke up with him."

"Why did you do that, Ellie?" she asked gently. "Your eyes practically sparkled every time you mentioned his name, when you looked at him... There's no doubt in my mind you love him."

"Oh, more than anything. It's just... *Fuck*." I blew out a breath. "I did something dumb with school, picking a major I don't love just to annoy my mother, and now it's too late to get in anywhere next year, plus my credits won't transfer, and I applied to medical school but my mom did something to fast-track it so I'm kind of stuck doing something else I don't want to do and now I'm even more miserable than before and I can't think of any way to get out of it!" Once I'd started, I hadn't dared to stop talking until I let it all out.

"Oh wow." Renee let out a soft chuckle. "I'm not laughing at you, sweetie, but it sounded like you needed to get that off your chest."

"Yeah, kinda." I giggled a little too.

"So would you like some unsolicited advice?"

"I would love any and all advice because I don't want to disappoint my mother, but I miss Patrick and I'm so lost."

"Do you love Patrick? Like with all your heart, the kind of love that might last forever?"

"Absolutely, but—"

"No interrupting. Just yes or no."

"Okay, then yes."

"Have you given any thought to what it might be like to be married to him? Meaning, married to a professional athlete."

"Yes."

"Does it scare you?"

"A little. So…yes?"

"Believe it or not, that's a good thing. It means you're thinking beyond how it feels right now, with a freshly broken heart. It means you're not looking for a quick fix to the current situation."

"Renee, there's no fix. I don't know where I'm going or what I'm doing…"

"You're nineteen—why on earth should you know the answers to all those questions? I'm a bestselling author and didn't figure out what I really wanted to be when I grew up until my thirties. Considering that you already have not just one degree, but two, puts you way ahead of the game."

"But what do I *do*?" I whispered. "Like, literally. What do I do next?"

"You breathe. Let your body heal. Give yourself a week or two to get your head together."

"And then?"

"Then we'll talk again. But there are no quick fixes to broken hearts, broken relationships, or recovery from surgery. Take some time to just be. Don't think so much. Don't stress over every little thing. Cry. Eat chocolate. Study a little, but don't overdo it, and do not, under any circumstances, make any big decisions. Don't agree to go to medical school, don't apply to any more colleges, just let it all simmer."

"Okay." I wasn't sure I could do that, but I would try.

"Trust me, you need time to heal. Inside and out. Once you're on your way, you'll have a clearer head and be able to make more thoughtful decisions."

"I'm going to give it a shot."

"And call me any time. Okay? Promise?"

"Yes. Promise."

"It's going to be okay, Ellie. One way or another."

31

PATRICK

The Frozen Four tournament was the culmination of everything we worked for in college hockey. We hadn't won one since I'd been at Moo U and this was supposed to be our year. I'd taken everything Toli said to heart and put absolutely everything but hockey—and a modicum of studying—out of my mind. Regionals were this weekend in Detroit and I couldn't afford to be distracted. Not even by the woman I loved more than anything.

The tournament was composed of four groups of four teams in regional brackets: Northeast, West, East, and Midwest. The winner of each regional bracket would advance to the Frozen Four, which would be held in two weeks in Philadelphia. It was a huge deal, the tickets often going for more than two hundred dollars apiece, and arenas selling out. We'd lost during regionals last year, so this year I couldn't afford to let myself think about anything else. Especially now that I'd made the decision to go pro.

I'd spent the last few days studying statistics and working on my final paper for my global business class, so I'd been in a much better headspace until my dad showed up in Detroit. It was approximately an eleven-hour drive from where he lived outside Minneapolis, and he'd been sitting in the hotel lobby when we got there. My stomach automatically clenched and my chest tightened; he always did that to me. No matter how good I was playing, he'd tell me exactly what I had to do to be better. And sadly, he was usually wrong, completely at odds with what my coaches were telling me.

"Patrick! Paxton!" He stood up, grinning broadly, holding out his arms as if hugging was something we did in our family. It was all a show because we were with the team, so I gave him a half-hearted hug just so there wouldn't be a scene.

"What are you doing here, Dad?" Paxton could ask questions like that because they didn't fight the way Dad and I did. He typically treated Paxton like an afterthought, which was both good and bad, but he'd started paying more attention to him once Paxton announced he was going to Seattle in the fall.

"It's a big weekend. How could I not come? Especially since it was within driving distance." His eyes twinkled as he said hello to Coach Keller and a couple of our teammates, who mostly ignored him.

"Hey, Mr. Graham." Tate knew how I felt about my dad but was polite anyway, a testament to both his manners and our friendship.

"How's it going, Adler?" Dad grinned, as if Tate was his new best friend.

Jesus, I didn't think it was possible to like my dad any less than I already did, but apparently it was.

"Boys, I need you to check in and get ready for the meeting," Coach Keller called out, eyeing me pointedly. I'd had a few run-ins with my father at games over the years and he knew it was never good when Dad showed up unannounced, so he was obviously running interference.

Most of the guys scattered and I cut a glance at Paxton, who was doing something on his phone.

"Can I sit in, Coach?" Dad asked him, his face as beguiling as a four-year-old asking if he could pet his puppy. "This is my last chance now that the boys are going pro."

I grimaced, but kept my mouth shut, hoping Coach would turn him down, but he didn't.

"That's fine, but I'd appreciate it if you didn't interact at all. You're just an observer." Coach Keller was using his no-nonsense voice, the same one he'd used to tell me I needed to get my grades up or he'd bench me, and my dad was too self-absorbed to notice.

"Yes, sir. Absolutely. Quiet as a church mouse."

"We're meeting here in the lobby in thirty minutes." Coach Keller turned and headed for the elevators.

Dad automatically started following us, slinging his duffel over his shoulder.

"Dad, we're just going to drop our things off, freshen up, and come right back down," I told him.

He shifted uncomfortably. "I thought maybe I could crash with you guys. The hotels are really expensive this weekend."

I gritted my teeth to keep from saying something obnoxious, so Paxton jumped in. "Dad, they're full-size beds. No way you'll fit with either of us."

"No problem at all. I already asked at the desk and they can send up a cot."

I nearly cried in frustration but Paxton nodded. "Okay, that works, I guess. But you can't watch TV all night, Dad. We have to rest."

"Promise." He held up a hand as if making some kind of oath.

Fuck.

So much for having my head on straight.

Despite our father being up our asses, Paxton and I had a great first game. With our usual connection stronger than ever, we scored a goal each and skated all over the other team. With one game down and one more to go to earn our spot in the finals, I felt good, but of course, my father had to shit all over my good mood.

"You could have scored at least twice more," he said when we got back to the hotel. "You had so many opportunities... What were you thinking?"

"I was thinking about hanging on to the lead and not worrying about jacking up the score just so I could say I got another hat trick," I replied.

"The Sidewinders are watching!" he snapped. "You need to shine out there."

"We won," I said dryly. "How much more do I need to shine?"

"All right, I need to get some rest," Paxton interjected. "Let's save that arguing for after the tournament, okay?"

Dad looked unhappy but merely grunted and turned on the TV.

"Dad, we can't sleep with the TV on."

"I can't sleep without it."

"Then you probably should have coughed up the money for your own room."

We glared at each other.

"I'm still your father," he growled. "You wouldn't be on the verge of the big leagues if I hadn't pushed you."

"That has nothing to do with us needing our rest."

"I'll keep the volume low."

"Dad, you promised."

"It's just a little TV. Jesus fucking Christ."

"You're an asshole, you know that?" I said, putting my hands on my hips.

"You watch how you talk to me, boy."

I arched my brows. "Boy? Who are you calling boy?"

"Okay, knock it off." Paxton stood between us. "Let's not do this. Dad, the deal was no TV if you stayed with us."

"You're both a bunch of pussies," he hissed. "How I raised—"

"Would you be talking like this if Mom was still alive?" I challenged.

He was momentarily startled into silence and then he went into the bathroom and shut the door behind him.

"Fuck." I blew out a breath. "I need him out of here. Can we afford to get him his own room?"

"This place is sold out and I think most of the hotels around here are."

"I'm going for a walk," I said. "I can't sit here and fight with him all night."

I grabbed my wallet and room key and left, taking the stairs down to the first floor just to walk off a little nervous energy. Why did he have to show up? Wasn't it enough to have not one but two sons going to the pros? Jesus, I'd happily send him money every month in exchange for him to just shut his mouth and stay away from me.

For the first time since my talk with Toli, I let my thoughts drift to Ellie. If things had been different, I'd be on the phone with her now, letting her calm my chaos. That was one of many things that had been special about what we'd had. And with each passing day, I missed it more and more.

"You have me and I have you," she'd said.

I would've done almost anything just then to hear her voice telling me I had her and she had me. 'Cause I needed her more than I'd ever thought possible.

Eye on the prize, I reminded myself as I walked outside. I'd allow myself a few minutes to miss Ellie, and then go back to focusing on hockey.

Dad continued to make a nuisance of himself but he turned off the TV and kept his mouth shut that night, if nothing else. Paxton had obviously had a talk with him, but I didn't give a shit anymore. I'd been loath to articulate it, but deep down I was slowly but surely pushing my father out of my life. He was toxic and brought nothing to the table. I was grateful he'd given me life and helped me achieve my dream of playing professional hockey, but the trade-off was too much. My sanity was too important, and from an emotional perspective, he destroyed everything around him. I'd battled with the guilt of not "liking" my father for years, but I was done now.

I'd write him a check once in a while after I started getting paychecks from the Sidewinders, and hopefully that would be all he needed from me. I truly didn't give a shit anymore. And once I'd made that decision, I played like a guy going to the pros. The final game was a blur of skating, shooting, and passing. My brother and I were a well-oiled machine when the stars were in alignment, and everything fell into place that game. Two goals and an assist later, we were headed to the Frozen Four. Now I just had to come up with a plan to talk Ellie into giving me another chance.

Something told me that was going to be way harder than a hockey championship.

32

ELLIE

I did my best to take Renee's advice, keeping my mind free of anything to do with Patrick, medical school, or even my ectopic pregnancy. Mostly I focused on the present, which was finishing this semester with good grades. Even though I wasn't going to continue in the program, I wanted to make sure my grades reflected my overall work ethic so that when I decided which direction I was going, I had something impressive to show whatever academic institution I chose.

My mother was being surprisingly patient with me since I hadn't yet accepted the offer to go to Harvard, especially after I told her my body needed two weeks to heal and rest. For some reason, that resonated with her, so our phone calls were lighthearted and more frequent than usual.

"You sound so sad," she said about a week into my two-week timeline. "Are you sad about the baby?"

"I'm sad about Patrick," I admitted. "I miss him."

"Have you heard from him?"

"Not since I told him I wasn't ready for something as serious as the relationship we had."

"It's probably for the best, honey. If he's going to Las Vegas and you're going to Boston, how would you be together?"

"Mom, what happens if I don't go to Boston?"

She didn't reply for a long time. I mentally pictured her counting to a hundred or something, with my dad making a slashing motion with his hand to keep her from saying something to upset me.

"Mom?"

"I don't know how to answer that," she said. "This has always been the goal. You already tried deviating off course and look what happened. You could have been well into medical school by now, moving into the next phase of your life. I understand you needed to do something your way, explore something different, but you've done it. Why are you fighting this so hard, Ellie?"

Her words made me want to cry, something I'd vowed I wouldn't do anymore. Why was this so complicated? I wasn't ready to make a decision this big and it was like no one understood.

Well, Patrick did. He'd understood all my struggles and never pushed me to go one way or the other. He'd said it too, the night we'd broken up. He understood that my parents pushed me all the time and he refused to add to it. That was why he hadn't asked me to go to Vegas with him. I'd been too hurt that night to really listen to what he was trying to tell me, and I'd done some-thing rash. Breaking up with Patrick had been stupid. Really, really stupid. Just like when I'd chosen to get a doctorate in computer science.

"Mom, I'm not you," I said softly. "I know your dreams were squashed by your unplanned pregnancy and marriage, but I've got to live *my* life, not yours. I don't want to be a medical doctor."

"You have the potential to do anything, Ellie. Absolutely anything—why not go for it?"

"I will. Once I decide exactly what I want."

"I knew what I wanted at nineteen. Heck, I knew at seventeen."

"And yet, you veered off course," I said.

"Like you said, you're not me and I don't want you to be me. I want you to do all the things I didn't get to do. I have so many regrets."

"And I hate that for you," I said sympathetically. "Truly. I know this isn't what you want to hear, but I'm simply not ready to make any big decisions. I promised myself I'd take a couple of weeks to heal, both physically and emotionally, and during that time I'm not making any decisions beyond what to wear and what to eat every day. Medical school is too much of a time and financial commitment to be rash."

"I suppose you're right about that. I just don't want you to miss the deadline. What are you going to do next year if you don't go to Harvard?"

"I don't know, but I'm working on it."

"All right." She seemed to want to say something else but then changed her mind. "Let's talk soon, okay?"

"Love you."

"Love you too."

Though I'd been trying not to think about Patrick too much, I ran into him in the dining hall the following week. He was going in as I was coming out and we paused in the doorway. He was with his friends Tate and J.D., from the team, and they said a casual hello to me before continuing on their way.

We stood there for a minute and my tattered soul was momentarily soothed, as if his very presence made everything better.

"How are you?" Patrick asked after we'd stared at each other quietly a little too long.

"Better," I replied. "The doctors said it would take four to six weeks to fully recover, so I'm getting there."

"I'm glad."

There was an awkward silence and I hated that it had come to this. "So you guys did amazing last weekend. Chastity, Dylan and I watched the game at Tito's and you looked great. That goal in the second period was epic. You and Paxton do that psychic thing on the ice and it's like watching magic."

He smiled, though it was a little sad. "I'm trying to enjoy every minute left of playing with my brother because after this we'll be playing against each other."

"It'll be an adjustment, but nothing will ever change the bond you have. Don't forget that."

"For sure."

"Do you—" he began.

"I guess I—" I said at the same time.

We both stopped and he nodded at me. "You first."

"I was just going to say I guess I need to go so I can study."

"Oh. Yeah. I didn't mean to hold you up."

"What, um, what were you going to say?" I asked.

"Nothing." He shrugged. "I'll let you go."

"Well, take care." There didn't seem to be anything else to say so I turned and headed out. As I walked away, it was like I'd left a piece of my soul behind, and it hurt just as much now as it had the night we'd broken up.

"You just let him go?" Chastity demanded that weekend when I told her about running into him. "Why didn't you sit with him so you could talk?"

"And say what?" I asked.

"How about being honest with him?" she asked. "How about telling him how scared you are but that you love him and want to try to make it work? Or how about just saying you need him?"

I shook my head vehemently. "I can't. It wouldn't be fair. Plus, he doesn't love me back."

"You won't know unless you try. What if he's just trying to protect you? You said he didn't want to push you in any direction because you didn't need any more people telling you what to do —so what if that's the real reason he let you go?"

"Well, that and the fact that you told him you needed him to," Dylan interjected. He'd come into the kitchen to get a snack and obviously overheard our conversation.

"What do you mean?" I asked, glancing up at him.

"You said when he tried to work things out, you told him you were overwhelmed and weren't ready for a serious relationship. What was he supposed to do? What else would any guy that cares about you do but let you go? You essentially told him that being together hurt you—and if he does love you, he's never going to intentionally do something to hurt you."

"But what if he doesn't?" I whispered.

"Then you'll be no worse off than you are now," Dylan said amiably. "I mean, you're not together, you're miserable, and you still have no idea what you want to do academically. Seems to me it can't be any worse, but it definitely could get better."

"You're so smart, honey," Chastity said to him.

"I try." He placed a soft kiss on her upturned face and then walked out of the room.

"He's given you something to think about, huh?" Chastity's face was full of sympathy.

"Is it always this hard?"

"Love or life?"

"Both?"

"Yes."

We chuckled together.

On my way home, I called Renee. Her advice had been stellar when I'd asked her what to do and now I needed to run something by her.

"Ellie, hi!"

"Do you have a minute?"

"For you? Of course."

"So…I need advice."

"Shoot."

"What do I do next? I did what you told me to do and took a little time to get my head on straight but I'm starting to realize that all that other stuff—school and my mom and my future career—don't matter without Patrick. My life is an empty shell now that he's gone."

"Oh, honey."

"I saw him earlier this week at the dining hall and for those brief moments where we talked, my life was full again. As soon as he walked away, I went from color back to black and white."

"What do you need from me?"

"I need to know what to *do*. Like the next step. I'm still terrified, but he's too important to walk away from. I realized that when I saw him the other night. I need him, Renee, and I don't know how to make it happen."

"That's easy. You show up at the Frozen Four tournament next weekend and show him you're there for him, even though you're going through a rough patch. Even though you're technically not together. You show him how you feel, how you'll support him through thick and thin."

"But then what? I don't know where I'll be going to school, and once I start a doctoral program, I can't leave in the middle, so how will I support him when I can't even support myself?"

"You figure it out together."

"I don't know how to do that. I'm scared…"

"I know, honey." She paused. "What if I came too?"

"What? Came where?"

"To the tournament. It's in Philly this year, right?"

"Yes."

"I'll book us a hotel room and meet you there. Can you drive to Philly by yourself?"

"Yes, I suppose."

"You know what? Forget driving, why don't you fly?"

"I can't afford it."

"I'll buy your ticket and we'll go together."

"Oh, no, Renee, I couldn't let you do that."

"Sure you can." She laughed gaily. "I love playing matchmaker and as the head coach's wife, it's my job to make sure all the WAGs are happy. In fact, I might round up a couple of the other girls to come too. Okay, I have to go. Lots of plans to make!

I'll text you in a little while with the details. Now go rest so you can build your strength back up."

"Renee, are you—" I cut off because I was talking to myself; she'd hung up before I could say anything else.

Holy hell, what had I just agreed to? I took a deep breath and slowly let it out.

She'd told me to breathe and that was exactly what I was going to do. Right now, it was all I *could* do.

PATRICK

For the first time in a long time, I was nervous *as fuck* the morning of a game. We'd arrived in Philadelphia yesterday for the Frozen Four tournament and I'd barely slept last night. I was excited, because I loved hockey and this was going to be the climax of my college career, but I was worried. There was a lot of pressure on the team in general. We hadn't come this far in the tournament in a long time, since before any of the current players had gotten to college, so we had something to prove.

My father had made some noises about coming, but Paxton told him rooming assignments had changed and we had nowhere for him to stay. That had been a lie, but we'd talked to Coach Keller about it and he was happy to move us around so I was rooming with Tate and Paxton was rooming with Lex. We couldn't afford a distraction like Dad, so we'd tried to be proactive in keeping him from showing up. The tickets were expensive and we knew he couldn't afford them, but he was wily when it came to hockey.

I stretched out when we got to the arena, loosening up my muscles and clearing my mind as best I could. Seeing Ellie a few days ago had thrown me off-balance again. She'd seemed so sad, even more so than I was on the inside, but she wasn't as good at hiding it. Plus, I knew her well enough to see the hurt that practically radiated out of her. And it fucking gutted me. I wanted so much to soothe her, to take away whatever demons were haunting her soul, but she was keeping me at an emotional distance and I hadn't wanted to push it.

"Good news/bad news, boys." Coach Keller came over to where Paxton and I were still stretching. "Which do you want first?"

"Bad news," Paxton replied automatically.

"Your dad is here. We just got a request for a ticket to the game."

"Jesus fucking Christ." I put my hands on my hips and stared up at the ceiling, counting to ten.

"Fuck." Paxton shook his head. "Sorry, Coach. You don't have to get him a ticket."

"It's all right." He gave us a brief smile. "He's still your dad, even if he's a pain in the ass, so I get wanting to see you play the biggest games of your college careers."

"Then what's the good news?" I asked dryly.

"The Sidewinders and the Sockeyes both reached out to let us know they sent representatives to attend the games."

"*Shit*. Dad and the pros." I glanced at Paxton. "No pressure, huh?"

"Nah, I'm good. I'm going to text Naomi and sic her on him. He won't know what hit him."

I nodded but I really didn't need this kind of distraction. What was my dad thinking to show up like this? We'd tried so hard to discourage it, but he was nothing if not persistent. I was done letting him get under my skin, though. I didn't need or want him in my life, but breaking all ties was harder than it sounded.

"Head into the game," Coach Keller said quietly. "Don't worry about him—I'll handle it. I'll get him a ticket and make sure security knows he's not to be allowed back to the locker room, no matter what he says."

"Thanks, Coach. I'm sorry he keeps doing this."

"Like I said, he's your father, so I get it. When we win the whole thing tomorrow night, he can gloat and brag and annoy you all he wants. But until then, I'll handle it."

"Thanks." I walked out of the locker room and into the tunnel toward the ice. It was early, so no one was in the arena but the staff, and I stood there staring out at it. This was one of those moments I might never have again. The calm before the storm of the tournament, my final games as a college hockey player. They didn't have to be, because I still had the option of staying in school, but I was so torn. When it was all said and done, going pro meant leaving Ellie and I was having serious second thoughts about that.

What would be the harm of staying in school another year? Especially if it gave us the time to deepen our bond and come up with a plan. Maybe if she stayed at Moo U and started her doctorate there, she could go back and forth from Vermont to Vegas while she worked on her dissertation. It would all depend on the program, of course, but I knew she wanted to move into biotechnology and a quick internet search told me they had a biotechnology department at UNLV too. Whether or not it was a good one or whether she could get in were separate issues, but another year at Moo U together might buy her the time to figure it out.

I'd come to the conclusion I'd do whatever I had to do to get her back, to show her I was serious, that I loved her. A huge part of me had been missing since she'd left me and I needed her. Physically, emotionally, sexually—I needed it all. Whether that meant staying in school or taking her with me or even offering to do a long-distance thing, I had to try. My dad would kill me, the Sidewinders would undoubtedly be disappointed, and I might be taking a huge risk by waiting, but if that's what it took to have Ellie, I was going to do it.

I breathed in deep, the scent of a hockey arena moving through me with familiarity. I could and would do this. One step, one day at a time. Today, I would put it all out of my mind and do everything in my power to win this game and eventually the tournament. On Sunday, I would fall at her feet, tell her how I felt, and beg her to give me, give *us*, another chance. I'd make all the sacrifices—whatever it took—as long as she was happy and loved me the way I loved her. And I was pretty sure she did.

Coach Keller was true to his word, keeping Dad away from us during and after the game. We snuck into the hotel through a side entrance and took the stairs up to our rooms so we wouldn't run into him, and Coach made the whole team go digitally dark that night anyway, asking us to turn off our phones and computers and get some rest. We were going to need it, and no distractions were allowed. Personally, I was grateful. I got out my global business textbook and read until I fell asleep, determined to stay on track as much as I could.

We had a morning skate after breakfast and then spent the afternoon in our rooms, relaxing until it was time to leave for the arena. I turned on my phone for the first time in twenty-four hours and there were at least a dozen texts from my dad, but I ignored them. I went to Instagram instead, planning to mindlessly skim my feed.

"I'm going down to see Maggie for a little while," Tate told me. "I'll be back in a bit. You need anything?"

"Nah, thanks."

I sighed, wondering what Ellie was up to. Was she studying? Hanging out with Chastity? I wanted to reach out, maybe call her, but I'd promised Toli—and myself—I'd focus on nothing but hockey until this tournament was over. Distractions could be dangerous and I didn't need that.

I was just about to close my eyes and take a nap when someone pounded on the door.

"Patrick?! Open the door, son!"

Jesus. Fucking. Christ.

I got up and steeled myself as I faced my father. "I'm trying to nap, Dad."

"Fuck that. We need to talk." He brushed past me and then turned, folding his arms across his chest. "What's this bullshit about you knocking up some girl?"

I froze. I had no idea how he'd found out, and that terrified me. Paxton and Naomi wouldn't tell anyone and I was fairly certain Ellie hadn't even told her professors. For my father to know, it could only have come from Toli, and the fact that they'd talked was bad.

"Dad, it's none of your business."

"Are you fucking kidding me? After how hard you've worked, you're going to ruin your life over some broad who's after your money?"

"Dad, there's no baby, no girl, no nothing." That was true, at least, even though I planned to do everything in my power to change the last part of that statement.

"Don't lie to me. And what the hell are you doing airing your dirty laundry to Toli Petrov?! Man, it's a good thing you've got the athleticism because you really aren't big in the brains department."

Fury was slowly racing through my veins and it was taking control I didn't know I had not to lay him out.

"How did Mom marry a prick like you?" I mused aloud. "I mean, she's been gone eleven years and no one else can stand you, so either she saw something the rest of us don't or she was blind."

"Don't you talk about your mother that way!" He moved toward me but I laughed. He was twice my age, overweight, and out of shape. I was in no way, shape or form intimidated now, though I had been when I was younger.

Another knock on the door interrupted us and I stepped around him to answer it, grateful for a reprieve. Coach Keller stood there and he looked past me with a frown.

"No guests," he growled, as if he was mad at me. I knew him

well enough to know he wasn't, that he was just protecting me, but it was a little disconcerting nonetheless. I was a thousand times more afraid of my coach than I was of my father.

"I didn't know he was coming," I said quietly.

"I'm leaving," Dad grumbled, brushing past me. "But this conversation isn't over. You're not going to ruin your life over some knocked-up bimbo!" He stalked down the hall and I slumped against the wall.

"He's tenacious," Coach Keller said when he was gone. "I'll give him that."

"All I want to give him is a broken nose."

Coach scowled at me. "Do I need to babysit you today, Trick? I'm serious. We're on the verge of winning the whole damn thing —you better not fuck it up getting in a fight with your father or girlfriend or whoever."

"No, sir. I'm good."

"Why don't you take your things and go on up to Lex and Paxton's room? You and Lex can change places and your dad won't know where you are."

"Thanks. I'm really sorry he's here."

"It's not on you. I'm just trying to keep my team on an even keel. Three hours until we leave for the arena. Can you stay out of trouble until then?"

I really fucking hoped so.

ELLIE

I hadn't told Patrick I was here in Philly but I was getting antsy on Saturday. Though they'd won easily last night, tonight's game was going to be rougher. North Dakota was a tough team and they had a stellar lineup. Not that Moo U was anything to sneeze at, but it wouldn't be as easy to beat North Dakota. In the meantime, though, I was having a great time with the WAGs from the Sidewinders.

Renee had brought Chelsea and Tessa with her and we'd gone out to breakfast this morning and then gotten pedicures. I rarely took time to do stuff like that but Renee was spoiling me on this trip, saying she could afford it and anyway, she was invested in getting Patrick and me back together. I thought she was wonderful, and though I wasn't sure Patrick and I could make it work, I was going to try.

"I say we go down to ice level during the warm-up," Renee suggested as we got ready to go. "He needs to see you, know you're here."

I shook my head. "I don't want to mess with his game mojo until after."

"Are you sure?" Tessa asked. "According to Toli, Patrick's father is here making a nuisance of himself. He texted me a little while ago and said that Donald Graham approached him in the hotel lobby."

"Patrick's *dad* is here?" I grimaced. "That's not good. He hates his dad."

"Yeah, and I think Toli opened his mouth about something he wasn't supposed to. He, Jared and Nate are meeting us at the arena so we'll find out in a little bit."

"Shit." I ached to text Patrick and make sure he was okay, but he'd probably locked up his phone already. Coach Keller had strict rules about technology in and around game time.

I didn't know what his father's appearance meant, but it couldn't be good. Impulsively, I texted Naomi on the way to the arena.

ELLIE: *Are you at the arena?*
NAOMI: *I'm in Philly, yes. Why? Are you here?!*
ELLIE: *Yes. I'm going to try and surprise Patrick after the game.*
NAOMI: *He's going to be so happy to see you! Are you going down to ice level before the game?*
ELLIE: *No. I'm waiting until after. I don't want to mess with his head. Where are you sitting?*
NAOMI: *There are some WAGs here from Seattle, so I'm sitting with them.*
ELLIE: *Okay, cool. Look for me in the concourse toward the end of the game and we can go find the guys together.*
NAOMI: *Will do.*

I felt better after talking to Naomi, and I followed Renee and the others inside. Toli, Jared, and Nate were already in the concourse and came over to greet us. Toli looked upset as he kissed his wife.

"What did you do?" she asked him.

He sighed. "I think I fucked up. I had no idea..." He looked at me. "I didn't realize Patrick and his father weren't close. I assumed he knew about..."

"The baby?" My eyes widened. "You told Patrick's dad about *the baby*?!"

"He was bitching about Patrick's playing a few weeks ago and I was trying to defend him, so I said something about him having a lot on his mind, that an unplanned pregnancy was distracting, and he went storming off before I even had a chance to explain." He shook his head. "I'm so sorry."

"Patrick's dad is a total prick." I turned to Renee. "I changed my mind—I'm going down to watch the warm-up."

"Let's go this way," Toli said, touching my shoulder. "We can stand by the tunnel, so maybe you can say hello."

I glanced at him curiously, wondering why he cared about Patrick and me. It made sense that he cared about Patrick, since they were going to be teammates later this year, but what did they care about me? Patrick was a good-looking, talented man who would undoubtedly have all kinds of women after him. He'd certainly had his choice on campus at Moo U, and the numbers would be tenfold in Vegas. It made no sense that they were all essentially rooting for me. For us.

It made me feel good despite how up in the air everything was, but I couldn't dwell on that now. If Patrick's father had gotten in his head today, he would need something to calm him down and that was me. No matter what we'd been going through the last few weeks, I had that effect on him and he had it on me, and right now he needed me. He might not even know it yet, but I wasn't going to let his father derail everything he'd been working for the last three years.

The teams hadn't come out yet and we crowded around the railing that flanked both sides of the tunnel, waiting for them. Toli, Nate and Jared had baseball caps on and kept their heads down, not wanting to attract any attention, but I was grateful to have them here with me.

"Here they come," Renee whispered, nudging me.

Toli pushed past a few people and lifted me up and over the seats so I could lean against the rail. The closer I was, the easier it would be to get his attention. I just wanted him to see me, so he would know I was here. That was all. I hoped it would be enough to keep him focused, and not have the opposite effect, but it was a chance I was willing to take. No matter what, I had a more positive impact on him than his father ever did.

"Hey!" Naomi tapped Toli on the shoulder and scooted past him so she could stand next to me.

"Hi." I hugged her with one arm.

"Here they come," she said, her eyes twinkling. "He's going to be *so* surprised…"

I unconsciously reached for her hand. "I'm so nervous. What if he's not happy to see me?"

Naomi smiled. "That's not even possible. Trust me."

The team's starting goalie, a senior named Josh Gruber, led the team out onto the ice with a few guys like Tate, Lex, and J.D. behind him. No Paxton or Patrick yet, though. They were a pretty superstitious group, going out in the same order every night, with the twins usually right behind Josh, but it didn't matter at warm-ups, only for the actual game.

Then I saw him. Even side-by-side with his twin, he was easily distinguishable to me. Paxton was more serious; there was no other way to put it. Patrick always had a tiny bit of mischief on his face, no matter what the situation was, and a cleft in his chin that was deeper than Paxton's. It didn't matter, though, because when I said his name, his eyes snapped to mine and he faltered.

"Ellie…" His voice was a whisper and he stopped in front of me.

Our eyes locked and for a moment in time, everything stood still. Like we were back at the hockey house, some mythical energy drawing us together in exactly the same way it had that first night. But we weren't actually at the hockey house, and so much had happened since that night. He also had a game to play.

"Go," I whispered back. "I'll be waiting."

A grin slowly spread across his face and he tapped his stick against the wall beneath me before skating out onto the ice.

"Uh-oh." Naomi's voice had a weird edge.

"What?" I glanced at her in alarm.

She surreptitiously motioned with her head and I looked across the tunnel to the other side, and a middle-aged man was staring at me with a scowl of disgust.

"His dad," she murmured.

"Crap."

"Come." Toli took my elbow. "Let's go find our seats."

"See you later," I called to Naomi.

I ignored the man shooting daggers at me and followed Toli and the others. Something told me Patrick's father wasn't going away any time soon and it scared me far more than everything else Patrick and I had gone through put together.

The good news, of course, was that Patrick had definitely been happy to see me. I tried to focus on how that felt instead of letting his father's obvious distaste upset me, but it was hard to ignore.

"It's going to be okay," Renee whispered to me as we got to our seats. They were in the lower level, a few rows back from the glass, close to center ice. Honestly, these seats were amazing, much better than where I usually sat for Moo U games, and I was so excited to be this close to the action.

"Have you thought any more about what you're going to do about school going forward?" Renee asked me as we waited for the game to start.

"I have." I met her gaze. "I'm going to move into biotechnology. I don't know where or when, but I can't go to medical school. So I'll get a job teaching or working at the mall, it doesn't matter to me, until I find the right program. I'm only nineteen—I have plenty of time—and Patrick's career is more important at the moment."

"There's nothing wrong with taking a gap year," she said gently.

Though that had been in the back of my mind, I'd never articulated it, not really, and hearing someone say it aloud made me as excited as it did uncomfortable. "It's not part of the plan I had for myself, but neither was Patrick, and what we have is special. School isn't going anywhere, but finding someone like Patrick doesn't happen every day."

"It definitely does not."

PATRICK

Ellie was here.

As I skated around the ice during the warm-up, my heart pounded a little faster and I couldn't stop smiling. I was trying to play it cool but my twin noticed immediately. He'd seen Ellie and Naomi, of course, and skated up next to me as we waited to take a few shots on goal.

"She's here," he said, as if I didn't know.

"Yup."

"You better not fuck it up this time."

"Oh, I have no intention of doing that." I grinned at him and stepped up to take a shot. I put it right over Gruber's shoulder and he gave me a nod.

After Paxton had shot, he skated up behind me again.

"You're going to stay at school, aren't you?"

"I think we need more time together, and honestly, I want the degree. I would've gotten it eventually, but maybe this is better. And being with her is definitely better."

"You could just ask her to go to Vegas with you," he suggested mildly.

I frowned a little. "I don't think she can. School and all that. I mean, we'll probably end up being apart for months at a time, but working on a doctorate includes a lot of research and paper-writing, so my hope is that she gets into the program she wants and we live apart some, but then she can spend chunks of time in Vegas too. But we'll have another whole year to figure it out."

"I'm happy for you," he said, holding out his fist for me to bump it. "I mean it."

Knowing Ellie was nearby calmed me. It had since the first night we'd met, and I was able to put everything but hockey out of my mind. My dad, the Sidewinders, my uncertain future, everything just faded away. This game was all that mattered, winning the whole damn thing.

And North Dakota didn't make it easy on us. Every time we scored, they came right back with one. By the end of the third period, we were tied at six apiece and going to overtime. For me, it was a dream come true because overtime was where I excelled. I had a sixth sense in that post-regulation period, something inside of me that turned on and gave me an edge. It was hard to explain because it didn't happen every time, but I'd say about ninety percent of the time.

The connection with my twin intensified during overtime as well, and Coach Keller knew it, so he had us on the same line, which gave us an almost unfair advantage. But I was all over it, looking for anything that would get me or the puck to the net. I faked around to the outside by the boards, watching the other team's defenseman's skates to see if he would cross over, since that would prevent him from easily changing directions to follow me. The moment he did, it gave me the half step I needed to cut back to the middle and drive toward the net.

I didn't have to look to know Paxton had been watching and waiting, ready to get me the puck as soon as there was a shot. The North Dakota D-man had already recovered and was back on top of me, but I had my stick out in front of me and on the ice, waiting for Paxton to put the puck on it. Then I saw it, my twin sending the puck my way, and I got just enough of the blade on it to deflect it up and over the goalie's shoulder.

That red light was the most beautiful thing I'd ever seen and my arms shot up in the air in victory. The first person to reach me was my brother and he wrapped his arms around me, lifting me off the ground as our teammates joined us, one at a time. Before I knew it, I was on the bottom of a pile, laughing as they continued to jump on top of us. I barely felt it, adrenaline and excitement surging through me.

We'd done it, won the whole damn thing, and I'd put that game-winning goal in the slot. It was what I did, what I hoped to continue doing for at least another decade or two, and I hoped like hell this would convince the Sidewinders I was important enough to wait for. I couldn't control that, though, and as I got to my feet, I searched the crowd for Ellie.

There she was.

She was whistling and yelling, arms in the air as she celebrated with the fans around her. God, she was beautiful. I wanted to run over there and touch her but there was too much going on. The coaching and support staff had joined us on the ice and we were getting ready for the handshake line.

I found it kind of a barbaric tradition, forcing the losing team to be good sports and shake hands with the winners. We were all on top of the world and they were dejected as hell. But that wasn't my problem, not today anyway, and I did my gentlemanly duty while trying not to gloat too much.

Once we were done, I took a minute to skate over to the glass close to where Ellie was, putting my palm against it. She practically vaulted over the people in front of her to get to me and her smile made everything that much better.

"Locker room?" I yelled through the melee.

She nodded, pointing to Toli, who gave me a thumbs-up. I took that to mean Toli would get her back to me and that's all that mattered. I winked and headed off the ice with my teammates.

The locker room was even crazier than the ice had been, with everyone yelling and partying. There was plenty of champagne and we made a big show of dousing Coach Keller, who endured it like a champ. The press was waiting outside to talk to us and friends and family had started to gather too. By the time Coach let everyone in, it was a fucking zoo, and I skimmed the faces, looking for Ellie.

And there she was. I pushed past throngs of people to get to her and she was already heading my direction as I held out my arms. She threw herself into them and nestled against my sweaty chest.

"Hi." I kissed the top of her head.

"I'm so proud of you," she said. "You were amazing out there."

"Thanks." I hugged her tightly. "But what are you doing here?"

"You need me and I need you. It's that simple."

"It really is, isn't it?" I hadn't thought of it quite that way, but it was so good to hold her again.

"I missed you." Her voice was barely discernible but I heard her and hugged her tighter.

"Me too." I looked down at her and she tilted up her face to me. There were people and reporters everywhere, but I didn't care, and I lowered my lips to hers. I kissed her sweetly, considering how many people were around, letting my tongue flick hers for a few seconds before reaching out to cup the side of her face. "I'm so fucking happy you're here."

"There was nowhere else I could possibly be this weekend." Her eyes met mine and what I saw there told me everything was going to be okay.

"Babe, can you—"

"Is this the little slut trying to get your money?" My dad's voice was worse than nails on a chalkboard and the growl that left my throat was deep and filled with more than a decade of fear, frustration, and hatred. I shoved Ellie to the side as I whirled to face him.

"What the fuck did you say?"

"You're not ready to be a father."

"Duh."

"You can fuck anyone!" Dad was on a roll, his face getting redder as his voice got louder. "She's nothing special—don't you see she's using the baby to trap you?"

"She's extremely special," I hissed. "And it's none of your business anyway."

"Why do you consistently do everything in your power to fuck up your career? Are you just fucking stupid?" He used both hands to shove me in the chest, sending me back a few feet.

I came back at him and my fist shot out before I could stop it, sending him sprawling. People started to yell and I sensed my teammates surrounding me, but I was laser-focused on my father. He got to his feet and charged me, but I was ready for him, catching him around his middle and throwing him back on the ground. He jumped up and swung, connecting with my bicep as I side-stepped him, and I hit him again, this time square in the nose.

"Patrick!" Paxton was pulling me off of him. "He's enough of a dick to press charges—don't do it."

"Patrick." Toli stood between me and my father, his eyes meeting mine. "Don't destroy your future over this guy. He's not worth it."

"Babe." Ellie's soft voice penetrated my haze of fury more than the others, her hand on my forearm, tugging gently. "Don't. *Please* don't. I don't care what he says about me. They're just words."

I didn't say anything, my eyes still locked with my father's, as blood dripped from his nose.

"Ungrateful little shit," he was saying. "I've sacrificed *every-thing* so you could be where you are today and this is the thanks I get."

"You're out of here." Coach Keller appeared with two security guards. "And you're officially persona non grata at any and all Burlington University sports events. Get him out of here."

Dad was still yelling insults and I dipped my head, ashamed I'd lost my temper and embarrassed to have done this in front of my whole team, the Sidewinders who were here, and the press.

"I'm sorry, Coach."

"You're fine, kid." He clapped a hand on my shoulder. "I think that was a long time coming and if he does decide to do something stupid like press charges, you have a whole room of people who'll say he started it."

I pulled Ellie close again. As always, the calm in my chaos.

"I'm sorry," she whispered. "I hate that you fought because of me."

"Baby, we've been fighting since long before I ever met you. What just happened could have happened at any time the last couple of years."

"I still hate it."

"I'm sorry he called you names."

She shrugged. "Sticks and stones and all that. Fuck him."

I laughed. She was so quiet and reserved most of the time, but when she let loose it was great.

"You okay, sweetheart?" Renee joined us, her eyes filled with concern.

"I'm better than okay." Ellie smiled at her.

"There's *so* gonna be make-up sex tonight," Tate chortled.

I took a playful swing at him, laughing. "I fucking hope so."

ELLIE

It was a long time before Patrick and I had any time alone, to talk or anything else. The team started partying almost immediately after the locker room altercation, and I let Patrick talk to the press and enjoy the win with his teammates. I hung out with Renee, Tessa, and Chelsea, watching, taking it all in. It was exciting, even though I technically wasn't part of it, and I loved seeing Patrick in his element, especially when journalists were falling all over each other to get to him. His game-winning goal had been epic and they wanted to know what was next for him.

"I'm only a junior this year," he'd said. "I think college is the best place for me. The Sidewinders aren't going anywhere and I'd like to graduate. I haven't made a final decision yet, but that's the direction I'm leaning."

"Patrick, have you talked to the Sidewinders about your decision?"

"They're super supportive," he'd replied calmly. "They haven't put any pressure on me to make a decision either way, so I'm taking my time to make sure I do the right thing for my future."

What was he talking about? He'd already decided to go pro

and I'd obviously missed something if he was leaning toward staying at school now.

"I have to go back to the hotel with the team," he said to me at some point in the evening. "Will you meet me there? Where are you staying?"

"We're at the same hotel."

"You two can totally have our room," Renee told me. "I'm going to stay with Jared tonight and fly home in the morning."

"Thank you." I reached out to hug her. "This was all because of you and I'm so grateful."

"Remember, communication is key. Don't hold anything back."

"Thank you a million times."

"You're very welcome."

It was after midnight before Patrick and I were finally in my room. The parties were still raging but we needed to be together, to talk and sort things out. I had no idea what he was thinking and I had so many things to tell him.

"You didn't have to cut out early for me," I whispered as he dropped his bag on the floor.

"Yeah, I did." He kissed me, lightly. "But before we do anything else, I need a shower. I'm sweaty and covered in champagne."

"Champagne is yummy," I teased. "I'm happy to lick it off of you."

He grimaced. "Not mixed with sweat and bacteria from my equipment. As a future biologist, you should know this stuff."

I laughed. "Okay, fine. Go shower."

Ten minutes later, he came out of the bathroom in nothing but low-slung sweats, and every part of me clenched in longing and anticipation. Those broad shoulders and muscular arms did me in every time, but his flat, rippled torso and bright blue eyes weren't bad either.

I unconsciously licked my lips and he quirked a smile in my direction. "Bet I know what you're thinking."

"Who, me?" I feigned innocence. "I have no idea what you mean."

"How about you turn over and let me take a bite of that luscious ass of yours?"

"I'm scandalized," I said, laughingly throwing an arm over my eyes and lamely faking a Southern accent. "I would nev-ah do such a thing."

"Come here, you." He yanked me up against him and wrapped his arms around me. There was so much unspoken contentment in his touch, in the way he held me, and I closed my eyes, letting it wash over me.

"You want to talk?" he asked after a moment.

"Yes."

"Let's sit over there." He motioned to the chair by the window and led me there by the hand. He sat down and pulled me onto his lap. "I need to touch you," he said.

"That's good because I totally need you to touch me."

"So, what are you doing here? I mean, really?"

"I…" I took a deep breath and tried to organize my thoughts in a way that would make sense. "My life was very structured before I met you. High school, college, graduate school—it was all a neatly ordered plan. I took a little detour after my undergraduate degrees and went into computer science instead of biotechnology because I wanted to piss off my mother, but in the end, all that did was waste time. What I didn't understand then was that my life was very black and white, both emotionally and in terms of the way I lived it. And then I met you." I smiled, touching his cheek. "The gray of my life turned to bright colors. Everything was better…even school. You made me see and feel things I'd never imagined, and when I left you, the darkness came back so fast it felt like I'd fallen into a deep well of despair."

"Oh, baby, I'm sorry." He stroked my hair.

"It was just so much, so fast," I continued softly, swallowing. "All the firsts happened in, like, two months, and adding the pregnancy on top of it, part of me shut down. The only way to sort through it all was to push you—and everyone else—away. I needed to find myself before I could let anyone else in."

"And now?"

"Now I realize that mostly what I need is you. Not because I can't manage on my own, but because everything is so much better with you at my side."

"And that's kind of where I'm at too," he said, his eyes meeting mine. "I realized going to the pros wasn't worth it if it meant losing you. I'm willing to give up the degree—even though I'd still like to finish at some point—but not you. So I'll stay at Moo U another year, get bigger and stronger and more mature, and that should give you time to figure out where you're going to be."

"But I don't want you to stay for me," I whispered quickly. "I have zero idea where I'm going to be in a year, so you need to go to Vegas."

"I don't want to go without you," he said, pressing his forehead to mine. "Ellie, I love you."

Tears burned my eyelids and I let them fall unchecked. How long had I waited to hear those words? "I love you too," I choked out, wrapping my arms around his neck.

"If you want to come with me to Vegas, I'm happy to take care of you," he said. "Take a year off, live with me, and use the whole time to pursue all the things you've wanted to try but never had time for. And when you find the right program, the place you want to be, if we have to do a long-distance thing until you finish, it's okay. We'll survive. My gut says we'll be married by then."

I crashed my mouth to his, overwhelmed with passion and emotion and romance. And he kissed me back like a man who owned me. His tongue pillaged mine, taking pull after pull until I was an aching, squirming mass of hormones. I needed him so badly, but I wasn't sure if we could.

"I need you," he whispered.

"I don't know if it's okay," I whispered back. "I never asked about intercourse because I didn't think I'd be having any."

"Oral?" His eyes glittered with intensity.

"Yes. Fuck yes."

He got up with me still in his arms and within ten seconds we were naked, our bodies close together on the bed. And somehow, the urgency faded, as if just being like this, back together, was enough.

"We don't have to do anything," he said after a moment. "I don't want to hurt you. You need to heal properly. I can wait."

"Oral isn't going to hurt anything and I need to come so badly, I might explode the second you touch me."

"Mmmm, I love hearing that." He stroked his hand down my back and over the curve of my ass. "But first, flip over and let me nibble on that ass of yours."

I turned onto my stomach and closed my eyes, losing myself in how it felt to have his hands all over me. He ran them down the center of my spine, the curve of my hips, the backs of my thighs. Then he nipped my ass cheeks, grazing me with his teeth, harder and then softer, squeezing and caressing, until my insides were tight with need. I wanted him inside of me so bad, but since we couldn't, I'd bask in his attention instead.

He lifted me to my knees and spread them apart, keeping my torso flat on the bed, and then he moved between my legs, running his tongue from my clit to my asshole. I moaned, deep in my chest, moving against him.

"Mine," he whispered. "This gorgeous body is all fucking mine. Say it."

"Yours," I said in a shaky voice. His tongue was inside of me now and I was so close I was going to embarrass myself. He was fingering my ass, something I'd come to love, and devouring me like this was his last supper or something.

"Patrick!" I squeaked out his name and then my world went white. Weeks of pent-up sadness, passion, and frustration exploded out of me in a series of waves so strong I stopped breathing for a few seconds. Then he pushed his finger deeper into my ass and I came again, bucking and writhing as he held me in place.

"That's my girl." He pressed a few light kisses on my lower back before my knees gave out and I landed flat on my stomach again.

"I'm calling the doctor first thing Monday morning," I said, still trying to catch my breath.

"Definitely." He collapsed beside me and I turned my head to look at him.

"Now what do we do?" I asked.

"We can get dressed and go back to the party or we can lie here and cuddle all night."

"Your choice," I said. "You're the champion."

"I've done a lot of partying since I got to Moo U. I'd rather spend tonight with the woman I love."

"So…are we going to Vegas?"

"That's up to you. Tell me what you want and I'll do it. I realized pretty quickly that my life didn't mean much without you in it. If you think some time off would give you the freedom to search for your true passion, then yes, let's go to Vegas. If not, I'll stay at school and we'll have a whole year to come up with a new plan."

"I've wanted a gap year for a long time," I admitted. "But I never dared say it or even really think it. The fact that you understood that even before I did is one of many reasons why I love you —and don't want to be without you."

"What's your mom going to say?"

I shook my head vehemently. "We are *so* not talking about her tonight."

"I love you, Ellie. I need to hear you say it."

"I love you too, Patrick." We smiled into each other's eyes and I'd never been more secure in any decision I'd made. Now if I could somehow salvage my relationship with my mother, things would be pretty damn amazing.

37

PATRICK

The week following winning the tournament was one of the best of my life. I had my girl back, I was a fucking hero around campus, and as far as I was concerned, my father was no longer part of my life. He'd tried calling, texting, and showing up at the hotel before we'd left, but security had kept him away from us and I'd blocked his number. A tiny part of me felt guilty, because he was still my father, and really the only family I had left other than my twin, but I couldn't take the toxicity he brought to my life. Paxton felt the same and we'd both washed our hands of him. We'd be there if he was ever sick or something, but unless and until he had a major change of attitude, we were done.

Which made officially meeting Ellie's parents today that much more important. She hadn't yet told her mother about us or our plans to move to Las Vegas, so today was either going to be really bad or surprisingly good. Ellie was a nervous wreck as we drove out to Brattleboro and all I could do was hold her hand and tell her I had her back, no matter what.

"How sad will it be if we lose all four of our parents?" she asked when we were almost there.

I sighed. "Pretty sad, but my gut tells me no. Your mom is overbearing but when you were sick, she was there in an instant.

My dad probably would've told me to suck it up and then would've asked how long until I could be back on the ice."

She wrinkled her nose. "Was he always this way?"

"Maybe? I think my mom was a buffer when she was still alive, but once she died, he just got worse and worse."

"Well, here goes nothing." She motioned to a long, winding driveway and I turned in.

"It's going to be okay," I told her. "And I'll be right there."

We walked up to the front door holding hands. I had a bottle of red wine in my other hand and hoped to make a good impression. I'd dressed up a little, in dress pants, a button-down shirt, and dress shoes, and Ellie had laughed at me. But it was Easter Sunday and I figured dressing up would both help celebrate the holiday and potentially make a better impression than jeans and a polo shirt.

Ellie looked adorable in a white peasant skirt and a pale green sweater. It was warmer now that it was almost mid-April, but there was still a chill in the air. We had heavier jackets in the car because it would be cold on the drive back to campus later tonight.

"Hi, guys." Ellie's father opened the door. "Happy Easter."

"Happy Easter, Dad." Ellie hugged him and I held out my hand.

"Happy Easter, Mr. McGinn."

"Please. Call me Russ."

"Thank you." I handed him the bottle of wine. "Ellie said Mrs. McGinn is making a pot roast, so I thought red would go well."

"Excellent. Thank you."

We walked through a warm, well-lit house and into the kitchen.

"Ellie." Her mother turned, a spoon in her hand. "Happy Easter."

"Happy Easter, Mom. Patrick, this is my mother, Abby McGinn. Mom, Patrick Graham."

"Nice to meet you." Her mother didn't look impressed with me and I just tried to look polite.

We made small talk in the kitchen as the ladies finished cooking and Russ set the table. I tried to help but they wouldn't let me do anything, which was probably for the best, and eventually they brought up the Frozen Four.

"So putting aside the fact that you're my daughter's boyfriend, I've got to go into fan mode for a minute," Russ said. "I mean, that overtime goal was…" He seemed to be fumbling for the word.

"Epic?" Ellie supplied, laughing.

"Amazing," he said, nodding. "How'd you do that?"

I chuckled. "It's what I've done since I was little. Hockey is what I do."

"What else will you do?" Abby asked pointedly. "When you're done with hockey?"

"Hopefully, that won't be for a long time," I replied. "I'm only three classes shy of my bachelor's in business, and I plan to take two this summer and one next fall if I can take it virtually. So I'll have options if my hockey career is cut short." I'd prepared for questions like this.

"Tell us about your family," Russ said, changing the direction of the conversation.

"My dad played professional hockey for one season before he had a career-ending injury," I said. "He's worked construction since then. My mother died in a car accident when I was ten so I don't remember her much, but I have an identical twin brother, Paxton, who's also going to play in the pros next year."

Abby arched a brow. "So you're leaving soon?"

"We need to talk about that," Ellie interjected slowly, moving closer to me. "Patrick is taking two classes this summer while I'm teaching, but as soon as classes are over, we're moving to Las Vegas."

Abby put down the spoon she'd been holding with a thud.

"You have got to be kidding me. Just what do you think you're going to do in Las Vegas?"

"Whatever I want," Ellie said softly. "I'm taking a gap year so I have time to decide where I want to end up."

"You just can't bear to break things off so you're going to give up everything to follow him! And I won't let you do it! I won't let you ruin your life, having babies while you're still practically a baby and—" She burst into tears.

"Mom." Ellie walked over to her mother and put a gentle hand on her arm. "Mom, listen to me. Patrick isn't your ex. I don't know who he is or what he did, but that's not Patrick and I'm not pregnant. Nor do I plan to be. My pregnancy was a fluke."

"But it happened!"

"Yes, but we weren't careless. And we're going to be super careful going forward. I'm getting a birth control implant and we're going to keep using condoms until we're satisfied that I'm protected. Neither of us is ready for a baby and I'm not giving up anything."

"If you leave school now—"

"Lots of people take gap years. What, you think I'm going to be happy sitting home doing nothing while he plays hockey? Mom, I'm going back to school. I just need time to grow up a little. I've been in college almost five years. I'm ready for a break. And Patrick needs me."

"I love Ellie." I finally spoke up, unwilling to interrupt the mother/daughter moment until now. "And I'm going to support her in whatever way she needs. Emotionally, financially, whatever it takes."

"You're going to support her?" Russ finally joined the conversation. "Will you be able to?"

"I'll be making almost a million dollars next year," I said quietly. I hated talking about money but I understood her parents would want to know that she would be okay. "I've already spoken to the team and they provide health insurance for domestic partners. I'm getting a signing bonus this summer that will help us get an apartment, so we'll be fine. Ellie can take all the time she needs to find the right school, the right program…"

"But what about Harvard?" Abby sniffled.

"I don't want to go to medical school," Ellie whispered. "Please, Mom, don't make me choose between Patrick and the career I really want, and you. *Please*."

"That's never going to happen." Russ reached out to put an arm around his wife's shoulders. "Abby, it's time to let her go. And to let go of the past. She's not making your mistakes; she's making her own. Like this computer science thing she had to do. But she's okay. We raised a brilliant girl with a good head on her shoulders."

"But Las Vegas is so far away…" Abby started to cry again.

"We can go visit," Russ said, hugging her.

"And we'll be here most of the summer," Ellie pointed out. "We're not going anywhere yet."

"I think we need wine," Russ said, turning to open the bottle.

Dinner was great. The food was good, Ellie seemed happy, and her parents actually seemed interested in knowing all about me and my plans with the Sidewinders. Once they accepted the idea that Ellie was taking a year off to grow up, and going with me to Las Vegas, they warmed up to it, talking about coming to help us get settled and Ellie and her mom going shopping for some necessities since even modern young women needed at least some semblance of a dowry. I didn't know what a dowry was so I discreetly looked it up on my phone.

Property or money brought by a bride to her husband on their marriage.

I almost laughed but kept a straight face as we continued discussing my future in hockey, Ellie's plans, and how we'd spend our summer up until we left for Vegas. It was nice in a way I hadn't experienced in a long time. Not since before my mother died, and I barely remembered those holidays. Dad had always been drunk on the holidays, ordering food instead of cooking, and throwing us a twenty-dollar bill or new hockey sticks instead of wrapped gifts at Christmas. Having a sit-down meal while all dressed up on an actual holiday felt like the kind of normal I'd unconsciously longed for all my life. My only regret now was that Paxton wasn't here. And with him in Seattle, chances were we wouldn't spend many holidays together going forward. I hadn't thought about that until just now.

"Babe?" Ellie's voice was soft as she searched my face. "You were a million miles away just now."

"Thinking about how Paxton and I probably won't spend another holiday together for a really long time."

"But we can spend summers together. Maybe in a few years, when we're a little more settled, we can buy some kind of beach house or condo, a place we can stay in together for parts of every summer. Maybe even big enough to enjoy when we all have kids."

I reached for her, kissing her forehead. "You really do understand me like no one other than my twin ever has."

"I'm your…*sexual* twin," she said, straining to keep a straight face.

"I don't even know what that means," I said, chuckling.

"Well, he's your physical and biological twin. I'm your emotional and lifetime twin."

"My soul twin," I amended, smiling down at her.

"Your forever twin."

"Forever is right."

ELLIE

A few months later …

We moved into our new apartment in Las Vegas in mid-August, a month before Patrick had to report to training camp, and a couple weeks after finishing our summer semesters of school. Patrick had done the unthinkable—with the help of his advisor—and taken all three classes over the summer, so he'd be graduating in December. The third class technically hadn't been available, but the school had worked with him to make it a project-type class, and with the help of the Sidewinders' back office, he'd gotten it done.

The summer had been brutal. He'd taken both summer sessions, which were six weeks each, and he'd been nonstop the whole time. He'd been in classes all day five days a week and then did nothing but study at night and on the weekends. I'd taught one class in each of the summer sessions, but it hadn't been nearly as much work for me. So while Patrick had busted his ass trying to graduate, I'd had free time. For the first time ever.

I read, did yoga most mornings, and even began swimming regularly in the university pool. I spent a week with my parents since Patrick was so busy, and it had been nice to just hang out with my mom. We'd gone shopping for tons of things Patrick and

I would need in our new apartment and she'd taught me how to cook a few things since I didn't know how.

Patrick and I had taken ten days to drive across the country from Vermont to Nevada, making it a mini-vacation since he hadn't had any kind of break yet. We'd stopped in Chicago, Des Moines, and Denver and did a little sightseeing, so it hadn't been nearly as tedious as we'd thought it would be to spend that much time in a vehicle. I'd never been to any of those places and he'd only been to Chicago for hockey-related events, which made it fun for both of us.

We'd gotten to town yesterday, and thanks to the Sidewinders, had an apartment we could move into. There was no furniture but we'd ordered a few things online and we were currently waiting for our bed, mattress, and bedroom furniture to arrive. I'd hung up our clothes in the master bedroom closet while he'd emptied my SUV. My parents had really gone overboard in getting us things we'd need to start our life together, which was a huge help and really sweet of them, considering everything that had happened during the school year.

"Where do you want this stuff?" Patrick asked, coming in with three more boxes.

"Kitchen," I said, grinning at him. He looked hotter than ever in shorts and a tank top, a trickle of sweat sliding down one side of his face. I had an urge to lick it and playfully tugged him over to me.

"Gross," he laughed as I kissed his sweaty face.

"I seem to recall a guy who likes kissing when we're sweaty."

"It's a different kind of sweaty!"

I pressed my lips to his. "But it's your sweat, so I like it all."

"God, you're sexy." He lifted me onto the kitchen counter and planted himself between my legs so he could kiss me properly. Lots of tongue and lips, until I was completely out of breath.

"I wish we could take this to the bedroom," I moaned, "but you know that's when the delivery will arrive."

"We'll be christening the new bed all night," he said, laughing.

He was just about to kiss me again when there was a knock on the door.

"Who could that be?" I asked. "Isn't this complex gated?"

"Several of the guys on the team live here," Patrick said. "They must be coming by to say hello." He walked over to the front door and opened it.

"Hi, guys!" Renee walked in looking around. "Congratulations on the new place and welcome to Las Vegas!"

"Thank you!" I ran over to hug her.

"I made scones and muffins." She handed me a basket. "I figured you wouldn't feel like baking until you get settled and—"

"I don't know how to bake," I told her, laughing. "It's one of many things I plan to learn while I'm not in school."

"I give lessons!" Renee said. "We'll work on it once hockey season starts."

"Hey!" Anton Petrov walked in carrying something that looked like a casserole. "My stepmom said you'd probably be too tired and busy to cook dinner today so she made this. Just put it in the oven at three-fifty for thirty minutes."

"Oh, wow." I took it from him. "Thank you for bringing it by. I'll have to call her."

Nate and Chelsea came in behind him, also carrying bags filled with food and groceries. "I know how hard it is to start from scratch," Chelsea said, "so consider this a housewarming gift."

"Thank you!" I hugged her, a little overwhelmed at how nice everyone was being.

"You need help with anything?" Nate asked Patrick.

"I was going to go pick up the barstools we ordered for the kitchen island but we're waiting for the bedroom furniture to get here."

"Why don't we run out and grab the stools then, and the ladies can wait here for the delivery guys."

"Okay, cool." Patrick leaned over to brush his lips across mine and then he, Nate, and Anton were gone and I was in the kitchen with Renee and Chelsea.

"What can we do?" Renee asked, looking around.

"I'm unpacking all the boxes of stuff my parents got us," I said. "Trying to figure out where I want to put everything. There's a Keurig coffee maker, a toaster, a blender, and one of those George Foreman grills."

"I love my George Foreman grill," Chelsea said. "It's great for nights when we're in a hurry."

"And grilled cheese sandwiches," Renee added. "It's perfect when Braden has friends over." She'd told me she had a ten-year-old stepson.

"Since I barely know how to cook anything, I think this will be a lifesaver," I replied, putting the grill on the counter.

"Do you have pots and pans?"

I shook my head. "Just a few. A frying pan, a small pot to boil water, and a larger pot to make things like spaghetti. My mom said I'd want to buy my own, that it's personal when you start cooking."

Renee nodded. "That it is."

We talked as we put everything away.

"I have a list of things I need to buy," I told them. "Sheets, towels, all kinds of stuff."

"Shopping for that kind of thing is fun," Chelsea said, grinning.

"I don't think Patrick agrees but we've been trying to do that stuff as a couple since it's our first place together."

A knock on the door announced the arrival of the delivery men and I directed them to where I wanted everything. I loved the furniture we'd picked out and couldn't wait to put on the sheets and comforter my mother and I had bought.

Chelsea sat on the edge of the mattress and bounced a little. "Nice and firm. You'll need it if Patrick has half the libido Nate does."

I snickered. "Oh, he definitely does."

They helped me make the bed and finish putting away everything that was left. By that time, the guys were back and we put the three stools by the island.

"It's coming together, huh?" Patrick asked me, sliding an arm around my shoulders.

"It is."

"Jared and I would love to have you over for dinner this week," Renee said. "I'll text you, okay, Ellie?"

"Thank you, that sounds great."

"We're having a cookout in a couple of weeks," Nate told us. "So don't make any plans the first Saturday in September. It's an end-of-summer party and it's always a blast."

"Sounds fun." Patrick shook his hand, thanked Anton, and then everyone took their leave.

"Come on," I said, tugging him toward the bedroom.

"Oh, wow, babe, this looks amazing." He smiled when he saw that the bed was already made and I'd put some of our things on the dresser and nightstands.

"Wanna break it in?" I whispered.

"Uh-huh." He scooped me up and carried me across the room. "What do you think? Ready to begin the biggest adventure of our lives?"

"So ready." I wrapped my arms around his neck. "You?"

"Beyond ready."

"It already feels like home," I said softly.

"Anywhere we're together, that's home." His eyes met mine.

"I love you, Patrick."

"Ditto." He kissed me and then we toppled over on the bed.

THE
END